EFA

By
R P Salmon

Grosvenor House
Publishing Limited

All rights reserved
Copyright © R P Salmon, 2025

The right of R P Salmon to be identified as the author of this
work has been asserted in accordance with Section 78
of the Copyright, Designs and Patents Act 1988

The book cover is copyright to R P Salmon

This book is published by
Grosvenor House Publishing Ltd
Link House
140 The Broadway, Tolworth, Surrey, KT6 7HT.
www.grosvenorhousepublishing.co.uk

This book is sold subject to the conditions that it shall not, by way of
trade or otherwise, be lent, resold, hired out or otherwise circulated
without the author's or publisher's prior consent in any form of
binding or cover other than that in which it is published and
without a similar condition including this condition being imposed
on the subsequent purchaser.

A CIP record for this book
is available from the British Library

This book is a work of fiction. Any resemblance to
people or events, past or present, is purely coincidental.

ISBN 978-1-83615-172-2

*for my amazing daughters
Elizabeth and Helen*

PART ONE

BOYHOOD

1

Aberfor, South Wales: 6th March, 1984

It was raining heavily, but it was not the pelting torrents against his bedroom window that had woken Bryn; it was the sound of raised voices coming from the kitchen. Kraig's bed was empty, its Iron Maiden duvet thrown on the floor in an untidy heap. Bryn's older brother had clearly got up in a hurry.

Breakfast before school was usually a quiet affair because the men of the house would either be on earlies or lying in. Something was up. He dressed hastily and descended the steep cottage stairs. Still a little bleary-eyed, cocooned in that half-awake state between dreamland and reality, Bryn had forgotten yesterday's big news: the miners had been called out on strike.

He opened the kitchen door. Mam was not baking bread or doing laundry. Cadi did not have her coat on waiting to be picked up for Day Centre. She was crouched in the corner, nervously clutching Reesa Rabbit. Her favourite soft toy was seemingly the only embodiment of normality in a suddenly topsy-turvy world.

It was Mam who was shouting loudest. 'It's not right,' she was saying. 'There's been no vote. How can Scargill just call you all out with no vote? You've had no choice.'

'We don't need a vote, Ma, everyone's behind this. We're solid. We'll take the Thatcher bitch down same way we took that fucking dork before her. Bring it on! She'll be finished by Easter,' pronounced Kraig.

'I've told you till I'm blue in the face,' retorted his mother angrily, 'I won't have that kind of language in my kitchen.'

'Your mother's right, son. Show some respect. If you live in this house, you live by our rules,' said Huw more mildly than his wife, but levelling a steely gaze at Kraig until the younger man averted his eyes.

'You're out of touch, Ma. You spend too much time at that fuck… that stupid chapel and not enough in the real world. I'm out of here. Going up to Megan's. Her dad will be putting a picket plan together and I, for one, want to be on the front line.' With that, he grabbed his cap, and instead of stepping over the dog, lying between him and the back door, he kicked it out of the way. The dog yelped and limped to a safer place by Bryn's feet.

'For pity's sake!' exclaimed Wynne at the retreating figure of her eldest son. 'I don't know what's wrong with him these days,' she moaned. 'It's since he started courting that Megan and spending time at theirs. It's like he has this devil furnace raging inside him, always spoiling for a fight.'

'He's just trying to find his way, Wynne. He's still young. He'll come right in the end.'

'You're too soft with him, Huw. He's twenty-one, not twelve. All man and no boy. He should have found his way by now.'

'Kraig mean, Kraig very mean,' muttered Cadi, pulling Reesa closer to her chest, in case her favourite cuddly toy might be next in line for a kicking.

Bryn's father was deep in thought. He felt troubled and wretched. His powerful sixteen stone build would have been sought after for a rugby front row if he had ever shown any talent for the sport. Just skimming six feet, he was not quite tall enough to warrant the moniker 'gentle giant' that often attached itself to Huw Ellis because of his size and mild temperament. He was a man of few words, who preferred to read poetry and exercise his baritone voice singing hymns at chapel on a Sunday morning than charge after a mud-soaked rugby ball or throw arrows in a smoky tap room. After thirty-one years down the pit, he had seen it all. A loyal union man, Huw had stayed solid throughout the strikes in the seventies. The government was the enemy, but his heart was sore that it had been ordinary folks who suffered most. Now it was starting all over again.

This time the moral ground was higher because it was not about pay; it was about the threatened closure of twenty collieries. The pits were not exhausted, the rub was in the rising costs to extract what was left. In the end it always came down to money. Well, he would stand with his union, as he always had. This was now about livelihoods and whole communities. It still sat uneasily with him.

All the while, Bryn looked on, stroking his whimpering dog. She was the runt of a litter born three years ago on a local farm where Wynne got her eggs. Runts were no use to farmers, who needed strong working dogs. Wynne, sensing the runt was destined to be drowned, had asked if she could take her. 'I expect it'll be dead inside a week,' said the farmer, 'but if you're daft enough to want it, I'll not stop you.' Bryn had been ecstatic at the prospect of a puppy. Huw had taken more convincing.

'What were you thinking, Wynne?' he had quizzed her when she returned with more than the two dozen eggs she had set out for. 'I thought we'd agreed that if we have a dog, it can't be a puppy. Cadi won't understand the difference between a cuddly toy and a puppy. It'll likely end in tragedy.'

'But she's older now. She's fourteen and understands more than you give her credit for,' argued Wynne. 'She might not have the words, but she has the feelings. She's kind, Huw. That girl is pure kindness. The pup won't come to any harm, Bryn will see to that. He's missed out on a lot because of Cadi. We have to think of him, too. He's growing up fast. Let's not deny him what most of his friends have long had.'

'Alright, Wynne. You generally have a feel for these things, but it will end badly if the runt dies.'

'She's not going to die.'

'It's a bitch then?'

'Yes, and Bryn has called her Efa. You mark my words, Huw, that dog's not going to die.'

Huw stroked his chin and smiled. Efa had been one of the names they had considered for their daughter. After complications at birth, she had survived against the odds, and its Hebrew meaning of 'life' had seemed apt when Cadi's precious life was spared. In the end, they had settled on Catrin after Wynne's mother. They had shortened it to Cadi when she was little, and it suited her still. 'Does Bryn know what the name Efa means? It's a good name for a runt if it survives.'

'Shouldn't think so, though you never know with that boy. He's only eleven but he has hidden depths. Takes after his father!'

In those early weeks, Bryn had spent every spare moment attending to his tiny charge. He went with his mother to get advice from the vet, who sold them a special milk formula for orphaned puppies. Bryn tipped up some of his pocket money to help pay for it, and Wynne was wise enough to take it. He lined a boot box with straw, which he changed daily, and hand-fed her the warm milk formula. Cadi donated one of her doll's blankets, 'Keep puppy warm,' she smiled.

Three years on, Efa was as firm and fond a fixture in the Ellis household as the timeless frying pan that had belonged to Wynne's mother. It was made of cast iron, with a diameter as large as the boiling plate on the Aga. Now blackened and rather scratched, it had become associated with wholesome vittles lovingly prepared by two generations of devoted mothers. Wynne poo-pooed the modern non-stick versions and swore it would go with her to her grave. Bryn would like to think that Efa would go with him to *his* grave, but he knew enough to understand that dogs, unlike frying pans, did not live outlive humans.

The NUM were bullishly confident they were going to win after their successes in the seventies. This time, it was different. The Government had been stockpiling coal in anticipation of expected industrial action. Easter came and there was no sign of any let-up. In Aberfor, the miners' cottages were fuelled by coal. Coal allowances were stopped for striking miners, so there was no central heating, no open fire, no hot water – and no Aga to cook on. Huw was grateful that it was late spring not mid-winter, although his savings were dwindling fast. Another dent had been made in them to buy a portable two-ring electric hob and an electric kettle. At least these appliances would enable them to have hot food and drinks – as long as they could still pay the electric bills.

The strike dragged on into the summer and became more bitter. Kraig became increasingly fired up. He joined the flying pickets and was away from home much of the time. As winter deepened, things got desperate. By then, Huw had been without a wage for nine months. There was no strike pay; only the £1 a day for picketing miners.

The Ellis savings were all but gone. They wore three layers of clothes and still couldn't shut out the cold. The only thing worse than the cold was the gnawing hunger. Huw and Wynne went without to give Bryn and Cadi more. Although he missed the company of his eldest son, Huw was thankful Kraig was away such a lot. It was one less mouth to feed.

There was no shortage of well-wishers for the flying pickets, often hot vittles and a barn to sleep in. In the towns, sympathetic publicans let them put their bedrolls down on the bar floor after closing time. On those occasions, there would also be whisky to keep out the cold.

Cadi was often ill, but Huw could not help out with his only daughter. If he did not join the local picket line, he would not get his £1 per day from the union. Fridays had long become the highlight of the week. It was the day the miners' wives distributed a food parcel to every colliery household from the donations they collected. Wynne had to stay home with Cadi and could no longer help, but the wives made sure the Ellis family still got their quota.

The days shortened. Bare trees and grey skies made the coal-blackened landscape even starker. Bryn had to pass the colliery on his walk to school, and in the early days he would try and spot his dad on the picket line with their waving placards and rousing chants. After a few weeks, the novelty was stale. Nothing ever changed.

Wynne tried her best with the extras that came in the seasonal food parcel, but Christmas was a grim affair. Kraig came home briefly. He was thinner and angrier. His face and body bore the bruises of police truncheons. He berated his family with endless tales of the violence and brutality he had encountered on the flying picket lines.

'They're not regular coppers, you know. They're drafted in from every county in the land. Fucking brutes and thugs, the lot of them. My mate Lloyd recognised some ex-Forces guys in the mix, too. It's dog eat dog, but we're holding our own. We won't give in. Arthur says hell will have to freeze over first.'

'Can't you give it a rest, Kraig?' pleaded Wynne. 'It's Christmas. Let's at least *try* and be cheerful. How about we sing some carols?'

'You're pathetic, Ma,' replied Kraig scornfully.

'Don't talk to Mam like that, she's doing her best,' shouted Byrn, squaring up to his older brother who was almost a foot taller.

'You're pathetic, too,' sneered Kraig, shoving his little brother out of his way.

Kraig left the day after Boxing Day, and the Ellis household breathed more easily.

'I never thought I'd say this about my own son, Huw, but I'm glad he's gone. He puts everyone on edge. I don't like how extreme he's become. He thinks violence is the only solution. I'll pray for him.'

'I don't like the violence either, Wynne, but it's dragged on so long now, folks are getting desperate.'

'We're desperate, too, Huw, but I don't see you throwing bricks at coppers.'

'It's complicated, Wynne. There's fault on both sides. Let's not be too quick to judge.'

'I pray every day for an end to this madness. Cadi's not strong like Bryn. She's wheezy with the cold, and her arms are so skinny – I'm scared they'll break if she falls over. I don't know how we'll keep her warm when the worst of winter bites. If only she was well enough to go to Day Centre. There's heating and hot food for her there.'

'I think the New Year will bring a resolution, Wynne. We just have to hold on.'

New Year came and went with no resolution. It was unlike Huw to be demonstrably affectionate, but on a bitterly cold mid-January Friday morning before Bryn left for school, he pulled his youngest son into a bear hug and then knelt down to face him so their eyes were level.

'We're going to have to let Efa go, Bryn. My picket pay only just covers the little electric we can afford, and there's barely enough left to put a crust in our bellies. Cadi needs warmth and hot food. I can't feed Efa as well out of the little we have.'

'No! No! You can't! You can't! I won't let you. She can have half my food. I'll go without. Oh please, Dad. You can't send her away.'

Huw put a large hand on each of Bryn's bony shoulders. 'I'm sorry, son. It's decided. Your Mam will take her back to the farm today. The farmer says he'll have her until we're on our feet again. It might not be for long, Bryn,'

'But she's not a farm dog. She only knows how to be a house dog. She'll have to sleep outside in a kennel. She'll be miserable. *I'll* be miserable. Please, please, Dad, don't do this.'

'I'm sorry, son, I wish there was another way.'

When Bryn got to school that morning, he sought out his friend, Ronnie, at first break. For the past few Saturdays, Ronnie had been sneaking up to the coal tip at dawn and coming back before breakfast with a sack full of scavenged coal. He'd asked Bryn countless times if he wanted to come along, but Bryn had always resisted, knowing his father would disapprove of any kind of stealing or law breaking.

'Are you still going up to the tip Saturday, Ronnie?'
'Yeah. You wanna come?'
'What time?'
'I'll wait for you, bottom of your road, ten before six. Don't be late. We need to be in and out with first light. I can get you a sack, but you'll need to bring a spade.'
'Okay. I'll be there. Thanks, Ronnie.'
'What's changed your mind?'
'Stuff.'
'Stuff?'
'Stuff. Same as your stuff. Same as everyone's round here.'

The next morning, Bryn met with Ronnie as agreed. The moon was waning. Faint streaks of light filtered eerily through the branches of bare trees.

'Watch your step,' said Ronnie. 'The ground's uneven, and it's too risky to shine a torch. There's enough light if you let your eyes adjust.'

'Aren't you afraid of getting caught?' asked Bryn.

'Nah. That's why I come at this time. The cops change shifts at six. They'll be too busy clocking on and off to worry about an odd sack of coal disappearing. Besides, we'd see them coming a mile off. Plenty of time to run or dive into a coal hole.'

'Coal hole?'

'You'll see when we get onto the tip. They're all over. Holes left from where folks have dug out their coal. Most of them are big enough for someone our size to hide in.'

The two boys crawled through barbed wire that had been erected around the perimeter of the tip. Bryn was surprised to see half a dozen scavengers already busy, taking turns to dig and keep watch – mothers, grandmothers, children. Some were already dragging their sacks home, others managing full ones, the young and the old pulling as much as they could manage on a mile-long trek back to safety.

'Are we late?' asked Bryn.

'No, these are the early birds; they'll be others after us. I like to get here when there are others around. Extra pairs of eyes to keep watch for the cops.'

'I thought you said the cops never come at shift changes.'

Ronnie shrugged his reply, 'Always a first time for everything. Best to be prepared.'

Bryn looked around him as his eyes adjusted to the growing light. With its coal holes dotted around, the tip looked like a giant black Swiss cheese.

'No time to stand there gawping, Bryn, you need to get digging. We need to be out of here in twenty minutes tops.'

Ronnie started to dig and had shovelled half a sackful when he heard someone shout, 'Cop alert! Cop alert!' Dozens of scavengers dropped their sacks and started to run.

'Jump into a hole, quick, Bryn,' shouted Ronnie. 'Pull your sack in with you.'

Bryn watched as Ronnie disappeared down a coal hole, complete with sack and shovel. Bryn stood frozen to the spot. This was all alien to him. Fear or lack of guile, or perhaps a little of both, immobilised him. Try as he might, his legs would not move, his arms were glued to his spade. All the while, he could see a torch sweeping and scanning ahead of him and hear the clomping of heavy boots approaching.

'What have we here then? Trespassing and thieving coal. Theft's a crime, lad, you know that don't you?' said the stern voice of PC Owen Edwards. He turned the boy's face up into the beam of his torch and smeared away the streaks of black coal dust. 'It's young Ellis, isn't it? Does your father know you're here?'

Bryn's limbs might not be working, but the same could not be said of his mouth. 'I don't care what you do to me or how hard you hit me with your truncheon. I'm not sorry. My sister's cold. She's sick. Sick real bad. They've sent my dog back to the farm cos we can't feed her. Mam cries every day. We need that coal. I don't care if it's stealing.'

'You'd better come with me, lad. Anyone else here I should be marching off the premises?' he asked, casting his eyes about him in the growing light. Bryn shook his head. 'The others ran away. It's just me.'

Wynne wept when she saw PC Edwards escorting her youngest son into the house. He dumped the half-full sack of coal in the empty dog basket. Huw was stoic. PC Edwards' eyes fell on Cadi, huddled in a duvet by the empty fire. She was coughing badly. He went over to her and felt her forehead.

'The lass has a fever,' he said gently. 'Do you have any kindling?'

'Oh sure, a whole shed full! As if!' replied Huw bitterly.

'There's a crate that came with the food parcel,' said Wynne, rallying. 'I'll get it.'

PC Edwards broke it up into kindling, set it alight and then banked it up with some of the coal from Bryn's sack. 'Not a word about this to a living soul or I'll lose my job,' said Owen Edwards. 'And you, Ellis junior,' he said, prodding Bryn's chest with his finger, 'you stay off that tip, y'hear me? Next time, it might not be me, and some of my drafted colleagues are a bit too handy with their truncheons. They'll have you in the back of their van faster than they can blow their whistles. You must be ten by now, I'm guessing?'

'I'm *eleven*,' insisted Bryn, outraged.

'Ten's the age of criminal responsibility, so you'll be in serious trouble if you get caught.'

Before he left, Owen slipped a £5 note onto the table and said quietly to Wynne, 'Get some hot food into the lass.'

Ronnie had stayed hidden the whole time, and once the coast was clear managed to fill his sack. He came round later that morning and handed it over to the Ellis household.

'It's to say thanks for not giving me away,' he said, throwing Bryn a grateful glance.

Huw would not take it, but Wynne grabbed hold of it eagerly and put it by the hearthside. 'It's for Cadi, Huw. We can take it for Cadi,' she pleaded.

'It's stolen goods, Wynne. There's no getting round that,' he said defiantly, at which point Ronnie thought he should make a hasty exit.

'See you at school Monday, Bryn.'

'God will understand,' continued Wynne.

'*He* might, but I won't,' replied Huw. 'Enough's enough! I'll not see Cadi get any weaker. I'll not see my son turn into a common thief, and I'll not see my wife barter her principles with her God. First thing in the morning, I'm going back to work.'

'Oh Huw – are you sure? You'll be the only one. You'll be a scab. We'll be a scab family. We'll be ostracised!'

'It will be what it will be.'

Wynne was right. The Ellis family became the dog shit on the village shoe. No taxi driver would take Huw across the picket line, so he had to be taken in and brought out in a police van. Bricks were thrown through their windows, turds pushed through their letter box, and graffiti scrawled across their walls. They might have a warm house, a working Aga, Cadi well enough to attend Day Centre, and Efa back in her basket, but it came at a heavy price. Overnight, Huw went from loyal union man and upstanding member of the community to dirty, stinking scab.

Wynne found herself castigated as a scab squaw. Only the farmer and the minister befriended her alongside the occasional cloistered visit from PC Owen Edwards.

Bryn was not spared either. Not all the pupils in his class were miners' children, but there was a big enough majority to deter others from associating with him. No-one wanted to sit next to him on the bus, nor in class, if they could avoid it. They called him Scabby – even some of the teachers.

When Kraig heard about his father's defection, he hot-footed it home. Bryn came back from school to hear angry shouting coming from the kitchen.

'What the holy fuck do you think you're doing, Dad?' bellowed Kraig. 'You're a union man! All your life you've been a union man. You can't do this! You can't do this to our family. You've made the Ellis name blacker than the coal in that grate. You've turned us into scabs. What do you think it's like for me trying to hold my head up on the flying picket lines with a scab for a dad. Are you fucking crazy, dumb, or just blind stupid! You *have* to come back out on strike.'

'What's done is done, Kraig. I'll not undo it.'

'I'm going to round up the lads and bring them back to talk some sense into you.'

'The same lads who put turds through my letterbox and daubed graffiti across my door? They'll not step foot in my house till they apologise to your mother and learn how to act like human beings not animals.'

'You shame me, Dad. You hear me! You shame me. I'm going over to Megan's. That's if her dad will still let me in their house now I'm blood-tied to a scab. But I'll be back. I'm not leaving till you're out on that picket line with the rest of us. Till we win!'

'There are no winners, Kraig, not on any side.'

Efa had the misfortune to be lying in her favourite spot near the back door. Kraig kicked her savagely out of his way.

Bryn ran at his brother, screaming at him, his fists pummelling Kraig's back. 'You brute. Leave her be, you bastard brute, bastard bully. Leave her be.'

Kraig turned on his brother, who was not much above half his size, picked him up by his shirt collar, and pushed him against the wall.'

'If I ever hear you call me a bastard again, I'll knock you senseless, you hear me? I'll break every bone in your body, fucking Scabby.'

Efa snarled at the sight of her owner being manhandled and hurled herself at the larger brother, sinking her teeth into his leg. Kraig howled and kicked out at the dog, grabbing the kitchen broom that was leaning against the wall and began beating Efa with its long handle. She jumped out of the way, yelping in pain.

'Fucking scab dog!' he shouted, throwing down the broom and marching out, leaving the back door wide open behind him. He got astride his motorcycle, revved the engine as loudly as he could and drove off.

'You mean, cruel bastard. Bastard! BASTARD!' Bryn screeched after him.

Kraig, on hearing his brother's taunts, turned his bike round and rode menacingly back towards his little brother, eyes hot with fury.

'What did you call me, you fucking scab squirt?'

Efa had followed Bryn outside. On seeing the bike tearing towards her master, she bolted into the path of the motorcycle, barking furiously. Kraig swerved, but the dog had come at him too quickly and too unexpectedly to avoid a collision.

'Fucking mongrel scab!' snarled Kraig. He did not stop to check what damage had been inflicted on the collie. Yelling profanely, he turned his bike around and sped off.

'Efa! Efa!' cried a distraught Bryn as he ran to the injured dog. Wynne and Huw came dashing out from the kitchen, and Cadi peeped out from the open doorway.

Bryn knelt down and lifted Efa's head onto his knee. He could see instantly that she was dead. He wailed and wailed, stroking her broken body, tears gushing unchecked down his cheeks. Huw and Wynne tried to comfort him, but he pushed them away.

'Best let him deal with this in his own way, Wynne,' whispered Huw to his wife, pulling her back towards the house.

'Kraig bad,' muttered Cadi. 'Kraig very bad.'

Minutes later, they watched as Bryn picked up Efa and, staggering under her weight, carried her into the kitchen. He placed her in her basket and then lay down next to her with his head against her back, his hair and her fur tangled into one matted, bloodied mane.

Cadi disappeared upstairs. She came down clutching Reesa Rabbit. 'Bryn have Reesa,' she said, offering her favourite cuddly toy to her younger brother. 'Keep,' she said. 'Call Efa.'

The tears that Wynne had been holding back broke loose at the spectacle of her seventeen-year-old daughter, with a mental age of two, giving up her most precious belonging to her more precious kid brother.

Bryn accepted Reesa and held out his arms to Cadi. She lay down with him, her head on his chest, Bryn's head on Efa's back, and one hand each on the newly named cuddly rabbit huddled between them. Even stoical Huw could not keep his eyes dry.

Bryn wrapped Efa in his Dr Who bath towel. 'Perhaps Efa can be regenerated like the Doctor,' he said as he sank a spade into the cold garden turf – the same spade he had used to scavenge coal from the colliery tip. The ground was hard, and he struggled to make a deep enough hole. Wynne wanted Huw to help him, but Huw knew there were some things you just had to do – wanted to do – yourself. Afterwards, Bryn went up to his bedroom. He didn't come down to eat supper.

'Leave him be, Wynne,' said Huw. He needs to deal with this in his own way.'

Next morning, Bryn came down for breakfast, already dressed in his school uniform. It seemed he was determined to pick up and carry on. He said nothing. Wynne saw more and more of Huw in him every day. Quiet, thoughtful, stoic.

Knowing how hungry he must be, having missed supper, she got out her cast iron frying pan to make him eggs. Huw was on earlies and had left over an hour before. Cadi had finished her cereal and was looking hopefully at the appearance of the frying pan and the promise of hot vittles.

'I didn't hear Kraig come back last night,' said Bryn, 'and his bed hasn't been slept in. Just as well. I might have kicked his head in if he'd been in the bed next to me when I woke up.'

'Don't talk like that, Bryn. What Kraig did was very wrong, but violence never pays. It always ends in tragedy.'

Bryn, hungrier than he dared admit, polished off two eggs and four doorstep slices of toast. His mother was busy at the sink washing the dishes when the back door opened and Kraig strode in.

'I don't know how you've the gall to show your face in here, Kraig,' said his mother. 'You realise you killed that poor dog. You broke your brother's heart. You have to make this right, son, or there's no place for you round this table.'

'Fucking hell, Ma. It's only a dog. It ran at me like something demented, there was nothing I could do to avoid it. Anyone would think Arthur had died.'

'I don't want to hear that Scargill man's name in my kitchen. Save it for the picket line.'

'You've all gone fucking soft, that's the rub of it.'

'I'm warning you, Kraig. I *won't* have that language in my kitchen.'

'It's just a mutt, for fuck's sake. You're pathetic, Ma, soft in the head. Must be where the mongol kid gets it from.'

When Wynne heard the words 'mongol kid', it was as if something snapped in her head. Her breathing almost stopped, and her heart felt like it was going to burst. 'What did you just call your sister?' she hissed at him.

'The fucking mongol kid. Soft in the head like you. Get over it, Ma.'

Wynne flew at him. The large heavy frying pan was still in her hand, soap suds and half congealed lard dripping from its rim. She lunged at him, but Kraig grabbed the pan from her and in a moment of fury whacked it across her head. 'Soft, sick cow!' he shouted.

Not much more than half his weight, the blow knocked her off her feet and she fell sideways onto the kitchen floor.

Bryn rushed to her. 'Mam! Mam!' He could see blood beginning to trickle into the quarry tiles. 'Call an ambulance, Kraig! NOW, Kraig, call an ambulance.'

Kraig was looking on horror-struck at what he had done. He dropped the frying pan like a red-hot poker. 'She came at me!' he howled. 'She came at me!' he repeated, panic overtaking him. 'She... she...'

He stared at the reddening tiles as if punch-drunk, then sped out the back door. Bryn heard the motorbike fire up and a screech of tyres as his brother raced off.

Cadi was intermittently screaming and sobbing, unable to make sense of what had just happened. Bryn dialled 999 first and then he went to comfort her. He realised he didn't know how to get a message to his dad at the colliery.

'I'll be back in two minutes,' he said to Cadi, holding up two fingers. 'Two minutes, okay?'

'Not leave me! Not leave me!' pleaded Cadi.

'Two minutes, Cadi,' he repeated, holding up two fingers again. 'I'll be back, I promise.'

With that he raced across the garden path and banged loudly on Mrs Matthews' back door. None of their neighbours had spoken to the Ellis family since Huw had broken strike, but surely this was different. This was an emergency, and Mrs M had always been like an auntie to him until Huw's actions had made them outcasts.

Mrs Matthews answered the door. 'I've nothing to say to you, Scabby,' she said, about to close the door on him.

'Please, please,' he begged. 'Mam's unconscious, bleeding bad. I've called an ambulance. You have to help me. Please, please. I don't know how to get a message to my dad…' Bryn didn't like to add 'at the colliery' or 'at work', in case it riled her such that she wouldn't help.

'Lord Almighty!' screeched Mrs Matthews, grabbing her shawl and running after Bryn, all thoughts of scabs and strikes gone in an instant.

'We have to try and stop the bleeding,' she said when she saw her neighbour and long-time friend prostrate on the quarry tiles. 'Bandages if you have them, Bryn. If not, some tea towels.'

Mrs Matthews did her best to stem the bleeding with torn strips of tea towels. She wound them round Wynne's head and instructed Bryn to hold them as tight as he could, while she rang the colliery.

It took twenty minutes to get a message down to Huw and another half an hour to get him back through the tunnels and up the cage. He did not stop to shower or change. He ran the whole way home, arriving just as the paramedics were lifting Wynne onto a stretcher and into the ambulance.

Cadi didn't recognise her father in his dirty orange pit clothes, black coal dust smeared across his face, and she screamed anew. Bryn, who had never seen his father in pit gear either, hugged her close and tried to reassure her about the identity of the 'scary orange black man'.

PC Edwards was already on the scene.

'What's happened here, Owen?' asked Huw.

'You need to go with Wynne to the hospital. I'll stay with your young 'uns until we can get a WC up here, and then I'll come to speak to you at the hospital. But before you go, I need the licence number of Kraig's motorbike. Bryn didn't know it.'

'R198 EBL. Why do you need it?'

'I'll explain when I speak with you at the hospital. You must go now, Huw. The paramedics are ready.'

Bryn ran out after his father and grabbed his arm as he was about to climb into the ambulance. 'Kraig did this, Dad. Kraig, did it! He belted her across the head with the frying pan.'

Huw couldn't take it in. He looked bewildered as Owen pushed him gently into the ambulance.

'There's no more time, Huw. You *have* to get Wynne to the hospital,' urged Owen.

'Look after your sister, Bryn. Look after Cadi. She'll be confused and frightened,' shouted Huw to his son as the ambulance doors closed.

The ambulance sped away, lights and siren flashing. Owen picked up his police radio to call in Kraig's licence plate number and then turned back to go into the house. He didn't know what was going to be more heartbreaking, taking a statement from an eleven-year-old boy about his brother grievously assaulting his mother, or having to notify a father that his son had almost killed his wife. There were some days when this job weighed very heavy with him.

Wynne was taken straight to theatre. Huw accepted the nurses' offer of a shower and the loan of some scrubs to change into while he waited. His wife came out of theatre and was placed in intensive care. He sat by her bed, holding her hand and looking desperately at all the tubes and wires poking out of her and the machines and monitors beeping and humming around him. The doctors had told him to expect the worst.

Wynne Ruth Ellis died at a quarter to four that afternoon.

When Huw got home, Bryn was down on the kitchen floor scrubbing furiously. The police had finally finished taking their samples and photos from the crime scene and permitted him to clean up the blood stains from the tiles. He was struggling to get it all out of the grout in the grooves. He wanted it to be spotless for when his Mam came home.

'Leave that for now, Bryn. We can finish it later. I need to talk to you about your Mam.'

'She's gonna be okay, isn't she, Dad? I held the tea towel round her head as tight as I could to stop the bleeding. She'll get better, won't she, Dad?'

'Your Mam died two hours ago, Bryn. She never regained consciousness. She didn't suffer.'

Bryn fell back onto his haunches in shock. Huw lifted him to his feet and held him close. A man of few words, his reservoir was empty.

Bryn finally pulled out of his father's arms, tears still streaming down his face.

'Cadi!' he cried. 'Cadi! How do we tell Cadi? How can she possibly understand what's happened?'

'I know, son, but she has to know. It would be crueller to try and keep it from her. Where is she?'

'She's up in her bedroom. She didn't want to look at this,' he added, pointing to the wet patch on the floor.

Huw climbed the stairs wearily, only to return moments later. 'I thought you said Cadi was in her bedroom?'

'Yeah, she is. Maybe she's gone for a pee.'

'No, I checked. She's not in any of the other rooms either.'

'She must be up there, unless perhaps she's in the garden? Mrs Matthews has been looking in on us while you were

22

gone, but I don't see how she could have taken Cadi next door without me knowing.'

Father and son walked out together and knocked on their neighbour's door. Cadi was not there. Mrs Matthews addressed her response to Bryn, unwilling, still, to converse with a scab.

'Thanks for helping earlier, Mrs Matthews, it meant a lot,' said Bryn. 'Mam died two hours ago,' he added quietly, trying not to sob in front of her.

Gracie Matthews took a sharp intake of breath. Her neighbour, her long-time friend, snuffed out by her own son. In an instant, maternal feelings took over, surpassing all other hatreds and prejudices. She put her hand on Huw's arm. 'I'm so sorry, Huw,' she said and then pulled Bryn into the kind of hug only mothers know how to give.

'I had my back to the stairs when I was scrubbing the floor. She must have passed me without me hearing,' said Bryn miserably. 'It's my fault. That's all you asked me to do, Dad. Look after Cadi, you said. It's all my fault.'

'It's not your fault, son. We'll find her, don't worry.'

'Wait there while I get my coat. I'll come and help you find Cadi. She can't be far away,' said Gracie.

Huw went back inside to get a torch and coats for himself and Bryn. It was mid-January, and the heavy rain was starting to turn to sleet and hail.

The trio must have walked over a mile before they found her. She was on the main road heading away from Aberfor. 'Going hospital,' she said, when they caught up with her. 'See Mam. Give her Pengy, make her better.' She held up a bedraggled cuddly penguin to show them.

Cadi was not wearing a coat, and she was just as wet and bedraggled as Pengy. Her hands were so cold that the toy slipped from her grasp and landed on the mud-splattered road. Bryn picked it up and hung onto it for her.

Huw took off his coat and wrapped it round his daughter. 'I'll take you to the hospital tomorrow, Cadi. Mam's sleeping just now. I'll take you tomorrow. Let's get you home and into a nice hot bath.'

He and Mrs Matthews took an elbow each and steadied Cadi between them. The last quarter of a mile, Cadi could hardly put one foot in front of the other. Huw picked her up and carried her the rest of the way.

By morning she had a high fever, and the doctor diagnosed pneumonia. She was admitted to the same hospital as her mother. And suffered the same fate. The only mercy was she had been too unwell to be told of her mother's death.

'It's my fault,' wailed Bryn. 'I was supposed to look after her. It's my fault she's dead!'

'It's no-one's fault, Bryn, least of all yours.'

It was hardly credible how fast the Ellis world had imploded. In a matter of days Huw had lost a wife and daughter and gained a criminal for a son. In a matter of days Bryn had lost a mother and a sister and gained a sworn enemy for a brother.

The sympathy for the plight of the Ellis family caused a slight softening of village ill will. But precious few attended the funeral or the burial of mother and daughter in a single grave. However, there were no more letterbox turds or scab graffiti. Some of the miners still held onto their deep-seated resentment, others were prepared to at least hold a civil conversation with the Ellis widower.

Their wives were kinder, mainly because of the young, motherless boy. An innocent who now had to grow up too fast in a brutally harsh world.

The Police caught up with Kraig, and he was arrested. A trial date was set. Deemed a flight risk, he was refused bail. Huw, a shadow of his former self, visited his elder son regularly in the months that preceded the trial, trying to make sense of the horror that had unfolded. His younger son was hell-bent on seeing his brother incarcerated for a very long time. Huw's attempts to convince Bryn that Kraig had not acted out of malice fell on deaf ears.

'You weren't there, Dad. You didn't hear the poisonous things he said about Cadi. And he left Mam lying there bleeding out. HE LEFT HER! HE ABANDONNED HER! Our mother – he MURDERED our mother!'

'Murder is a very strong word to use, Bryn. You need to mean to kill someone for it to be murder. I don't think Kraig meant to kill your mother, not for a moment.'

'He left her to die. It's the same thing. How can you say it's not?'

'I think he panicked, Bryn. Try to find it in your heart to forgive him.'

'Forgive him? Never! I hate him. I hate every hair on his head. I hope they lock him up and throw away the key. Even that's too good for him. He killed Mam. Cadi died because of him – and Efa, too. I HATE him.'

At the trial, Bryn had the option to give evidence in court via a video link because he was a minor, but he chose not to. He wanted to see and hear it all for real. As the only eyewitness, he was determined to be the one to put his brother away. The prosecution wanted a murder conviction, but Kraig pleaded not guilty on the grounds of temporary insanity and self-defence.

Huw Ellis looked on desolately as Bryn's testimony systematically trashed the defence case and, with it, all hope of rebuilding any sibling affinity. Under oath, Bryn claimed Kraig had already been fired up against his mother, that it had been building up since the previous day. He testified that his mother had never hit any of her three children, and Kraig would have known he was not in danger. The frying pan just happened to be in her hand when she was shouting at him for calling his sister a 'fucking mongol kid'.

Bryn was not reticent to flag that Kraig used the offensive term not once but three times. This and his description of Kraig fleeing the scene, leaving his mother to bleed out on the kitchen floor, was more than enough for a shocked jury. The prosecution got their verdict of murder, and the judge gave out a mandatory life sentence with a fifteen-year minimum term.

As the prisoner was taken from the dock, the two brothers eyeballed each other, steely, unblinking, oblivious to the torment being heaped upon the broken man who had sired them.

The miners' strike officially ended on 3rd March, 1985, with no settlement. The hardship of the year-long dispute had finally taken its toll. When they returned to work, Huw was still ostracised by most of the miners at his colliery. They had no option but to share a cage ride with him, but few would work on the same seam as him unless they were forced to. More often than not, Huw chose to volunteer to work at the far end of the tunnel line, keeping himself to himself and getting on with the daily grind of digging out the coal.

Easter came and went. The days got longer, and the black earth got warmer. It was towards the end of April when the colliery siren was heard blaring out across the valley. It was the sound every miner's wife dreaded. All the women dropped whatever they were doing and hastened to the colliery. News was emerging that a roof had collapsed in one of the new seams. The men were gradually being pulled out; most of the injuries were from the debris of the flying rock. There was only one fatality: Huw Ellis. He had been working at the furthest end of the line and been caught in the rock fall.

Huw Ellis's funeral was a different affair from that of his wife and daughter some months earlier. A colliery death was a village bereavement. It mattered little who it was or how much he was liked; the whole village would come together in collective mourning. They all knew that someone had to work the end of the line, if it had not been Ellis, it would have been one of their own kin. Latterly denigrated and reviled in life, it was his death that precipitated the reclaiming of Huw Ellis by the mining community as one of their own.

'That poor child,' said Ffion Edwards to her PC husband, shaking her head sadly. 'Such a slight boy. Takes after his mother, bless her soul. His shoulders just aren't broad enough for this. It's too cruel. It makes me question how there can possibly be a God. What will happen to him?'

'His only living relative is his older brother, and he's banged up for a long time, so I'm afraid Bryn will have to go into care. It'll be a Children's Home first up, and it won't be easy to find a foster home for a boy on the cusp of his teenage years.'

'Couldn't we do something, Owen? Couldn't we offer to foster him? Would he come to us? Our own two have flown the nest. We have the room.'

'We have the room, sure enough, but do we have the energy, Ffion? I've only ten years to retirement, and I was looking forward to an easier life. I want you to have an easier life, too. I hadn't factored a troubled teenager into the equation.'

'He's not a teenager *just* yet, and I doubt he'd be much trouble. He seems such a quiet, studious boy.'

'All teenagers are trouble, Ffion. Remember what ours were like!'

'Pssh! A bit of rebellion is no bad thing. It's character building. We've been blessed with good fortune all our lives, we should give som—'

Ffion did not get to finish her sentence because Owen had taken her in his arms. 'You're a good, kind woman, Ffion. It's why I love you so much. I can see there'll be no shushing you on this, so I'll ring social services tomorrow and see what might be done. It will be Bryn's decision, mind.'

'Of course. I wouldn't want it any other way,' she replied, as she planted a kiss on his forehead. 'You're a good, kind man, too, Owen Edwards. Mighty good.'

PART TWO
Thirty years later

London: Saturday, 17th May, 2014

Jarrad was already seated at *Vera's Vegan* when Mia arrived. They had taken to meeting up most Saturdays for a coffee whenever his hospital shifts permitted. It was six years since he had come to London from Canada to study medicine at Kings.

Theo had asked if she could keep a watchful eye out for the once shy teenager he regarded as his 'almost grandson'. And there was nothing she would not do for Theo Kendrick – the man who had rescued her from an orphanage in war-torn Iraq twenty-four years ago. Not that watching over Jarrad had been a chore. She'd come to cherish him like the kid brother she wished she had not lost.

'Sorry if I'm late,' said Mia, bustling to the window table he had secured. 'Hope you haven't been waiting long.'

'Only just arrived,' he fibbed, getting up from his chair to greet her. At six foot five, he had to stoop to avoid banging his head and stoop even further to plant a kiss on the cheek of his diminutive friend. 'What can I get you?'

'I'll get it, Jarrad. Do you want a cake to go with that Americano?'

'No, *I'll* get it, Mia. You've got to let me pay my way. I'm earning decent money now. Besides, I still haven't touched my inheritance from Grandma. I'm perfectly solvent. You can't nursemaid me forever. I'll be twenty-five in a couple of weeks.'

Mia was about to protest that being ten years older and earning several times his salary entitled her to spoil him, but she had caught the hurt in his voice so gave way graciously. 'In that case, a green tea and a slice of carrot cake, please.'

'Coming up,' beamed Jarrad.

'So, how's A and E? Wildly hectic, I imagine,' she asked when he was seated again.

'Yes, it's pretty full on. I'm certainly getting experience at the sharp end.'

'Only two weeks left on this last rotation and then you're fully qualified. Will you go back to Canada and join your dad in general practice?'

'No way! I love London, and I like the buzz of the hospital environment. I get a chunk of leave when I finish, so I'll probably fly back home for a quick visit. But I'd like to save some of the time to get out on my bike, exploring more of England. I've hardly been out of London these six years.'

'Good for you. Do you know what you want to specialise in?'

'My heart's still with surgery, especially if there's any opportunity for research. There's so much we can do now with robotics. I need a lot more basic experience under my scrubs first.'

'It's good to have an ultimate goal, though. I was like you. I knew pretty early on that I wanted to specialise in human rights, but I still had to work my way through the generic stuff.'

'That's new,' he said, glancing out of the window and inclining his head to a nail bar across the road. 'Wasn't there last week.'

'JUST HANDS' read Mia from a makeshift sign on the door. *Express Manicures, Bargain Prices* was sprawled across the window in large, ugly lettering.

A little perturbed, Mia gazed intently at the new salon. 'Hmm. Looks a bit dodgy to me.'

'Dodgy as in…?'

'Not legit. Exploited immigrants working for peanuts. Or could be a front for sex workers. I'm probably being overly suspicious. Hazard of the day job. All the same, I think I might wander over there later and nose around a bit.'

'Do be careful, Mia. I don't like the idea of you going poking about if you really think it might be dodgy. They won't take too kindly to some legal snoop descending on them.'

'I'll be careful. I can blend into a crowd and play dumb when I have to. No-one would guess my occupation. James always says after 'the nose', my greatest asset is that people habitually underestimate me.'

Barely scraping five feet, wearing a pair of jeans slashed at the knees and a sweatshirt with two long-necked, plant-eating dinosaurs sporting a *Team Herbivore* slogan, Jarrad had to agree with her Head of Chambers. Off-duty, no-one would guess that Amira Saleem QC was a hot-shot human rights barrister.

'Well, just be careful, that's all I'm saying. There are some evil bastards out there. We had a case came in last week, a battered woman dumped in a skip. Despite our best efforts, we couldn't save her. The Police couldn't do anything. They assumed she must be an illegal immigrant. No-one came to claim the body. It was heartbreaking.'

'Possibly trafficked,' added Mia. 'I see too much of it in my line of work. It's what makes me suspicious of places like that,' she said, nodding to the nail bar over the road.

'So, how's Theo?' he asked, turning the conversation.

'He's doing a swansong keynote presentation at Princeton. He's winding up his practice in Birmingham and moving to London. He's sold his house and bought an apartment in Hammersmith.'

'Theo retire? I didn't see that one coming. And to the Big City, too. I thought if he retired anywhere, it would be to his Cumbrian paradise. It'll be great to see more of him. He's been a wonderful support to me since I came to England. Best "almost granddad" a guy could wish for.'

'Best "almost dad" a girl could wish for,' chipped in Mia. 'Darling Theo, the "almost dude". Almost a father, almost a groom, almost a grandfather. He wears the mantle very stoically. I know he misses Beth terribly, even after ten years. She left a hole I'm not sure anyone can fill.'

'It was really tragic what happened. Grandma being taken from him just two weeks before their wedding. I wish I'd got to know her better; she was a really spirited lady. So sad.'

'Yes. And very sad for your mum. Being estranged from her mother for thirty years then, when she finally found her, losing her again in no time at all.'

She paused and then added a little sheepishly, 'Theo's not planning to retire exactly. He's not dropping the sessional work he does for the Met—'

'I didn't know he was attached to the Met?' interrupted Jarrad.

'He's not. He has an old friend there he helps out from time to time – mainly traumatised victims. But his main reason for giving up his Birmingham clinic work is so he can help me in a venture I'm putting together.'

'Sounds intriguing. Tell me more.'

'I was going to tell you once the final pieces were in place, but as we've just been talking about it, I might as well spill the beans.'

'We've just been talking about that nail bar. It's nothing to do with manicures, is it? I can't see Theo running a beauty salon!'

It was a comical image that made Mia smile momentarily. 'No, although thinking about it, one of its outlets *could* involve manicures.'

'You've completely lost me, just cut to the chase, will you?'

'Trafficked victims.'

'Trafficked victims?'

'I had a sizeable sum of money languishing in a dusty bond. You might not know this, but Theo was a foreign correspondent – investigative journalism – before he became a clinical psychologist. That's how he came to rescue me in Iraq all those years ago. The obliteration of my village was an atrocity committed by the allied forces and covered up. I was the only survivor. I lost my entire family. Theo threatened to go public with graphic evidence of the atrocity unless the Home Secretary agreed to a compensation package for me: British citizenship, international school fees, and a monthly allowance until I turned twenty-one.'

Jarrad whistled his astonishment. 'I knew about some of that from Mum, but I don't think even she knew about the Home Secretary part. He's one cool dude is our Theo.'

'I was only ten at the time. I never touched the allowance. It felt like hush money at best, blood money at worst. Theo invested it for me. After nearly twenty-five years, it was worth a tidy sum and I wanted to put it to good use. So, I've set up *The Lotus Hub Foundation* and am hoping to open the first *Lotus Hub* soon. I've bought a property in Finsbury.

'It will be a place of refuge and opportunity for women who have survived being trafficked. One part of it will be a residential wing to house victims for at least the duration of their statutory recovery and reflection period. The other part will be a hub offering all manner of support they might require to rebuild their lives. So, you see, there's no reason to discount manicure training if there was a perceived need for it.'

'What's a statutory recovery and reflection period?'

Mia slipped effortlessly into legalese. 'The Council of Europe's Convention on Action Against the Trafficking of Human Beings specifies a minimum period of thirty days when trafficked individuals are treated as victims. It allows them to experience a period of security and safety away from the influence of their traffickers while they receive assistance and support. Crucially, during this statutory period they can't be deported.'

'What's with the reflection bit?'

'It protects them from undue pressure and enables them to make informed choices about whether they want to cooperate with the authorities. Most of them do, but not all. Some are so badly traumatised they can't face having it all raked over. Many distrust the authorities and are terrified of being deported. I've represented dozens of trafficked women appealing against deportation. It's a very harrowing process for them, housed in overcrowded asylum holding units which do little to alleviate their already traumatised lives. Attempted suicides are not uncommon.

'It may be a drop in the ocean, Jarrad – the first *Lotus Hub* will only be able to house eight women at a time – but if it can provide an oasis of tranquillity and help rebuild the lives of even a few, it will be a good thing. A fitting use of the blood money. And if I can make a success of it, I'm hopeful that other *Lotus Hubs* will spring up elsewhere.'

'Wow, Mia, that sounds awesome. If we'd managed to save the woman from the skip, I'd like to think there might have been a *Lotus Hub* for her.'

'Yes. She's exactly the sort of woman we would hope to be able to help. It's the hubbing that's important. Having the contacts and the access to a host of opportunities for them. Theo and I have been gathering quite an army of illustrious volunteers willing to offer their expertise once we're up and running. I've cleared all the legal hurdles and am just waiting for planning consent to go through on the property. The initial response from the Council has been very positive, but there's the public consultation to navigate yet. If that goes well, we should be ready to take our first ladies very soon.'

'I don't know what to say, Mia. Part of me is so proud of you; it's such an awesome thing to do. And part of me is mega pissed.'

'Pissed? At me?'

'Yeah, Mia. Seriously pissed. I thought we were friends—'

'But we are, Jarrad. *Good* friends,' she interrupted.

'So why haven't you told me about this before, asked *me* to help? Why haven't you asked *me* if I want to volunteer?'

'But you've got your work cut out at the hospital. You get precious free time as it is, and you should be spending it out with friends your own age. Clubbing, partying – wheeling. That's what you say in Canada, isn't it – 'wheeling'?'

'Don't wriggle, Mia. Just come out and say it.'

'Say what?'

'That I'm not *illustrious* enough. Too young, too inexperienced to have anything to offer. Perhaps you should come down to A and E one of these days and see just how much grown-up shit I wade through.'

Mia was a little taken aback by the ferocity of this outburst from the generally mild-tempered Jarrad. 'I'm sorry. I didn't realise you felt this strongly. I guess I still think of you as a kid brother, and I've somehow missed the—'

'Can we agree to ditch the baby bro shit?'

Again, Mia was a little taken aback by the rancour she detected but did not want to fan the flames. 'Yes, of course. Yes, noted. I'll try harder.'

'I'm sorry, Mia, that was crass of me. You've been so good to me, *are* so good—'

'It's fine, Jarrad. We all need to let off steam sometimes. Of course you can volunteer at the *Lotus Hub*, if that's what you want. But please understand that most of these traumatised women only trust female doctors. It's not personal, it's—'

'I *know* that, Mia. I'm not completely insensitive, however green you think I am. I don't have to volunteer as a doctor. I'm pretty handy with a paintbrush or a garden spade, and if you're offering life skills training, I could help with IT or such like.'

'That's terrific, Jarrad, but I meant what I said, you really should be out playing hard as well as working hard.'

'You talk as if you're some grand old aunt in her dotage when you're only just hitting thirty-five yourself. I don't see *you* out playing hard.'

'Well, it's different for me.'

'Different how?' grilled Jarrad.

'I've never wanted that kind of life, I—'

'Pots and kettles,' he insisted, with a slight raise of his eyebrows.

Mia smiled and held up her hand in appreciation of being outmanoeuvred. She eased back into her chair to study him more closely. She had enjoyed having a 'pseudo kid brother' so much that she'd clearly missed his promotion to the big league. A resolute set of his jaw and a steeliness in his deep brown eyes belied the lanky slenderness, the large hands, and long slim fingers she had previously associated with the callowness of youth.

'Does the lotus have any special significance for you?'

'More it's significance for the trafficked women I am trying to help.'

'How do you mean?'

'The roots of a lotus can survive the filthiest water and still produce exquisite flowers.'

'Ah yes, I see how symbolic that is. As I said, I think it's wonderful, Mia. I have some news of my own.'

'Oh? Do tell.'

'Anna is coming to London. In fact, she's probably arrived by now.'

'Anna! How come? I thought she was in New York?'

'Yeah, she was. Apparently, some London theatre owner spotted her on Broadway and has offered her a starring role in his new production.'

'Do theatre owners do that?'

'From all accounts, he's a pretty hands-on owner – likes to call the shots. He underwrites all the productions, so I suppose he's entitled to have a say. Or that's what Anna told me anyway.'

'That's great for you but sad for your parents. They must have been hoping she'd go home after the Broadway run. I'm sure they were hoping you'd go home after you qualify, too. Now they might lose both of you to London.'

'Mum and Dad still have the cottage in Cumbria that Grandma left them, so I imagine they will come over more often now.'

'It's been lovely as always, Jarrad, but I have to get my head round a brief before Monday, so should be heading off. I'm going running Thursday evening if you want to join me.'

'Sorry, I can't. I'm on lates.'

'Ciao for now, then. I'm going to drop in for an express manicure before I head home.'

'Do be careful, Mia.'

'I will,' she replied, planting a kiss on his cheek.

Jarrad felt uneasy and decided to hang around until he saw Mia had safely navigated her express manicure. He ordered another Americano and took up his vigil by the window. Ten minutes later he jumped out of his seat and sped out, knocking over a chair in the process, and spilling some unsuspecting customer's honey rooibos into her lap. A startled waitress followed him to the door.

He had spotted a pregnant woman dash out of the nail bar in some distress and run into the path of an oncoming telecoms van. The sound of screeching brakes was deafening as the van swerved to try and avoid her but couldn't. She was thrown by the impact and landed headfirst on the pavement.

Jarrad was first to reach the scene. Mia, who had rushed out from the nail bar, was close behind him.

'Ambulance, Mia!' ordered Jarrad, as he knelt down to attend to the casualty. A slick of blood was already seeping out from her head.

Mia dialled emergency services from her mobile while Jarrad checked for a pulse and shook his head gravely. Shocked crowds had gathered around in no time.

'She's gone, I'm afraid,' he pronounced, pointing at the rapidly growing pool of blood. 'CPR can't help her now and would waste valuable minutes when I could try and save the baby. The mother's head has taken most of the impact. There might still be time.'

He pulled away her dress just enough to expose her pregnant belly. Taking a Swiss army knife from his pocket, he flicked open the blade. He took a few seconds to assess the contours of the womb, feel the position of the baby, steady his hands, and then he made a clinical incision large enough to pull the baby out.

Within seconds of making her undignified entry into the world, the tiny baby girl let out a feeble cry that drew spontaneous cheers from onlookers. Just as spontaneously, the cheers died to a respectful hush as people realised the miraculous birth was accompanied by a tragic death.

'She's very prem,' said an anxious Jarrad as he cut the umbilical cord.

Mia pulled off her sweatshirt to wrap it around the tiny infant.

'Do you have some towels?' he asked, turning to the waitress who had followed him out. She came back with an armful of towels with which to swaddle the newborn and a tablecloth to afford the corpse some dignity.

The Police arrived first, an ambulance moments later. Jarrad sat at the side of the road, wiping his blood-stained hands on one of the towels. The paramedics checked there was nothing they could do for the mother and then sped off with the infant. It was only then that Mia remembered the nail bar.

'The other girls!' she shouted at the two constables. 'We have to help them. There are three others in there. I think they are being kept against their will,' insisted Mia.

PC Zabhir Ahmed followed her to the salon, but the shop door was locked. 'Stand back,' he ordered as he kicked the door open.

There was no-one inside. Four manicure stations were positioned on a work bench. A receptionist podium stood empty. The occupants must have left in a hurry, because two of the chairs had been knocked over, and there were lurid puddles splattered across the floor where jars of nail varnish had smashed onto the floor.

Pulling out his truncheon, PC Ahmed slowly turned the handle of a door located behind the manicure stations. It opened onto a lobby with a windowless utility station off it, with a sink, washer-dryer, kettle, and microwave. Inside a wall cupboard were a few pieces of mismatched crockery. There was a rear door and a flight of stairs.

The rear door was partially ajar and he kicked it wide open and peered into an alleyway where somebody – or somebodies – had likely made a hasty retreat. He climbed the stairs cautiously. Off the landing was a small shower room and one bedroom. It housed four narrow beds. A few clothes were folded on top of a chest of drawers next to a compact wardrobe. There were bars on the window.

Zabhir flicked open his radio. 'PC Ahmed reporting in with an update on the incident at Hepworth Road. This is no ordinary RTA. I think we're looking at a human exploitation set-up of some kind. Can you pass it up asap? The victims are not long gone so the trail is still warm.'

He returned to the salon where Mia was crouched down, looking at the broken nail polish bottles scattered across the floor.

'Please don't touch anything, Miss. This is a crime scene. Forensics are on their way, and it's being passed up to SCD9 – er, sorry, Human Exploitation and Organised Crime Command.'

'New Scotland Yard?'

'Yes.'

'I suspected the girls might have been trafficked – I'm a human rights barrister, so know a bit about this sort of thing.'

'You might be right, Miss, but we can't be sure yet. The trail is still warm, so if you wouldn't mind hanging on until SCD9 get here, they will want to interview you.'

It was thirty minutes later when two detectives arrived from the Specialist Crime Directorate. Zabhir made himself known to them. 'Me and WPC Blackwell were first on the scene, sir.'

'DCI Bryn Ellis, SCD9,' replied the senior officer, 'and this is my sergeant, Jake Freeman.'

'My station DS is over there, sir, talking to the doctor, and my colleague is interviewing the van driver. The back-up team have cordoned off the area and are taking statements in the crowd and surrounding properties. The nail bar witness is inside the shop, sir. It's warmer for her there. She knows not to touch anything, and Chrissy – er – WPC Blackwell is with her.'

Bryn nodded his thanks and walked purposefully to the site where the dead mother was lying. Kneeling on the pavement, Bryn slowly lifted the tablecloth to inspect the corpse.

'The pathologist should be here before too long, sir,' informed Zabhir, as he launched into a summary of what had happened that morning.

Bryn replaced the tablecloth respectfully. 'Let's take a look inside, Jake,' he instructed his sergeant.

Bryn saw her immediately. She was standing near the reception podium, eyes cast down, deep in thought. Despite the ambient temperature, she was shivering in a thin bloodstained T-shirt sporting a *Powered by Plants* logo. His slight misstep was imperceptible to all but his beating heart which was now pounding in his chest. In seconds he had recovered his composure. He introduced himself to WPC Blackwell and then pulled some change out of his pocket.

'I think Ms Saleem could do with a hot drink, Chrissy. Perhaps you could get one from that place across the road, please. Is it still green tea, Mia?' he asked, turning to face her.

She looked up with a start at the sound of her name from a voice she recognised.

'Jake, could you check upstairs first while I take some details from this witness.'

Chrissy Blackwell headed towards *Vera's Vegan*. She did not know what was more surprising: that a DCI from a Scotland Yard special unit had addressed her by her first name; that he had used the word 'please'; or that he appeared to know the witness.

In contrast, Mia's surprise was not a pleasant one. After the trauma of the morning, the last thing she wanted was to come face-to-face with a ghost – nay, a demon – from her past. They were suddenly alone in the room, and it unnerved her.

'Hello, Mia,' he said, as he emptied his jacket pockets before draping it round her shoulders, holding her gaze a fraction longer than necessary. 'How've you been?'

'Don't you have a job to do? Isn't that more important than inane chit-chat?' she answered cuttingly.

'Same old Mia, I see. It's been almost seven years. People can change, you know.'

'*Some* people,' she replied coldly.

She was spared a response by Jarrad appearing at the door with PC Ahmed, just as Jake Freeman returned from upstairs. 'I think you'd better come and see this, Guv.'

'You two stay put,' said Bryn addressing Mia and Jarrad. 'I have questions for both of you.'

Upstairs, he took in the woeful sight that awaited him.

'This doesn't look good,' said Jake, pointing to the bars on the window. 'Do you think they've been trafficked?'

Bryn nodded bleakly. 'Most probably. We'll need our own forensics on this one. We can't afford to let the trail go cold. Looks like it's a small operation, possibly a splinter group – or the crumbs from a bigger cell. The more amateurish, the better for us. They're more likely to make mistakes.'

'I'll get onto it, Guv. Pretty awesome what that young medic did, by all accounts, don't you think? Saving the baby that way.'

'Maybe. We still have to establish that the woman was actually dead before he launched into his heroics. A postmortem will tell us all we need to know. I'd like you to see where that alley leads, Jake, and check if they dropped anything behind.'

'Right-o. I'm on my way.'

Returning to the ground floor, Bryn approached the two civilians now waiting just inside the broken door. Jarrad had his arm protectively round Mia, who was still shivering despite Bryn's jacket.

'Detective Chief Inspector Bryn Ellis,' he announced, showing his lanyard to the lanky young man who dwarfed him by about half a foot.'

'Jarrad Adams.'

'I'm going to need you to go down to the station with WPC Blackwell, sir, and make a statement under caution.'

'WHAT!' screeched Mia. 'Under *caution!* What the hell do you mean? His quick thinking just saved an infant's life. How can you talk of interviewing him *under caution?*'

'Until we have the results of the postmortem, we can't know definitively if the woman was dead before Dr Adams cut her open. He may have contributed to her death.'

'She was *definitely* dead. I saw it. Her head was smashed against the pavement, there was a pool of blood the size of a lake. He checked her neck pulse first. I saw him. I saw him check her pulse and shake his head. She was definitely dead, I tell you.'

'It's alright, Mia. Don't fret,' said Jarrad. 'It'll be fine. It's just procedure. I'll go with your officer, Chief Inspector.'

'If you're being interviewed under caution, I'm coming with you. You're entitled to legal representation,' declared Mia angrily.

'You can't represent him, Mia, you're a material witness,' said Bryn. 'We'll get the duty solicitor onto it.'

'Well, I'm coming with you, Jarrad. Even if I can't sit in on the interview, I'm coming with you. I'll be camping outside the door until you're released.'

'I need you here, Mia. I need you to go through every detail of what happened in this room before the tragedy occurred.'

'It's okay, Mia, really,' assured Jarrad. 'You need to do what the chief inspector says.'

'That would be a first,' muttered Bryn, and Mia shot him an indignant glare.

'You're doing this to spite me.'

'Don't be ridiculous, Mia. I'm just doing my job.'

When Chrissy had taken Jarrad away, Bryn's tone became gentler. 'Jarrad will be okay, Mia. Sounds like he did a heroic thing, but we have to follow procedure. I'm sure the postmortem will clear him. Are you two an item?'

'Excuse me!' she retorted angrily. 'What do you take me for? He's ten years younger than me and the nearest I have to a kid brother.'

'He's clearly besotted with you, that was plain enough.'

'Don't be absurd. We're just good friends. Can we just get this over with? This is a very uncomfortable situation, not of my choosing.'

'I'm sorry, Mia. I have a job to do. I don't mean to cause you distress.'

'Distress! What would you know about distress! You humiliated me in front of all the people who mattered in my life.'

Bryn bit his lip. He had no answer.

'Is this why you're back after ghosting me for nearly seven years? To taunt me, humiliate me some more?'

'No, no, of course not! I thought it was long enough for me to be away, that you'd have moved on.'

'You disappeared off the face of the earth. No-one knew whether you were dead or alive! Although I, for one, hoped it was the former.'

Bryn winced, trying not to show how much the jibe stung. 'Given what happened, I thought it best to apply for a transfer. I've been with Manchester Vice Division until eight months ago when I was approached about this post at New Scotland Yard, heading up a project unit in SCD9. It was a big opportunity for me, and I didn't expect our paths to cross. It wasn't like I was coming back to my old station or would be bumping into you in Crown Court every few months. This job is more of a specialist co-ordinating role. You being here, this case, well it's… it's… just a "happenchance", an unexpected happenchance.'

'You wanted to know if I'd moved on. Yeah, sure I have. Do you think I would spend six years mooning over a loser like you? The day you *abandoned* me, I wiped you, Bryn Ellis, like those *Men in Black* with their memory-erasing widgets.'

'I've moved on, too. I'm getting married in six months.'

It was Mia's turn to try to disguise her injured feelings. 'Who's the poor sod who's going to be saddled with you?'

'Her name's Susan. She's a receptionist in an estate agents. She's… she's uncomplicated. She's down to earth, grounded, wants the ordinary things in life, a nice house, a couple of kids, a cat purring on her knee. I want a shot at those things, too. She's good for me.'

'And I wasn't?' she retorted, hating herself for giving into a momentary twinge of jealousy.

'You were *too* good for me, Mia. I didn't deserve you. Anyway, water under the bridge and all that. Perhaps we could be friends.'

'We can't ever be friends, Bryn Ellis. Not ever.'

'Okay, if that's the way you want it,' he replied sadly. 'Let's get on with the task in hand. Talk me through every detail.'

'I'd been having a coffee with Jarrad at *Vera's*. Jarrad is Theo's sort-of grandson.'

'Theo! How is he? Top man, Theo. One in a million.'

'He's fine, good, not that it's anything to you now...'

'*He* might still want to be my friend. Not everyone is—'

'He's not the one who got humiliated,' she interrupted him hotly. 'Do what you like. What do I care.'

'You were saying... you were having a coffee with Dr Adams.'

'Yes. We noticed a nail bar had sprung up across the road, out of nowhere. My nose was telling me it might be dodgy, so I wandered over on the pretext of getting a manicure, to see what I might find out. It was busy. These low budget pop-up places often are. All four manicurists were occupied, so I sat down on one of the waiting chairs. That suited me, as it gave me more time to observe.

'I'd only been sitting there maybe ten minutes when one client's treatment finished, and she went to pay the receptionist. A bit of an altercation ensued because she wanted to pay by credit card and the receptionist was insisting it was cash only. I got up and waded in. I started quoting chapter and verse on retail and consumer law and requirements to clearly display cash-only notices, etc. It was getting quite heated. Our manicurist must have seized this opportunity while her minder was distracted to make a run for it.

'By the time I clocked what was happening, it was all over and Jarrad was sprinting out of *Vera's*. Until then, I hadn't realised she was pregnant. I don't think the van driver had a chance. He must be in bits, poor guy. You know the rest. Jarrad was awesome. It's despicable you treating him like some criminal.'

'We're not, Mia. We're just trying to establish all the facts. Would you recognise the receptionist woman again if you saw her?'

'Oh yes! Absolutely!'

'Good. We will need you to come down to the Yard this afternoon and look through some mug shots,'

'Why not now?'

'Because you need to go home and put on some warm clothes and recover. You may get delayed shock from an incident like this. Would you like an officer to take you home?'

'Don't baby me, you condescending prick. I can get myself home. Here's your jacket,' she added, pulling it off.

'I think you need it more than I do just now. You can return it when you come in this afternoon,' he said, replacing it gently around her shoulders. He pulled a business card out of his wallet.

'You've got to be kidding!' she exclaimed as he tried to offer it to her.

'Please, Mia, don't make this personal. You're a material witness in what might be the bottom rung of an organised vice racket. Take it… please… just in case. If you think you're in any danger, call me. Day or night – *call me*.'

She was about to retort 'over my dead body' until she realised the sinister black humour it inferred. Instead, she took the proffered card and crumpled it theatrically before pushing it into the back pocket of her jeans.

Back in her apartment, showered and dressed in warm clothes, she rang Jarrad to see if he had been released. Then she made a long-distance call to Theo.

'It's outrageous, Theo! Jarrad did an awesome thing, a wonderful thing. You should've seen him; you'd have been so proud. And he's got to wait till the result of the postmortem – God knows how long that will take! – to know if he's in the clear or facing a manslaughter charge. It's despicable. There must have been a dozen witnesses besides me who saw the pool of blood, saw that she was dead before he got the baby out.'

'Is he being kept in custody?' asked an anxious Theo.

'No, they released him under caution. He had to surrender his passport, though. Can you believe it!'

'I'm sure it's just standard procedure and the postmortem will clear everything up. Sorry, Mia, but I have to go. I'm on a flight from JFK tonight. I'll call round to see you tomorrow. Get plenty of rest. And stop worrying. It's going to be fine. I promise.'

Early that afternoon Mia made her way to New Scotland Yard, as instructed, and was shown to one of the interview rooms. It was DS Freeman who entered with a folder and a laptop under his arm. She had expected it would be Bryn and couldn't quite suppress a feeling of annoyance that she had been passed onto his sergeant. As it turned out, she was not able to identify anyone from their database.

'It was worth a shot,' said Jake. 'At least we have suspects we can discount. And we can mock up an e-fit from your excellent description of the receptionist. Thank you for coming in, Ms Saleem.'

7

Saturday Evening

Anna was peering over the balcony of her penthouse suite, dreamily taking in the London night vista, pinching herself that this was actually happening. Had she really been talent spotted from the chorus line on Broadway to star in a London theatre production? If it wasn't a dream, it must be a fairytale. Don had arranged for her to be flown over from New York and given exclusive use of his own penthouse suite in his apartment tower block just a stone's throw from the Pearl Theatre. He'd said he had other places to stay, and although he didn't volunteer it, she suspected one of them might be a large country pile somewhere on the outskirts of London.

He'd told her she had a great voice – he must have been listening attentively, because she only had two solo lines in the Broadway musical – and that she was the most beautiful goddess he had ever seen. Anna was used to men complimenting her on her looks and her six-foot model figure, though no-one had ever called her a goddess before. She was quite taken with Don Kavanagh. He was so *English*, with his Saville Row suits and silk ties – and a philanthropist, too. He had explained about The Pearl being a small, not-for-profit theatre where he was able to indulge his passion for the Arts, support lesser-known artists, and stage avant-garde productions. Don Kavanagh had promised to make her a star. An overnight sensation.

Anna was waiting for the clock to tick over a few more minutes so she could FaceTime Rosie. This seven-hour time difference to Canada was most inconvenient. She was dying to tell her bestie just how wonderful this all was. They had been buddies since Elementary school. As close as sisters; closer than she was to her nerdy kid brother.

She and Jarrad (she called him 'His Worthiness' even to his face) were chalk and cheese. Despite him being two years younger, he wore the mantle of a disapproving older brother, unapologetically dismissive of her stage ambitions. 'His Worthiness' had, of course, followed their father into medicine. No prizes for guessing that script!

Anna and Rosie had both majored in English, and although they had gone their separate ways – Anna to the stage, and Rosie to a less glamorous career in teaching – the expediency of social media enabled them to stay in daily touch. As the clock edged towards midnight, she reached for her mobile, confident Rosie would be home from school by now.

'Rosie!' squealed Anna when she saw her friend's face flicker onto the screen. 'Oh, Rosie, I think I've died and gone to heaven. I'm in a dream world.'

'Woah, Anna. Steady on. I can only cope with princess dreams on a full stomach.'

'Well, first up. This penthouse suite. Isn't it heavenly?' she said, panning her mobile round the room and out onto the balcony. 'And look, Rosie, these flowers. So *romantic*.'

'Nice,' came an unruffled response.

'And he's taking me to dinner tomorrow night to meet some of his friends. I expect they'll be theatre luvvies, perhaps famous ones, you never know.'

'Nice.'

'He's so attentive, so exquisitely turned out – a gentleman, Rosie. A real *English* gentleman.'

'How old is he?'

'Why is that important?' asked Anna sharply.

'Just curious. Married?'

'How would I know? What kind of question is that?'

'The kind a best pal asks when her friend has her head turned.'

'You're just jealous, Rosie Aldridge.'

'Not jealous, just curious. Be careful, Anna, that's all I'm saying. You don't know anything about him. Not really.'

'I know that he thinks I'm a goddess – he told me so.'

'So, tell me about the play and what's your part? Have you started rehearsals yet?'

'It's not a play, it's a musical. *A Clockwork Orange*. You won't have heard of it, but apparently it's a famous film from yonks ago by a famous director. I forget his name. It won lots of awards.'

'Stanley Kubrick.'

'What are you on about, Rosie?'

'Stanley Kubrick was the director of *A Clockwork Orange*. It was actually based on a famous book.'

'Okay. Right, well—'

'Anna, do you know what *A Clockwork Orange* is about?' interrupted Rosie.

'I haven't done a script reading yet, if that's what you mean. I get that day after tomorrow…'

'It's just that… well… didn't you say you were to have a starring role?'

'Don said he had a *special* role for me that would make me a star. It's a musical, so I get to sing.'

'I don't recall any big female parts in the film. The main characters are marauding punk youths… unless it's… I can't remember her name, the wife who… Anna, what part ARE you playing?'

'I told you I'll know that on Monday when I meet the Director.'

'Anna, seriously, don't do anything you're not comfortable with, PLEASE,' she begged.

'You're such a fusspot, Rosie. It will be fine. Better than fine. I'm going to be a star.'

8

Sunday, 18th May, 2014

When Mia's bell rang at 3pm, she rushed to the door thinking it was Theo, only to find Bryn standing there.

'Oh... I thought it was going to be someone else,' she said, unable to hide her disappointment.

'I'm returning your sweatshirt,' said Bryn. 'It's been laundered.'

'You could have sent a PC with that, or had it couriered. Somewhat below your pay grade, I would have thought,' she mocked.

'Yes, I could, but I thought it might be one of your favourites,' he said, fingering the graphic of a long-necked diplodocus. 'And because the results of the postmortem are in. I got it fast-tracked. I thought you might appreciate knowing sooner rather than later.'

Mia was so desperate to know the outcome that she flung the door open without thinking. Regaining her composure, she stood in front of an upholstered ottoman in her apartment entrance hall, and he moved just inside her front door.

He had inherited none of his father's or his brother's athletic good looks. His average height, averagely brown hair, and average build cut an unremarkable figure against the solid wooden door he had just closed behind him. She did not invite him to step in any further. The surroundings were unfamiliar. She had obviously moved from the apartment they had shared for nearly two years.

'And?' she demanded.

'Dr Adams is in the clear. The pathologist confirmed a massive brain injury. Death would have been instantaneous.'

Mia flopped onto the nearby ottoman with relief.

'There's something else,' said Bryn.

'What?' she replied impatiently. 'Do you *have* to work on a Sunday?' She realised what a fatuous remark it was. He was married to the job, worked all hours. She'd had two years of it.

'We haven't managed to identify her yet. DNA and genetic analyses will take a while longer, but we're pretty sure she was a trafficked victim. The pathologist's best guess at ethnicity is Syrian, given the huge exodus of refugees since the outbreak of the civil war there. Do you recollect any Syrian cases from your human rights work? Anything that might give us an early lead?'

'I'll look through my notes to see what I can turn up. Did the baby survive?' she added suddenly.

'Yes. She'll be in an incubator for a while yet, born at thirty-two weeks, but is doing as well as we can hope. The nurses have called her Miranda because of her miraculous birth.'

'You'd think they could come up with something more ethnically appropriate than *Miranda,*' she countered tersely.

'Give them a break, Mia. They're nurses, not genealogists. They do an amazing job in very challenging circumstances,' he admonished.

'If that's all, Chief Inspector, I have work to do,' she snapped, more affected by the rebuke than she cared to admit.

He placed her sweatshirt on the hall console, carefully smoothing it out. With one hand on the door latch, he half turned to face her.

'As I said yesterday, this was a happenchance. When the case is over, I doubt our paths will cross again. Have a good life, Mia. You're so driven, so unflinchingly fearless, so convinced you're always right. I'm not sure you know how to be happy, but it's what I wish for you – more than anything in the world, Mia. I want you to be happy.'

And then he was gone.

She was glad to be seated, otherwise her knees might have buckled. His impossibly tender voice with its soft Welsh overtones had caught her off guard and stung her to the quick. That firm jaw oozing integrity, that open stance that paraded confidence without any hint of swagger. She remembered it all. And she remembered how much it hurt to remember.

※※※※※

Later that afternoon

Theo's plane was delayed, and he did not make it to Mia's until five o'clock.

'Oh Theo, that poor woman. It was truly awful,' groaned Mia before he was hardly into her entrance hall.

'Are you really okay?' asked Theo.

'Yes, yes, I'm fine,' she answered impatiently. 'There were three other women, Theo. I fear there could be more.'

'Let the Police do their job, and we'll do what we can from our end – from the *Lotus Hub* end. I secured lots more donation promises while I was networking at the conference. Some quite substantial ones.'

'That's great, Theo. I think you said we were up to £720k.'

'If these come through, it should take it close to a million.'

'Oh wow! Amazing!'

'There's lots of support out there. I truly believe in time there will be more *Lotus Hubs* beyond Sycamore Avenue.'

'I do hope so.'

'Is Jarrad okay? I was going to call on him tomorrow. What shift is he on?'

'He's on lates this week. He's okay now the postmortem has cleared him. He wants to volunteer, too.'

'Volunteer?'

'At the *Lotus Hub*.'

'But he can't have any time, surely?'

'That's what I told him, but he seems determined. Have you heard the news about Anna?'

'Yes, her mother rang me while I was in the States – asked me to keep an eye out for her like I've done for Jarrad.'

'Hmm. Anna is a whole different kettle of fish! Extremely headstrong, as I remember.'

'She's still young. Enjoying life. Plenty of time to fold in her wings and get grounded.'

'Excuse me! She's twenty-seven. When I was twenty-seven, I was—'

'Not everyone's like you, Mia,' he interrupted.

She caught a hint of censure in his voice. 'Like how?' she challenged.

'Intense… intolerant…'

'Oh, but I…' she gasped and realised she did not know how to respond.

'Amazing and incredible, too,' he said a little more gently.

'I don't know how you can say such mean things, Theo,' she retorted, hurt stinging her voice.

'I can say them because no-one else will. Not since—' He was about to say *not since Bryn*, but stopped himself in time.

'Not since what?' she confronted him.

'Not since nothing,' he responded. 'I just wish you would let more people see the wonderful person hiding behind those porcupine prickles.'

'Not since Bryn. That's what you were going to say, wasn't it? Not since Bryn!'

'Let's not go there, Mia. I know you're still hurting, however much you pretend oth—'

'He turned up like a bad penny yesterday,' she butted in miserably.

'Bryn? Bryn Ellis? How come?'

'He's the DCI on this case. Some specialist new role at Scotland Yard. Back from a long spell on vice up in

Manchester. Getting married – to some estate agent person.' She could scarcely disguise the disdain in her voice as she reeled off this resumé as if it were a grocery list.

'Good for him. Sounds like he's turned his life around.'

'I'll believe it when I see it.'

'Give the guy a break, Mia, he's—'

'He broke my heart, Theo. I can't forgive him for that.'

Theo turned her to face him. 'Wasn't it you who gave me a lecture on Schopenhauer?'

'I think you're confusing me with Nasim, he was…'

'No, Mia, I'm not. Your foster father was my great friend and a fine historian who taught you well, but he had to have a willing pupil. Compassion has been your moral compass all your adult life. It's what makes you give half your time over to pro bono work. It's why you're using your compensation pot to set up the *Lotus Hub Foundation,* instead of buying yourself some luxury villa in the Caribbean. This is you, Mia, it's who you are, and more people would see it if you didn't work so hard to hide it. Forgiveness is part of the compassion package, too, isn't it?'

'Can't you give it a rest, Theo? Ever the psychologist, always analysing people,' she said angrily.

'You're not people, Mia, you're…' he stopped mid-sentence when he saw that Mia was weeping. He took her in his arms. 'What is it, Mia? Tell me? I hardly ever see you cry. What is it?'

'I miss them so much.'

'Nasim and Guita?'

She nodded. 'They were so gentle and kind. And they were so proud of me… and they… they understood my prickles. I don't suffer fools gladly, Theo, you know that. You say I'm compassionate, but you're wrong. It's only for the needy. I have no patience with incompetents, and I abhor weakness. I'm not a nice person, whatever your rose-coloured spectacles tell you.'

'I've never suffered with pink vision,' he replied, 'not even with Beth. I loved her in spite of all her faults – and they were many. This is more than delayed grief at the passing of Nasim and Guita, isn't it?' he asked gently.

'It's him coming back suddenly like that. It caught me off balance. I couldn't help feeling jealous that he'd found someone else. That he was going to play happy families with someone else. Have kids with someone else. It's ridiculous! I mean, the guy's a loser, a commitment-phobe, a weak spineless loser. And then I had these really mean, wicked thoughts.'

'What kind of thoughts?'

'Wishing he'd died. That he'd got shot in a heroic stakeout or the like, so that I could have something to feel proud of and finally lay him to rest, finally get him out of my head. You see, I told you I wasn't a nice person.'

Theo hugged her closer and stroked her long black hair. 'You're human like the rest of us, Mia. Try to forgive him. It will get easier if you can forgive him. It will help you move on. It's been nearly seven years. You're almost thirty-five. You need to move on, Mia. Promise me you'll try.'

She nodded and pulled out the handkerchief he housed in his left trouser pocket to blow her nose, careful to avoid the right because she knew it was where he kept Beth's toy soldier in a small velvet pouch. It was always with him. She suspected it even went under his pillow at night.

Mia took a deep breath, smiled at him and rested her head on his shoulder.

'I was always surprised that you never let Nasim and Guita adopt you, they were both very keen as I remember.'

'My family name, Saleem, is all I have left of my roots. My whole family, my whole village were wiped out in that atrocity. Our homes destroyed, our animals burnt to cinders, every man, woman, and child dead. Our whole way of life obliterated in minutes. If I hadn't been getting water from the well, I would have been obliterated, too.'

'But Nasim and Guita understood that. They wouldn't have asked you to change your name.'

'You've never understood, have you?'

'Understood what?'

'That I only ever wanted you as my father.'

'We went through that at the time, Mia. It wouldn't have been possible.'

'That was twenty-five years ago. Times have changed since then. I'm sure it would have been possible nowadays.'

'Perhaps, but it doesn't help to fret over what was out of reach at the time.'

'It's not out of reach now.'

'How do you mean?'

'You could still adopt me.'

'You mean as an adult?'

'Why not as an adult?'

'Are you serious, Mia?'

'Of course I'm serious.'

Theo pulled her closer. 'There's nothing in this world I would like more. You've been as close as a daughter to me all your life. It would be wonderful to make it real.'

'Then we'll do it. I'll set the wheels in motion.'

'This is turning out to be quite a day!' exclaimed Theo, beaming from ear to ear.

Mia smiled contentedly. 'Not a word to anyone, Theo, not until I have all the papers ready.'

'I'm in your hands,' came the reply.

'Anna can stay in my spare room until she finds her feet.'

'That's a kind offer, Mia, but Charlotte tells me her daughter is going to be staying in a fancy penthouse suite, courtesy of this theatre owner guy. Either he's filthy rich, or he's convinced Anna's a star in the making. Sounds too good to be true. I hope it doesn't come with strings attached.'

'Well, she is rather stunning – could be the next West End sensation.'

'Hmm... as l say, as long as it doesn't come with strings.'

'What would Beth think about it all?'

'She'd just want Anna to be happy. Same as she'd want for Jarrad, but she'd be wary all the same.'

'You miss her still, don't you?'

'Yep,' came the ready response.

'Would you ever want to start over with someone else?'

'Nope.' Theo shook his head resolutely. 'I'm grateful for what I had. I don't yearn for anything more – only the lost years with Beth.'

'Not even that feisty chief superintendent at the MET you're always doing favours for. She can't be far off retirement, as I recall.'

'Nope. I have a lot of good friends, Mia. I only have one Beth.'

She smiled and nodded understandingly. 'As long as you're not lonely.'

'A little,' he answered quietly, 'but it's a small price to pay for what I had. You are lonelier.'

'ME!' she countered hotly. 'ME! I'm not lonely, I have dozens of—'

'Dozens of pegs trying to fill the holes in a lonely heart. Perhaps now he's getting married, you can finally move on.'

'Why does it always have to be about *him*!'

'Because you can't let him go. Grief comes in many guises. You are still grieving for what you had with him – for what you lost.'

'Tosh!' she interrupted hotly. 'I didn't lose it; he trashed it.'

'It doesn't lessen the loss. It doesn't lessen the grief. Anger will not overcome grief, nor will hate. Acceptance and forgiveness are your strongest allies. Give them a chance to help you move on.'

'I've been thinking about freezing my eggs,' she said suddenly.

'Where's this come from, Mia? You've never mentioned it before.'

'She was so small, Theo, hardly bigger than a newborn kitten. She had these adorably tiny fingers. I was the first to hold her. I wrapped her in my sweatshirt.'

'This is the baby that Jarrad delivered in the street?'

'Yes. So tiny. So very tiny. She let out this weak little cry. I don't think I could bear it if she dies.'

'I'm sure she's in good hands, Mia. She'll get expert care in the neonatal unit.'

'I'm almost thirty-five. My eggs must already be depleting. I should freeze some just in case.'

'Just in case what?'

'Just in case Mr Right comes along, or just in case I decide I want to be a single parent. Who knows what the future holds, but by the time I find out it will be too late for my eggs.'

'So, that's the spiel for the masses, but this is Theo. Now you can tell me what *really* brought this on.'

'It shocked me.'

'What shocked you?'

'Him saying he was getting married, wanting kids and a purring cat, it... it made me remember all those hopes and dreams we had of having our own family, our own real family after both of us were orphaned as children. *He's* going to have that now. It feels so unfair.' She buried her head in Theo's chest to try and stifle the sobs which refused to be muzzled.

'You just do what's best for you, Mia. Oocyte cryopreservation might even be a good thing. It might help you move on.'

As soon as she felt in control, she lifted her head and steadied her voice. 'I should let you go, Theo. You must be jetlagged.'

'I'm okay. I will head off, though, if you're sure you're okay. I've not unpacked yet.'

He was just about to leave when, reaching for the door handle, he turned back as if he'd forgotten something. He looked long and hard at his soon-to-be daughter. She was dabbing at her eyes with his unrelinquished handkerchief.

'For what it's worth, Mia, I never did buy that bullshit of his about making a mistake, changing his mind. It was completely out of character. My antennae twitch when people act out of character. It never sat right with me. I'm convinced there was more to it.'

Mia was ready with a tearful rebuttal about how he couldn't possibly understand what it was like to be abandoned on your wedding day, till she remembered Beth had died two weeks before Theo's own wedding, and her face softened. But when she looked up her 'almost father' was gone.

9

Sunday Evening

It was after six when Bryn got back to his flat. Susan was setting the table and tossing a salad to go with the lasagne she would put in the oven as soon as he appeared. She handed him a gin and tonic as he walked into the kitchen.

'You look dead beat, Bryn. Rough day?'

He put his arms round her waist and hugged her. 'Kind of,' he replied. 'It's always nice to come home to you, though. You're so understanding of the job, my unsocial hours, and everything.' He hadn't quite got round to owning up that he was more of a beer guy than gin and tonic, but it was a small price to pay. It was part of her world, part of the ordered existence he was buying into, and maybe he'd get to prefer it in time.

'Let's have some supper and then I must show you a house that came on the market today. It's perfect.'

'Sure,' he replied. 'You sound excited.'

'It's the best one I've seen in weeks, and we really must get a move on. The wedding's only six months away.'

'Well, at least you're in the right place to pick them off,' he added.

'It's not actually one of ours, it's with Merrivales. But I got an early nod from my friend Marcus who works there.'

With the dishes cleared away, Susan got out her laptop and began to show him the photos and floorplan of a large semi-detached house in Finsbury Park.

'It's got four bedrooms and two bathrooms, and the garden is all of a hundred feet deep, with a garage at the bottom and rear access. It's an up-and-coming area. There's a primary school close by and a big green across the road. It would be perfect – and it's been reduced, look.'

Bryn was looking at the reduced asking price. 'But we can't afford this, Susan. It's still £70k over our budget.'

'We might be able to knock them down further. I'll get the lowdown from Marcus. And even if we can't, it would only be a stretch for a little while. You'll get promotion to Super soon, surely? You've been a DCI over three years.'

'I'm not sure I want to be a Super.'

'At least let's go and view it,' she pleaded.

'Alright, Susan, but I don't want you getting your hopes up, only to have them dashed when we can't get a mortgage for it.'

'Couldn't we take a thirty-year mortgage instead of a twenty-five?'

'We've had this out before. I don't want to be saddled with a mortgage until I'm seventy. It's depressing enough thinking I'll be sixty-five before we pay it off.'

'You spent too long renting, Bryn, instead of getting on the property ladder. Most men have bricks under their own feet well before they get to your age.'

'Well, I can't change that now, can I?'

'Shall I get Marcus to set up a viewing?'

'If it makes you happy, sweetheart.'

Susan smiled and kissed him. 'I know it's the house for us. I know it,' she breathed.

✼✼✼✼✼

Anna looked stunning in a sleek black cocktail dress that made the most of her six feet height and model figure. Her hair and make-up were impeccable. She had put away her high-heeled stilettoes and chosen a low-heeled court shoe that would not draw attention to Don being three inches shorter.

She was parading in front of the dressing mirror, practising her smile and coquettish toss of her long, glossy black hair when Don Kavanagh breezed in without knocking. It unnerved her. It was his penthouse suite, of course, but even so she was irritated that he felt he could just barge in unannounced.

'My, what a vision of loveliness you are, my dear. You will be a sensation tonight.'

Don had booked a table for six. The other four guests were all men, a little older than Don but equally smartly turned out.

'Anna, I'd like you to meet my good friends and business colleagues.'

They introduced themselves one by one. 'So, this is the beauty you've been bragging about, Don. You weren't exaggerating – she's a knockout,' said Mike Dewson, as he held her hand rather too long and rather too tightly, his eyes x-raying her beautiful body. 'Where did you find her?'

'In the chorus line on Broadway. She's going to be in our next production at *The Pearl*,' replied Don proudly.

'What's the play?' asked Guy Standon.

'*A Clockwork Orange*.'

'Oh my! Can't wait to see that!' said Keith Willoughby, sweeping his eyes up Anna's long legs all the way to her perfectly shaped brows.

'We're staging it as a musical,' said Don. 'Toby's got rehearsals well underway – he's just waiting for Anna to slot into her role. We're scheduled to open on Friday.'

'And do you sing, Anna?' asked Wayne Burrows.

'Yes. I do it all – sing, dance, act,' she replied, a little thrown at suddenly discovering she would have less than a week to learn her lines and the songs. Perhaps that's the way they did it in London.

Later that evening, fuzzy with champagne and riding high on her fairytale wave, Anna pulled out her mobile to FaceTime Rosie. It was 2am in London, early evening in Canada. Perfect timing! She couldn't wait to share all the details of her dreamy evening.

10

Monday, 19th May, 2014

'Hi Susan, it's Marcus.'

'Hello, Marcus, any more info on that lovely house at Sycamore Avenue?'

'That's what I'm ringing about. The owners seem to be in a hurry to move, and I think they would take another £20k off the already reduced price. If you don't have anything to sell, you'd be in a strong position.'

'Bryn rents his apartment.'

'There is one snag…'

'Oh?'

'There's a large, detached property a couple of hundred metres further up, number 149. It wasn't one of ours, but I remember it coming on with Jacksons. It sold to a cash buyer. Well, it's got a well-advanced planning application in for change of use to a refuge for trafficked women.'

'What!' squealed Susan. 'Surely the council wouldn't agree to that? It will attract all sorts of undesirables, it will affect the neighbourhood, it will – Christ, our children might bump into them. Are the residents doing anything? A petition or something?'

'There are a lot of liberals and academics living at that end of the road who probably won't object. Plus, councils are under increasing pressure to deliver on these kinds of projects.'

'But not there! Why a leafy avenue in Finsbury Park?'

'Perhaps precisely because it *is* a leafy avenue in Finsbury Park – somewhere peaceful and safe for a refuge.'

'It's outrageous. Well, I don't want to risk having trafficked women for neighbours. Someone else will have to buy it.'

'Shame, 'cos it's a beauty and, as I said, you might have got another £20k off an already reduced asking price.'

'Well, I suppose there's no harm in looking – just in case the planning permission gets rejected.'

'Do you want me to show it to you after work? I can arrange for the owners to be absent.'

'I finish at four.'

'Perfect. Shall I meet you at the property at four-thirty?'

'Oh, why not? Can't do any harm to have a peep at it.'

❁❁❁❁❁

The theatre was already a hive of activity when Anna arrived. 'Ah, Anna,' said Toby, 'good timing. We're just about to go through the solo song you will be singing. Take a pew. Jill, your understudy, will sing it through first and then you can have a go. I have the music here. You do read music?'

'Yes, of course I read music,' retorted Anna, feeling a little disoriented. This was not what she was expecting at all.

Clearly the production was well underway without her. She'd thought they would be building the show around her, not slotting her in. She took the music from Toby's assistant and followed it as Jill sang it note perfectly, throwing Anna a look that was sullenly smug.

'Your turn,' said Toby methodically, and he indicated to the practice pianist to get ready to go again.

Anna missed her entry and stumbled over some of the rhythms but managed to hit all the right notes, including the top G that Jill had trilled out effortlessly before her.

Toby looked less than impressed but managed to keep his professional countenance. 'Take the music home and practise, Anna. We'll run through it again tomorrow.'

'And my lines? Do you have a marked-up script so I can start to learn my lines?'

'Here's a script, Anna, but it won't take you long to learn your lines. Mrs Alexander only has a few words. You'll need to practise your screams, though.'

Anna looked troubled, and it dawned on Toby that Don had not prepared her for the part she was to play. He'd probably sold her a sucker line like he usually did with the chicks he pulled into these kinds of roles.

As soon as she had walked in, with those long legs and stunning Hollywood looks, Toby had got the measure of it. What he wouldn't give for a hands-off owner who let him run the show like a director should. But Don paid well, and it was regular work in the precarious world of stage directing.

Mercifully, the girl only had one song. She was no Jill. But then Jill was no Anna in the looks department, and that's what would matter. That's what would have the audience on the edge of their seats. He had to admit that Don had at least got that bit right. The scene would be sensational. And all publicity was good publicity.

'We are just about to do a rough run-through with scripts. Why don't you sit and watch this one out, Anna, then you will have more of a feel for your part and we can slip you in?'

Anna did as she was bid, but as the minutes ticked by, she became more and more uneasy. Her ears were soon ringing from loud renditions of crashing Beethoven music, and most of the early action seemed to be focused on – what had Rosie called them? – punks. Punk youths vandalising and maiming their way through the scenes.

Half an hour into the production, she spotted Mrs Alexander's name in the dialogue column of her script, so she renewed her flagging interest. No-one was in costume. Jill came onto stage in her jeans and cotton overshirt. She ambled around, dusting ornaments and lovingly fingering some of the fake antiques, before launching into the song she had sung earlier. The words made sense now.

As the strains of the final bars concluded, the raucous punks charged onto stage. Alex, the ringleader circled Mrs Alexander like a tiger taunting its prey. When she screamed, he hit her across the mouth – it was well done. Anna made a note that she would have to practise how to do that without getting hurt. More taunts from Alex in his menacing solo song. He took out a pair of stage scissors and made out as if he would cut through her clothing.

'We'll have a couple of rehearsals with the actual catsuit, but for now just mime it, Wayne.'

The Alex character made an elaborate play of cutting into Mrs Alexander's clothing before pushing her to the floor behind a sofa. A relieved Anna concluded the sofa had been strategically placed on set to avoid having to stage the intended rape.

Hurriedly she flicked through the remaining pages of the script and could not find any more lines for Mrs Alexander. *Was this it? Was this the extent of her starring role – one lousy song and a feigned rape scene?* She felt sick. She hardly heard or saw the remainder of the production. The scenes in the psychiatric hospital were a blur. All she wanted was to get out into the fresh air and phone Don so she could sort out this misunderstanding.

'Okay, we'll call it a wrap for today,' said Toby. 'Same time tomorrow. I want to do a first run-through in costume, and I'll need the musicians and full chorus.'

Anna did not hang around to chat with Toby; she sped out and headed back to her suite. The access to the penthouse via a separate lift in a private underground carpark had felt tawdry when she first used it, not quite the glamour entrance she expected for a starlet. Now, she was glad of the anonymity it afforded her. Once in her room, she let out the hot tears she had been holding back and blubbed into her pillow. Then she pulled herself together, telling herself there must be a mistake.

She rang Don's number, but it went through to voicemail. Two hours later, after her seven failed attempts to get through, he rang back.

'Anna, darling, I have missed calls from you. Is something wrong?'

'No, no, nothing wrong exactly. Perhaps a misunderstanding, but I'm sure you can sort it out.'

'What would that be?'

'The musical seems well advanced already.'

'I fucking hope so, we open on Friday.'

'I only have one song, three lines, and lots of screams. My part seems to be mainly… well, mainly a mocked-up rape scene.'

'And?'

'You mean you knew?'

'Of course. What do you think I brought you over here for? You're perfect for that scene. With your beauty and those deliciously long legs, you'll look magnificent.'

'But you said I was to have a starring role?'

'That scene will be sensational. Of course you'll be a star. You'll be the talk of London. I have to go, Anna. String of calls to make. Rehearse well tomorrow.'

❈❈❈❈❈

It was after eight when Bryn got home. He could smell the delicious aroma of a lamb tagine coming from the kitchen – one of Susan's signature dishes. There were candles on the table and a bottle of red wine breathing in a carafe. He let out a huge sigh and relaxed. Married life was going to be so sweet. His fiancée was an enthusiastic homemaker. An understanding partner who didn't balk at the hours he worked. She would make a lovely home for them.

'Hi Bryn, how was work?'

'Oh, the usual, you know. This is a bit grand. I've not missed a special date, have I?'

'No. Just wanted the man of my dreams to know how much I love him. Nothing wrong with that, is there?'

'Nothing at all,' he grinned, pulling her towards him and kissing her.

'Let's eat while it's hot.'

'Sure, I'll just go and wash up.'

As they were tucking into their raspberry frangipane, Susan said conversationally, 'I went to look at that house in Finsbury Park after work – you know, the one I told you about.'

'Yes, I remember. The one we can't afford. I thought we were going to look at it together at the weekend.'

'Well, Marcus offered, and I thought it would save a wasted journey for you if it turned out to be horrid.'

'And was it horrid?'

'No, the house is divine. Almost perfect.'

'Almost? You mean apart from it being £70k over our limit.'

'Apparently one of the big, detached houses further up the road has been bought by some do-gooders trying to set up a refuge for trafficked women. They've got a planning application in that's at an advanced stage.'

'Why would that be a problem?'

'You can't be serious, Bryn. We wouldn't want that on our doorstep; all sorts of undesirables coming and going the day long. And our children. Think of our children. They might… they might bump into one of them.' She shuddered.

Bryn put his dessert spoon down and looked intently at his fiancée. 'These women aren't lepers, Susan. They're victims of terrible atrocities. They deserve our pity, not our contempt. It's a good thing, surely, that someone wants to help them rebuild their shattered lives. Have you ever met a trafficked woman?'

'No, of course not. You know I haven't. Why are you being so mean about this?'

'Well, *I* have, many times. Only a few days ago, I was called out to an incident where a pregnant trafficked woman died in an RTA, trying to escape her captors. I'd like to think there could have been a haven for her. So, why not Finsbury Park? What the hell is your problem, Susan?'

'I didn't realise it was a problem to want a nice home in a decent area with a good school for our children,' she responded archly.

'Have you no compassion?'

'Well, of course I feel sorry for them, but why should I have to…'

'Suffer them in your own back yard,' he finished for her. 'You're a heartless snob, Susan.'

She gasped at the sharp reprimand in his words. 'If I'm a snob, then so are all my friends. I'm no different from them. None of them would—'

'Then perhaps you should reappraise your circle of friends.'

'How dare you!' she screamed at him. 'How dare you criticise my friends, you sanctimonious pig. You can clear the dishes. I'm going to bed.'

Bryn picked up the remainder of his coffee and slumped onto the sofa. It was the first time they'd had a full-blown row, and he felt wretched. Life was usually so calm and straightforward with Susan. No dramas, no rebukes, no barbs about his work hours. An oasis of tranquillity is what he was signing up for, wasn't it? He rebuked himself. He must concede some of the high ground; learn to compromise. He would apologise tomorrow.

11

Tuesday, 20th May

The SCD9 incident room was buzzing industriously. Bryn had requested the loan of two officers from Bancroft Road station, it being the nearest to the nail bar episode. Local knowledge could be invaluable in these early days before the trail cooled. He was offered two detectives, but Bryn specifically asked for beat constables Zahir Ahmed and Christine Blackwell by name. It was their turf, and they would have the best instinct for the intricacies of the neighbourhood. They had also been first on the RTA scene, which was another plus.

'Morning, sir. Can I get you a coffee?'

'Thanks, Chrissy, but I can get my own. I don't expect to be waited on – and can we drop the sir. Inside this incident room, it's Bryn, unless you want me to WPC Blackwell you the day long.'

She smiled in response. 'Just takes a bit of getting used to, sir… er, Bryn.'

On his way to the coffee station, Bryn stopped by Jemimah's desk. She was the SCD9 ace backroom researcher and could turn her hand to anything.

'Can you dig up some information for me, Jemi, that might prove fruitful? At the moment we're clutching at any straw that presents itself. Apparently, there's a late-stage planning permission for a new refuge centre for trafficked women on Sycamore Avenue in Finsbury Park. Can you get me the lowdown on it? I know these kinds of charities can be sensitive about cooperating with the police, but they could have access to a community of trafficked survivors who might give us some useful leads.'

Jemimah busily wrote down the details in her notebook. 'I'll get onto it straight away, Bryn.'

'Thanks, Jemi.'

With coffee in hand, he went in search of Jake. 'I'd like you to go with Zabhir and Chrissy this morning. They are your best eyes and ears. Suss out any nearby fast-food places, convenience stores, etc. Those women would have had to eat. A microwave and a kettle were hardly going to give them a lot of options. Someone might know something.'

※※※※※

Anna was hanging round the stage while everyone else seemed busily occupied, until Toby spotted her. 'Morning, Anna. You on top of your song today and your lines?'

'Given that I only have three lines, it was hardly going to be difficult. But yes, I've learnt the song.'

'Good, well I'll need you in costume today. Go to Jenny in Dressing Room 3. She's got your catsuit ready and will make any adjustments needed. You rushed off yesterday before I could get her to try it on you.'

Anna found Dressing Room 3, which was just as busy as the stage area she had left. Costumes were littered on backs of chairs, and a group of chorus girls were fighting for mirror space. The air smelt oppressively of perfume and hairspray.

'Ah, Anna, there you are. Slip into this, would you?' said a woman she assumed must be Jenny.

The woman reached for a hanging rail that housed dozens of identical scarlet red catsuits. 'Toby said you were about six feet and slender, so I hope I'm not far off, but I can make any necessary adjustments after rehearsals. I won't bother with this one for today, but at least I can get the others skintight by tomorrow. That's what Mr Kavanagh has asked for – skintight. You'll look stunning.'

Anna started to undress and put on the catsuit, when Jenny piped up, 'No, Anna, you'll have to remove your undies.'

'You mean everything? Even my thong?' she asked incredulously.

'Everything, dearie. Skintight, remember.'

The catsuit was a good enough fit, but Anna felt a long way from the lustrous star she had expected to feel.

The rehearsal got underway with numerous stops and starts as Toby eked out stronger performances from his cast. As the time for Mrs Alexander's song drew nearer, Anna's nerves melted away. In their place was a steely resolve. She was going to show these patronising gits just what calibre of star they were dealing with. She performed it note and rhythm perfectly, hitting the high G as sweetly as a nightingale.

'Terrific, Anna,' said Toby, hardly able to disguise his surprise. 'Just a bit more sass as you move around the set. Can you give it me one more time, please? This time we're going straight into the punk raid – and don't forget, as Alex and his gang enter from stage right you've to look frightened, but don't scream until he begins to circle you. Ok? You *have* been practising your screams, I assume?'

She hadn't but was not going to let on, so she nodded a weak assent. 'Yes, I've got it.'

The music was deafening as Alex and his punks swaggered in, kicking over furniture and smashing ornaments with their baseball bats. When Alex circled Anna's character menacingly, she screamed out in terror.

'Well, look what we have here, boys,' said Alex.

'CUT!' shouted Toby. 'Anna, we need a *scream,* not a whimper. You've got to give me more. Let's pick it up again from the entry of the punks.'

Mechanically, Anna screamed as the Alex character circled her. 'What have we here? A red goddess all dressed up and nowhere to go!' He brushed his baseball bat up and down her catsuit. 'Tie the old geezer up. This beauty's mine.'

Anna cried out her three solo lines, 'Do something, Frank. Stop them! Do something!'

'You heard the lady,' said Alex. 'Let's see what hubby can do for his Mrs with a couple of broken legs.' They acted out beating Mr Alexander.

Anna screamed again, and Alex approached her, putting his finger on her lips, 'Quiet now, baby, the louder you scream the harder we hit him,' before pushing her down behind the sofa.

'CUT!' shouted Toby. 'I still need more realistic screams, Anna. You're going to have to put more practice in. This is a pivotal scene, so I need three hundred per cent more volume and two hundred per cent more terror. Can we just run this again? Take it from the last clothing cut. Jenny, can you quickly tack the middle of the catsuit together again for me? Just a couple of stiches should hold it.'

Anna felt numb with shame at the prospect of repeating any part of this humiliating scene, but she did her best with the scream. She surprised herself how much volume she could produce when she used her singing breathing techniques, incentivised by knowing the sooner she got it right the sooner she could get off stage, as her character did not appear again in the production.

Anna rushed away as soon as she could. She still had to steel herself for tomorrow evening's meal with Theo and Jarrad. Theo was a darling, but His Worthiness would be his usual pain in the butt.

She'd brushed them off a couple of times with excuses of heavy rehearsal schedules but had finally agreed to a quick tapas supper. She could tough it out. She would sell it to them as a stepping stone. Rosie had said it was a famous book, so even His Worthiness couldn't take issue with that. There was a bit more flesh on display than she would have liked, especially with her kid brother sitting in the audience, but she had adjusted to it being plot-centric not gratuitous.

She would hint to them there were bigger parts in the pipeline, and she could cut the meal short on the excuse she had an early start the following day as it was the big

Thursday dress rehearsal. Yes, she could do this. She could tough it out.

Don was right. However small the part, it did put her centre stage, and it did give her a solo song. The hardest thing in her line of work was getting noticed. Lots of famous actors attested to luck playing a hand in getting their first break. Toby, too, had said this was a pivotal scene.

Okay, it wasn't the West End, as she had naively thought it was going to be, but it was a new progressive theatre with what Don called his avant-garde approach to showcasing new talent. Her photo was on the billboard, admittedly with all the others from the production, and not as large as she had hoped – but it was a great photo. It was duplicated in the programme with a small bio.

On Broadway she had had to be content with her name in tiny letters on the back inside page, grouped with nineteen others who made up the chorus. No photo. The only plus had been the alphabetical ordering: Anna Adams at least got her first onto the chorus list.

She looked at herself in the mirror, tossed her hair, and mouthed to her reflection, 'Pull yourself together, Anna Adams! This is a pivotal cameo role. It's your staircase to stardom. Embrace it!' She threw her arms wide as she articulated the last two words in theatrical fashion and reminded herself of that luvvie British actress who got an Oscar for eight minutes on screen as an English Queen. She'd forgotten the actress's name, but she would Google it before tomorrow's dinner so she'd have something up her sleeve if Jarrad got on His Worthiness soap box.

'Anything is possible, Anna Adams!' she mouthed to the mirror again.

There was going to be a press reviewer at the dress rehearsal, and although it wasn't some highbrow columnist from *The Times*, hopefully her singing would earn her a glowing review.

That evening, Bryn made a special effort to get home at a reasonable hour, bearing a large bunch of flowers. Susan was in the kitchen with her back to him. She did not turn towards him when she heard him come in. Evidently, she was still smarting.

'I'm sorry, Susan, can you forgive me? I shouldn't have sounded off like that. I expect too much of you. It was unfair.'

She turned to face him 'But you think me some kind of callous bitch, you… Oh, they're lovely, Bryn, thank you!' she declared, switching tacks seamlessly as she spied the flowers.

'I don't think you're a callous bitch at all, Susan. You've been so good to me, and I'm a heel for trying to impose my views on you. I can't expect you to think the same as me about everything.'

Mollified, she took the flowers and planted a kiss on his cheek. 'Let's not fight about it.'

'Come on, leave that, you can reheat it for tomorrow. Tonight, I'm taking you out.'

When their pasta main courses had arrived and they had chinked their glasses, a smiling Susan said, 'It was such a shame about that house. Marcus said we might have got an extra £20k off it. They want a quick sale.'

'We'd still be £50k short, and I thought you'd already discounted it.'

'I was wondering whether, you know, whether the planning permission might get rejected. I don't suppose the Police could lodge an objection, it being so close to a primary school and a park?'

'What are you getting at?' asked Bryn coldly.

'Well, you know, I just wondered, you being a DCI and—'

Bryn flung down his serviette. 'There is no way I'm interfering in due process. Not for you, Susan, not for anyone – and certainly not for a project I actually approve of. Now, can we just drop it, otherwise we'll end up in another fight.'

Susan picked sulkily at her pasta and gave a dismissive shrug. They ate the rest of their main course in silence.

Bryn took her hand when dessert was served. 'Let's not fight, Susan. This isn't like us. You're the woman I want to marry, spend the rest of my life with. Can we just put this behind us – please?'

'Very well,' she said, a little frostily. 'But it really is a beautiful house.'

12

Wednesday, 21st May, 2014

The evidence board was beginning to build up in SCD9 incident room. A square kilometre map of the nail bar area was surrounded by attached notes containing key pieces of information, including the e-fit image of the receptionist which Mia had provided. Down one side was a column headed by a question mark. It's where Bryn encouraged his team to write oddities, clues, and potential leads. All of this was on computer, of course, but Bryn had long favoured the additional prompt of the 'crazy wall' that so often expedited seemingly random connections.

Ahmed and Chrissy were a great addition to the team, and Jemi was on hand to process information they shared with her on any recent, unusual, or notable activity in the target locality.

A call had gone out to all London stations to be on the lookout for any new pop-up nail bars in their areas. Bryn was working to a hypothesis that the three manicurists were more valuable alive than dead. Their captors would keep a low profile for a while until they thought the heat was off and then start up somewhere else.

The team briefing that morning pulled together the different strands they were all working on. Jemi had done a forensic trawl of any recent or suspicious activity in the square kilometre vicinity. 'This might be a bit left field but—'

'Your left field hunches are usually gold dust, Jemi, so we are all ears,' interrupted Bryn encouragingly.

'This last year has seen a major reworking of a rundown theatre and a disused office tower block. A company called Pearl Enterprises bought them up and renovated them. The Pearl Theatre, as it has been renamed, opened six months ago. It does short runs of three or four weeks, billed as avant-garde experimental productions supporting up-and-coming actors—'

'I remember that theatre renovation,' cut in Zabhir. 'Word on the street is that the productions are on the risqué side of experimental.'

'That would fit,' agreed Jemi, 'given what I turned up on the renovation of the office tower block. It's been transformed into a boutique aparthotel. It needed planning permission for change of use to The Pearl Tower Aparthotel. I have a copy of the plans here,' she said, pinning a copy onto the evidence board. 'It makes interesting reading.'

'Why so, Jemi?'

'It has twelve floors. The top one is a penthouse suite. The bottom ten floors are studio apartments with small self-catering facilities. Floor eleven is laid out as single rooms, with ensuite toilets and one shared bathroom. They are probably the original offices. At first, I thought these might just be budget rate rooms for students or backpackers – except for three particulars.

'One: this floor and the penthouse suite all have industrial level soundproofing. Two: they are accessed by a separate lift located in a small underground car park. And three: they do not appear on the aparthotel website.

'I phoned them on the pretext of booking a budget single room and was told they were an aparthotel. They only have self-catering apartments, and they don't do single occupancy discounts. It's possible that the single rooms are used for peripatetic theatre staff, or perhaps musicians – hence the soundproofing. I followed that up, but the theatre retains only a small ensemble of musicians – five, I believe, all local, and they are only used if a musical is being staged, not for plays. There are eight single rooms on this floor.

'I did wonder if the high spec soundproofing which was added at the refurbishment stage was to disguise other kinds of activity going on, such as prostitution or temporary housing of migrants. If our nail bar victims were needed to be rehoused in a hurry, it could have provided an ideal temporary solution for their captors. But as I said, it's a bit left field, and I sometimes do get carried away.'

'Good work, Jemi. Get it pinned up, we'll put it on the watch list. Jake, perhaps you and your two trusty comrades might ask around discreetly, see what you can find out.'

'Will do, Bryn.'

'Are we any nearer identifying the victim?'

'Nothing's coming up on any of our international searches,' answered Jemi.

'What about DNA?'

'Again – nothing.'

'Do we have DNA results back yet on baby Miranda? It might throw up a match to the father from our databases.'

'I chased it up earlier this morning,' said Jemi. 'The pathologist has requested a repeat test. She wasn't satisfied there hadn't been a mistake made with the first one, so she wanted independent verification.'

'Keep chasing her, Jemi, and get them to me as soon as they come in.'

※※※※※

A little after three that afternoon, Hilda Simpson waddled into The Pearl Tower Aparthotel Reception, pulling a wheelie case behind her and a large handbag strapped across her chest. The pockets of her voluminous coat were stuffed to capacity. She pinged the bell and waited for a weaselly man to appear from a door behind the counter. He looked about mid-forties, slightly built, with greasy black hair that was thinning on top, and a moustache that hadn't yet decided if it wanted to be a David Niven or a Charlie Chaplin.

'Can I help you, madam?' he asked, a little surprised at his guest. Elderly grandmothers were not the usual clientele at The Pearl Tower. And this one was all of six feet tall, with the build of a warrior queen.

'Hilda Simpson – that's Simpson wi' a p. I'm booked in fer five nights in a studio apartment,' she announced, pulling out a fistful of papers from one of her bulging coat pockets.

'Very good, madam., if you could just sign the booking form, please, I'll get your apartment key.'

'Me ticker might not work so well these days, but there's nowt wrong wi' me lug 'oles, so no need to shout, young man,' said Hilda, aware that he was speaking to her like she was an old biddy in a care home. 'Unless, of course, it's you as is 'ard of 'earing.'

'My apologies, madam,' he replied in a quieter, chastened voice. 'The lift is just down the corridor to your left. You're on the fourth floor, in apartment 405,' he said, handing her the swipe card. 'Here's a street map. I've marked the nearest cafes and restaurants. There are several within a few minutes' walk. And the Pearl Theatre, of course, which is also only a five-minute walk. There is a small fridge and a two-ring hob in your room if you prefer to self-cater. The nearest tube is just across the square.'

'Not fer me, laddie. If I wer meant t' travel in undergroun' tunnels, the guid Lord wud a med mi a mole.'

'As you wish, madam,' he continued. 'Can we help you with anything else? Your luggage or…?'

'Nah, I'm good to go, an' I'm not over fond o' tipping sum bellboy just outta nappies fer wheeling a wheelie in an' out of a lift,' she added bluntly. Plain speaking was a Hilda speciality.

'Well, any problems, just dial 0. I'm only here 9 to 11 in the mornings and 3 to 5 in the afternoons; we're a self-catering establishment, you understand. Outside of those hours, the reception line is linked to my mobile. I'm never far away. If you leave a message, I will get back to you promptly. Enjoy your stay with us, Mrs Simpson.'

Hilda bundled herself into the lift. She located ten floor buttons underneath a sign which advised a maximum load of six people. 'Must be six pygmies then,' she muttered to herself.

The studio was decent enough and had a view of a bustling pedestrianised street below. *No traffic, that's good*, she thought. *Won't be too noisy at night.* She checked her papers to make sure she had her theatre ticket. Yes, it was there: stalls, row 3, seat 17. No doubt she would check it another dozen times before the performance.

Hilda liked a good sing-song and all that stage razzmatazz, but she was really here for Beth. It was Beth's granddaughter singing on that stage, and Beth would have been so proud. 'I'll be proud fer you, Beth. Proxy proud. I won't let yer down. I'll clap an' cheer an' 'oot an' whistle an' be dead proud. Dead, dead proud.'

As soon as she had unpacked and hung up her Sunday best dress, she collapsed onto the bed for her habitual forty-minute afternoon nap.

✽✽✽✽✽

That night Bryn made a special effort to be early. He felt there was still ground to make up with Susan, and he desperately wanted things back on an even keel.

Just as he was leaving, a call had come in about a suspicious death. Uncharacteristically, he sent Jake to investigate without him and headed home. It was not quite six when he pulled up outside the apartment and was surprised Susan's car was not there. He collected the local paper from the doormat and put it on the kitchen table. Susan would want to scour it later in case there were any private sales advertised that had not been picked up by estate agents.

It felt strange to come home to an empty flat without the strains of Justin Timberlake or enticing aromas wafting from the kitchen. He realised how much he prized this comfortable existence and how much he took it for granted.

'Hi darling,' he breezed, when she arrived not many minutes later.

'Oh. I...I wasn't expecting you so soon. I'm late. I... er, I... volunteered to stay back today. One of the girls called in sick so there was a backlog. I'll get dinner on. I'm afraid it's a shop-bought quiche with some salad. I haven't had time to prepare anything else.'

'No worries, Susan. I don't expect you to wait on me hand and foot. I've been taking you for granted far too much lately. We can always get a takeaway or eat out.'

'My, this is a turnaround! We already ate out once this week.'

'Do I need an excuse to treat my darling fiancée twice in one week?'

'Well, if you're sure? That would be lovely. I'll just go and change.' She dumped her car keys and handbag on the kitchen table and headed to the bedroom.

Bryn sat down at the table to wait for her. Perhaps he should look through the local rag himself. Show willing.

As he grabbed the local paper, he knocked her handbag, and her car keys fell on the floor. He picked them up and was about to put them back next to her bag when he spotted that a sheet of paper had fallen out of its side pocket. Thinking it might be details of another house, he unfolded it. There was half a page of typed text:

Dear Householder,

In case you are unaware, there is a planning application for the large house at the top of the avenue, Number 149, for change of use from a private residence to a refuge for trafficked women. The public consultation, to which we are all entitled to contribute, is almost closed. I would urge you to oppose this application. The undesirable comings and goings of such a venture would create an unsafe environment for our children. We have a school here. We have a park here. This is a low crime area. It's highly inappropriate to locate such a centre in the midst of our community. We need to protect our families and our properties. This would undoubtedly have a negative impact on the value of houses in this road. The planning application number is DF3719 on the council website, where you can also lodge your comments. I urge you to act with haste.

A concerned resident.

Susan swept into the kitchen fixing an earring and stopped in her tracks when she saw Bryn holding up the sheet of paper.

'Where did you get this, Susan?' he asked in a quiet, steely voice.

'It's none of your business. You can't interrogate me like one of your suspects. How dare you go through my handbag like I'm a criminal.'

'I didn't. It fell out. Did you write this, Susan?'

'What if I did! *You* weren't going to do anything to help.'

'How many of these did you print?'

'A hundred. That's the last one. I was keeping that one to show Marcus. I posted them through the doors on my way home from work. That's why I was late.'

'For fuck's sake, Susan. What were you thinking?'

'Don't use language like that with me. If you have to spend your days griming about in the gutter, you can at least leave the filthy lingo there before you come home.'

'What gives you the right to post these through residents' front doors? What gives you the right to call yourself a "concerned resident", to say "we" and "our"? "Our community", "o*ur children*". For fuck's sake.'

'I told you not to use lang—'

'I fucking heard you. And you think *this* isn't the fucking gutter?' he said, shaking the paper violently at her. 'It's sickening.'

'I did it for us!' she shrieked. 'If you weren't so sanctimonious, you'd see that.'

'This is about *you,* not *us.* I don't want anything to do with it, and I'm telling you, Susan, even if you manage to sway enough people to oppose this venture, we are NOT buying that house. After this, I wouldn't buy it even if it were the last available house in London.'

'I hate you, Bryn Ellis. Do you hear me, I hate you! You and your precious social conscience. Why can't you put me first for a change, instead of all those no-hopers. What about our children, Bryn, aren't you going to put them first either?'

'I hope any children of mine grow up with their moral compass pointing in the right direction.'

'And you think mine doesn't? Because I want to protect my own?'

'That's not protection, Susan, it's a straitjacket.'

It was then that Bryn's mobile rang. 'What is it, Freeman?' he snapped.

'I'm sorry to disturb you, sir,' said Jake, unused to his DCI snapping, 'but I think you need to come and see this. I'm at King's A and E. We have a woman resembling the e-fit description of the nail bar receptionist that Ms Saleem provided. She's had her throat slashed.'

'I'm on my way,' said Bryn. 'I have to go to work,' he announced brusquely to Susan, and left her sniffing into a tissue.

※※※※※

Bryn strode resolutely into the A and E department of Kings College Hospital, his fury not yet spent. 'Where was she found, Jake?'

'At a junction between Benton Road and an alleyway that runs behind a Chinese takeaway. It's only a couple of hundred metres from our nail bar incident. We've interviewed the takeaway staff. One of them heard a scuffle at the top of the alley when she was taking rubbish out to the bin. She thought she saw someone fall and someone running away. She went to investigate, and that's when she found the victim. I surmise the killer had followed his victim up Benton Road, pulled her into the alley, cut her throat, and would have been gone in seconds. If this is our nail bar receptionist, then it was a professional hit.'

'My thoughts exactly, Jake. If so, it puts a whole new complexion on the case. Was this a reprisal killing because she messed up, or because she knew too much? Either way, this is looking like a much bigger operation than we first thought.'

'I've got two officers doing door-to-door in the area.'

'Good,' said Bryn, just as two medics appeared from the scrub room.

'Bill Salter, duty registrar,' said the shorter man, extending a hand to Bryn. 'This is Jarrad Adams, my F2. He dealt with the incident and can give you the details. Senseless waste of a young life. Am I needed? It's just I have a patient waiting on a trolley who needs urgent attention.'

'Of course, do go and see to your patient, Dr Salter.'

'Thanks,' said Bill. 'Make sure you get off after the update, Jarrad. Your shift finished long ago.'

'We meet again, Dr Adams,' said Bryn. 'Not under auspicious circumstances, it would appear. Was she dead on arrival?'

'Yes. A clean slash to the carotid artery. She would have bled out very quickly. I couldn't find any other obvious injuries, but a pm will tell us more. I'd say your killer was clinical and knew what he or she was doing.'

'Any bruising or broken bones?'

'Not that I could detect, but again a pm will confirm that.'

'I think we have all we need for now, thank you, Dr Adams. We don't want to keep you later than we've already made you.'

'Unusual to have a DCI from a Scotland Yard special unit for something of this nature. Is it connected to the nail bar tragedy?'

'Too early to tell, but we have to consider the possibility. I'll see if I can fast-track the pm.'

'She had some kind of serial number tattooed on her inner left forearm. Could that be significant?'

'Possibly. Thank you, Dr Adams.'

Bryn went to inspect the body. He noted the tattoo Jarrad had referred to: BA3B27D6 – a seemingly random collection of four letters and four numbers. Deep in thought, he pulled out his mobile, unsure whether she would pick up.

'Mia, it's Bryn. I need your help with something,' he said, in what he hoped was a level voice.

'I can't imagine what that could be,' she replied icily.

'That nail bar incident – last week, remember?'

'As if I could forget.'

'You said you would recognise the receptionist again if you saw her, and you gave an e-fit description to my sergeant.'

'Yes.'

'Well, we have the body of a woman who resembles that e-fit. She's had her throat cut. Would you be willing to come down to Kings A and E to do an identification for us.'

'I'll be there in twenty.' She had forgotten to lay on the ice when she spoke, and Bryn rejoiced in the warmer tone he could hear in her voice.

Bryn showed Mia into a side room where the body had been laid out. She looked long and hard at the corpse before nodding her head. 'I can't be a hundred percent, but I'm ninety percent sure it's her. Does this mean the three manicurists might also be dead?'

'Not necessarily. This could be a hush killing. She's a minder who messed up and probably also knew too much. But it does suggest the three manicurists might have been moved out of the immediate local area, so speed is now even more vital. Your ninety percent is more than good enough for me. We'll proceed on that basis. Thank you for coming so quickly, Mia. We're very grateful,' he said earnestly.

Noting he had said 'we' and not 'I', she nodded her response and turned to leave. She did not look back. Bryn, however, watched her every step as she exited the hospital, his gaze fixed on her disappearing form until it passed through the revolving doors.

❦❦❦❦❦

The tapas bar was not far from Pearl Tower. Theo had considered Anna's busy schedules when booking it. Jarrad had only just arrived. 'Sorry, Theo, I was late leaving the hospital.'

'No worries, Anna's not here yet.'

'No surprise there.'

Theo was on the brink of defending the woman he thought of as his granddaughter when the lady herself appeared.

'Darlings, it's so great to see you both,' she breezed. 'I've been SO busy. It's a frantic schedule, and everything is so different over here from what I'm used to.'

'I'm glad we finally got to pin you down for a couple of hours then, Anna,' said Theo cheerily. 'Loads to catch up on. Mia sends her love. She's on her way back from Strasbourg. She's looking forward to your opening night on Friday. How are you enjoying London?'

'Busy, you know. Busy, busy, busy.'

'How's the play coming along?' he added.

'It's a musical, Theo.'

'Yes, yes, of course. Based on a thought-provoking novel, as I recall. I'm intrigued to know how the director will handle the psychiatric hospital scenes.'

'Typical psychologist, more interested in the case notes than the musical ones,' she teased him.

'Except for your notes, of course, Anna, which will be exquisite,' he replied gallantly.

'They haven't given you much time to learn your lines. How are you managing?' asked Jarrad.

'Oh, the main bit for me is singing, and that comes naturally. So it's not been hard, just busy, you know. Busy, busy.'

'Tell us all about your part, Anna?' asked Theo enthusiastically.

'Let's not have any spoilers before the opening night. It's no big deal, anyway; just a stepping stone. It's only a three-week run, and I have other parts in the pipeline. Enough about me. Tell me all your news. How is everyone up in Cumbria?' pressed Anna.

This was so unlike the self-centred sister he remembered that Jarrad wondered if he had misjudged her. He'd hadn't seen much of her in the six years he'd been in England. Perhaps he'd got her all wrong. He must make more of an effort while she was in London.

'They're all fine,' replied Theo. 'Rhianne has her hands full with her three. Beth is nine now, and tall like Eithan; Tommy is six, already showing off his ball skill; little Daisy is nearly three, cute as a kitten – and very bossy! You know Hilda is coming down for your opening night, don't you?'

'No, no, I… I… didn't know that. I… I… didn't think it was her kind of thing.'

Theo was surprised to see how disconcerted Anna was by the news.

'Hilda! You must be joking!' he replied with gusto. 'You're Beth's only granddaughter. Wild horses wouldn't keep her away. Mia offered to put her up, but she's booked herself into a studio apartment at your place, The Pearl Tower.'

'Oh,' repeated Anna, even more disconcerted. 'But they're self-catering studio apartments. I thought she would have wanted to be in a serviced hotel.'

'Not Hilda!' chuckled Theo. 'She likes her own space and making her own bed. Besides, she said she'd enjoy trying out different eateries. I invited her to join us tonight, but she said she needed her beauty sleep.'

'But how will she manage with her sticks? She's—'

'Don't you worry about Hilda, Anna. She's fiercely independent. I'm assuming The Pearl Tower must have a lift?'

'It has two actually,' replied Anna archly. 'There's a separate one for the penthouse.' She instantly regretted giving way to the temptation to show off and didn't add that the second lift was located in a grubby underground carpark.

'What's your penthouse suite like?' asked Theo.

'Fabulous! It has the most gorgeous views across London from its balcony.'

As the meal progressed, Anna picked at her food and made a show of looking at her watch.

Theo was alert to the hint, so he called time. 'Jarrad, I really think we ought to be going. Anna looks done-in. It must be a punishing schedule for her, and she's got the dress rehearsal tomorrow before the big opening on Friday night. We'll walk you back to your suite.'

'No need, Theo. It's just round the corner. I *am* pretty tired,' she admitted, throwing him a grateful glance. 'We can meet up again once the show is underway and I'm more into the rhythm of things.'

'Sure, Anna. We understand,' he replied warmly.

'Yeah. Ciao for now, sis. We'll be rooting for you on Friday night. The big reveal!'

Anna shuddered slightly and smiled wanly. 'Don't... don't expect too much. It's like I said, it's a stepping stone,' and hastily turned to leave. Jarrad was oblivious, but Theo had missed neither the slight shudder nor her eyes welling up.

There was nothing more to be done at the hospital, but Bryn could not face going home just yet. He grabbed a takeaway pizza and sat in his car, trying to quell the demons that were mustering inside him. A week ago, his life had seemed so clear-cut. Now it was all at sea. Did he really know Susan? What she did had shocked him. Should he be shocked? Had he any right to be shocked? Deep down, he knew he'd rushed into things. He'd been too impatient for a shot at a normal life.

It had all happened with consummate ease, like a carpet unrolling effortlessly across a marble floor. The estate agent assistant who had shown him round the flat, the well-groomed, attractive, uncomplicated woman he had asked on a date. Six months later she had moved in with him. In another six months they were going to be married.

He had felt lucky, repeatedly telling himself he didn't deserve this second chance. Yet he could not dispel haunting thoughts of Susan and the flyer she had authored. When the air had cooled, he would try and reason with her, explain his position. See if he could persuade her to think differently about the women he regarded as victims, and she castigated as undesirables.

Who was he kidding? This watershed had exposed just how far apart they were. They needed a circuit breaker, a time to reflect before they hurtled towards what might be the biggest mistake of both their lives. It would mean postponing the wedding. What did that say about him? It was scarring enough to have abandoned one fiancée on her wedding day, now he would be tainted with prevaricating over another.

Approaching forty, had he been too desperate to fill the family hole that orphaned him as a child? And then, out of nowhere, *she* was suddenly there. That elfin face with impossibly large brown eyes and glossy black hair that almost, but not quite, covered a burn scar to her upper left temple. That petite body his arms ached to envelop. The porcupine spines bristling with passionate indignation. A mind as sharp as a razor, and a heart as deep as a well. Yes, she was there, her hatred of him constantly throwing out angry sparks from the bonfire of their past. He could not get her out of his head. But he must. He must! He absolutely must or his head would burst.

It was only a little after ten when he got home, so he was surprised there were no lights visible in the flat and even more surprised that Susan's car was not there. He saw it as soon as he turned the kitchen light on, staring at him accusingly from the table. A white envelope, a yale key – and her engagement ring.

Bryn sighed. He picked up the ring and placed it in his palm, wrapped his fingers around it for a few moments, then placed it resignedly next to the yale key before opening the letter she had left him. It was short and to the point, no sorrowful regrets or allusion to what might have been. It was clinical and empty of emotion.

Bryn had to admit to an element of surprise that she had acted so swiftly but also to a growing sense of relief. This was a huge wake-up call for him, too. He had been about to sleepwalk into a marriage teeming with comfortable niceties and devoid of substance. He left the note, key, and ring languishing on the table and headed up to an empty bed.

13

Thursday, 22nd May

After a restless night and with no appetite for breakfast, Bryn left early for work. None of his team were in yet. On his desk lay some background notes Jemimah had prepared for him. A couple of sheets of A4, neatly folded with an identifying Post-It note.

He got himself a coffee, pulled a cereal bar from his bottom drawer, and settled down to read her report. The charity was called The *Lotus Hub Foundation*. It was new, only formed six months ago. Its patron was Baroness O'Neil, a Lords cross-bencher. The website listed a dozen eminent names who had pledged their support and volunteered their expertise. Names such as Richard Forrester, Professor of Linguistics at UCL; Tiwa Okocha, Chair of *Eradicate Modern Slavery*.

Scanning down the list, Bryn paused at a name he was very familiar with – Professor Theodore Kendrick, PTSD specialist. That made sense, given the trauma the women would have experienced, and he was glad it was Theo. No-one better.

The website's current donations stood at £720k. Pretty good for six months, and its founding director was listed as... Bryn's heart missed a beat... Ms Amira Saleem, QC.

Mia!

The *Lotus Hub Foundation* was Mia's undertaking! Once he had adjusted to the shock, he found himself smiling. This was so Mia. So very Mia. His heart swelled and ached in equal measure. Why hadn't she mentioned this new foundation when he asked her if she knew of any Syrian refugees from her caseload? Granted, it wasn't fully up and running yet, but she clearly had a passionate interest in helping trafficked women beyond her pro bono work. It needed no soul searching to answer his own question. She wanted him out of her life as quickly as possible; strictly necessary communication only. She had made that abundantly clear. Who could blame her after what he had put her through? His understanding did not lessen his pain.

Later that afternoon, Bryn took a call from the pathologist wanting to see him about the postmortem she had just undertaken on the throat-slashed victim. Bryn stopped off to buy coffees and blueberry muffins on the way, surmising that Fiona had probably missed lunch again, as she often did when it was busy.

'Have you got any further with the ethnicity profiling, Fiona?'

'My best estimate is Syrian, possibly Lebanese.'

'Syrian would fit with our working hypothesis. We believe she was the minder of four trafficked women working in a pop-up nail bar. She's probably an illegal immigrant who climbed her way into a survival niche. We think she was murdered because she messed up or knew too much – or both. Possibly trafficked we think?'

'I'd say probably.'

'Why so?'

'Interestingly, she only had one kidney. That puzzled me, because she looked to be mid-thirties and otherwise healthy.'

Bryn bowed his head and bit his lip. He knew where this was going. Six years with Manchester Vice had bruised his soul too often to doubt the inhumanity that some were capable of.

'It did explain what that serial number tattooed on her forearm was,' said Fiona, pointing to BA3B27D6 tattooed on the victim's forearm.

'I wondered if that was some kind of identifier to keep tabs on them when they were moved around – and to deter escape attempts. It's a dehumanising means of control; a statement of ownership like the branding of livestock. But it's an odd combination of letters and numbers. The Auschwitz tattoos were numerical, and black slave branding was more likely to be initials. Also, the RTA victim from the same nail bar didn't have this kind of identifier, as I recall.'

'No, I checked,' replied Fiona. 'There were no tattoos anywhere on her body, identifiers or otherwise. She also had both her kidneys. That's what set me thinking.' Fiona picked up pencil and paper and started to demonstrate. 'It seemed random until I spotted that numbers always followed letters. I missed it at first because I was working on BA 3, B27, D6, but when I separated the letters further, the numbers only came after the last three letters.' She wrote down what she meant B – A 3 – B 27 – D 6. 'That's when I spotted the connection.'

'It's still double Dutch to me,' said Bryn.

'That's because you're not a medic. I realised the first letter referred to blood group, and the following letters and numbers were tissue type and antigens.'

'Antigens? As in antibodies?'

'Yes. Organ transplants need to be matched on three categories: blood group, tissue type, and antigens. The best antigen match is when they don't work against each other, as it minimises the risk of the organ being rejected because the recipient's antibodies attack them. Your Jane Doe's blood group was B, which is rarer and more common in black and ethnic minorities. My best guess is she had been matched for a kidney donation. Since the explosion of Type 2 diabetes, we can't keep up with the demand for kidney transplants. The waiting lists are growing by the month, fuelling a profitable black market. Trafficked victims would be prime targets. Pretty ruthless. The tattoo would have been a fail-safe identifier in case she had to be moved in a hurry – or tried to escape.'

'So, not a philanthropic donor?'

'I think you know the gruesome answer to that better than I.'

Bryn nodded sadly. 'Brilliant work, Fiona. I owe you more than a blueberry muffin. I should shout you dinner.'

'No need to buy me dinner, Bryn. Just find the brutes behind this. That's all the thanks I need.'

That evening Bryn went home to an empty flat. He tossed his keys onto the table next to the engagement ring, still lying where he had left it. He picked it up to examine it more closely. The large solitaire diamond had set him back a pretty penny. Even though they had only been engaged for three weeks, it would not have mattered to him if she'd kept it and sold it. He had to give her credit for not wanting to profit from their failed relationship. Susan had her own moral code, just not quite in tune with his own.

He bore her no ill will. He did not want to profit from their failed relationship either. Perhaps the jeweller would give him a decent price for it, and he could donate the money to charity. His heart told him exactly which charity. He would make an anonymous donation to this new *Lotus Hub Foundation*. Mia need never know.

His doorbell rang. It was half past eight. He was not expecting anyone. Perhaps it was Susan coming back for something she had forgotten. Well, he would be gracious.

But it was not Susan standing at his front door; it was Theo Kendrick.

'Theo!' exclaimed Bryn, unable to hide his surprise. 'It must be nearly seven years! What brings you here? How did you know how to find me?' Then suddenly his expression turned to alarm. 'It's not Mia, is it? Nothing's happened to Mia. Please tell me she's alright.'

His obvious distress confirmed to Theo that he had done the right thing in rocking up on Bryn's doorstep. He was determined to get to the bottom of what had happened on that fateful wedding day. If he'd phoned, Bryn might have blown him off. It would be harder to turn him away in person.

'She's fine, don't alarm yourself.'

'How did you find me?'

'Oh, you know me. Investigative journalism is still in my DNA. Piece of cake. May I come in?'

'Sure,' replied Bryn, relieved that no ill had befallen Mia and that Theo still wanted to be on speaking terms with him.

Theo followed Bryn into the kitchen and spotted the remnants of his failed relationship sitting accusingly on the table.

'What happened here?' he asked, pointing to them.

'I messed up again. She's gone. She decided I was too much of a sanctimonious prig.'

'I've been accused of that often enough in my time,' said Theo with a wry smile.

'It's probably for the best. I rather rushed into things. I only latterly realised we didn't share the same values. We were never going to be soulmates; more like housemates with fringe benefits. Perhaps I'm just not cut out to be a family man.'

'Would this have anything to do with bumping into Mia again?' asked Theo, not letting his penetrating gaze wander from Bryn's face.

'Why on earth would you think that?' came the defensive response.

'Because I'm a psychologist, and I understand a lot about humans – particularly those in pain.'

'There's nothing to understand. I'm not in pain. I just got it wrong again. I told you, I'm just not cut out to be a family man.'

'Bullshit!' declared Theo sternly. 'I never bought all that rubbish about commitment phobia. That's why I'm here. I want to know the real reason you abandoned Mia on her wedding day, and I'm not leaving till you tell me.'

Bryn put his head in his hands. 'I *can't* tell you, Theo. You don't understand. She could still be in danger. I like you, Theo. I like you a lot, always have, but please don't press this.'

'Now I *really* need to know,' said Theo more firmly. 'If Mia is in danger, I *absolutely* need to know.'

'If I tell you, you can't ever tell her, you understand? I have to be able to trust you on this.'

'Alright. We will agree to trust each other. You tell me everything – and I mean everything.'

'It's a long story.'

'Just as well I brought some beers,' replied Theo, placing a four-pack on the table.

※※※※※

Saturday, 18th November, 2008

Bryn emerged from the hotel shower room on the morning of his wedding, high on a cocktail of excitement, nerves, joy, exhilaration – all those turbulent emotions that imprison grooms on the morning of their approaching nuptials. He had booked into a Holiday Inn near to the wedding venue to give Mia some space the night before their wedding. Mia had said he was being neanderthal about it. He'd been living in her flat for eighteen months, so what difference did one night make, but he had insisted. Whistling, with one towel draped around his waist, another rubbing his wet hair, he stopped in his tracks. There was a man sitting in the bedroom chair a few feet away, holding a gun.

Bryn would have known him anywhere, because he was the spit of their father. Tall and athletic with thick dark hair that still had no hint of grey.

'Morning, little brother. I see you're still as skinny as the little runt I remember.'

'*How the hell did you get in here, Kraig, and what the fuck do you want?*'

'*I was wondering why I hadn't had an invitation to the big event.*'

'*No list could be long enough to have your name on it. How did you know about it anyway?*'

'*You'd be surprised how much I know about you, bro – and that little Arab cunt of yours. Have a seat,*' *he said, indicating the bed with a wave of his gun.*

'*Fuck off, Kraig. I haven't got time for this.*'

'*Sit!*' *yelled Kraig. '*Unless you want the little woman to be a widow before she's a bride. Time for retribution. Time for me to be judge and juror. I've been waiting for the right opportunity for a few years now, and you've presented me with the perfect scenario. Lady Justice herself couldn't have balanced her scales better.*'

Bryn sat on the bed and Kraig threw a pair of handcuffs at him. '*One round your wrist, snap the other to the bed frame, then we can have a cosy chat.*'

Picking up on the menace in his brother's voice, Bryn did as he was bid.

Once Kraig was satisfied that his younger brother was securely handcuffed to the bedframe, he put the gun down on the dressing table next to him and pulled out a mobile phone from his pocket. It was Bryn's.

'*You really are pathetic, Bro. I got your password on the second attempt. Tried Ma's birthday first then Cadi's. Should have tried hers first, given how attached you appear to be to that pathetic soft toy she mooned over,*' *he said, pointing to Reesa Rabbit aka Efa propped up on the bedside cabinet.* '*Quite touching that you're so sentimental, Scabby Cop.*'

'*What do you want, Kraig?*' *asked Bryn through gritted teeth.*

'*A cosy chat. Set a few records straight. Get my revenge, that sort of thing. How about you, Bro – want to get anything off your chest?*'

'I've got nothing to say to you except fuck off. I hoped I'd never have to set eyes on you again.'

'Hmm, pretty damning, considering you have no idea who I am.'

'Of course I know who you are!'

'No! You don't,' interrupted Kraig angrily. *'You haven't the first clue. I'm fifty years of age. I was ten when you were born, and you got me sent down when I was twenty-two. Do the maths, kiddo. If you take off a few years for the incoherence of toddlerhood, you've only ever known me when I was a teenager. So don't come pretending you **know** me. Prison was hard, but there were some upsides. Would it surprise you that I have a degree in psychology, that I have my own haulage business? No boss, no Ma'ams and Sirs to answer to like you have.'*

'I told you I haven't time for this. What the hell do you want, Kraig?'

'I'm here to administer my own brand of justice. I have my own scales to balance. But first up, let's set a few records straight. It's about time you faced the truth you've always denied.'

'What truth?'

'That I did NOT murder our mother.'

'If the blow to the head didn't kill her, then running off, deserting her, leaving her to bleed out on the kitchen floor – what was that if not murder?'

'Like I told them, I panicked. I couldn't believe I'd hit Ma. It was a moment of madness. I just panicked... I just ran. Dad believed me. The jury would have believed me if you hadn't put the boot in, making out I meant to kill her, making out I'd been planning it. I loved her, for fuck's sake, Bible-spouting, soft mare as she was. I loved her, you idiot. Not in the soppy way you did, but I loved her all the same.

'Before Cadi came along, I was the apple of her eye. I was her clever, golden boy who could read by the time I was four, who could find half the countries in Europe in her worn atlas

before I started school, who sang all her favourite hymns up at chapel. Yes, don't smirk at the thought of me inside a house of God, you moron. The sermons and the prayers were pretty tedious, but I loved the singing. Pa with his deep baritone voice and me with that sweet angelic voice six-year-olds can lay claim to. And then she was born, the fucking retard, and everything changed overnight.'

'Don't dare call her that! Don't dare sully her memory. She would still be here if it weren't for you.'

'You always did have a vivid imagination, Bro. I didn't let her go roaming out on a freezing, stormy night. It was you who was supposed to watch her. If anyone's to blame for Cadi's pneumonia, it's you, Scabby.'

Bryn had no answer. Despite his father's constant reassurances, Bryn had never forgiven himself for not keeping Cadi closer that night.

'You robbed me of a dozen years of my life. I'd have got a manslaughter sentence and probably a heap of mitigation, too. Megan would have waited for me. I was going to start saving once the strike was over, and we were planning to marry as soon as we could afford a place of our own. She would have waited for me if I'd got a short sentence, but there was no way that was going to happen once they gave me life. I can't blame her. She's the love of my life. There's never been anyone else.

'I tried to get her to come away with me when I got out, but she couldn't do it to her kids – or him; said he was a good father and a good husband. I'm hoping she might change her mind when the kids are grown. But that's in the future; her youngest is only ten. Let's get back to Lady Justice and the business of the day. What do you think a suitable sentence would be for stealing a dozen years of someone's liberty?'

Bryn stayed silent. He was not going to dignify Kraig's taunts and game-playing with a response.

'On one side of the scales we have the additional years of incarceration, the stigma of a murder conviction, the loss of *earnings, a career – and crucially, the loss of the wife and family of my dreams. On the other side we have to consider you were only eleven at the time of the trial, so a chunk of mitigation has to be made for that. Prison was bearable. It spared me years of hard labour half a mile underground, possible injury, and the likely blight of emphysema. I gained an education – Ma would have been made up. She always said how clever I was. I'd have done well at school, if I hadn't been so disaffected. Understandable in the circumstances, as my psychology has taught me.'*

'Cut to the chase, Kraig.'

'Don't be so impatient, little Bro. You have to savour these moments. We haven't talked about your career yet. How could you, Bryn? Of all the jobs in the world, how could you choose the police force? After everything they did to me on the picket line. After everything they did to my mates, the brutality, the—'

'We all know they weren't regular police officers. Even I know they were paramilitaries, government plants in an orchestrated conflict, unholy cover-up that it was. Regular police do a stalwart job. My foster father was a stand-up guy, salt of the earth, moral integrity and fortitude. I was proud to follow in his footsteps.'

'Dad would turn in his grave.'

'Owen Edwards and our father had a lot more in common than you dare admit. Dad would have been grateful to Owen and Ffion for taking me in, or I'd have spent my teens in a care home.'

'That would have balanced the scales. I'd probably have considered the debt paid if you'd been incarcerated for years in some grotty kids' home. That was then and this is now, and there is still a debt to be paid.'

'I'm getting pretty sick and tired of this farce.'

'Shut the fuck up and listen,' said Kraig, starting to type into Bryn's mobile phone. *'That should do nicely,'* he added, *smiling roguishly at his brother still perched uncomfortably*

on the bed. 'So, to the small matter of your sentence. Mitigation and leniency are required in view of your youth at the time. However, we mustn't forget what it says in Ma's good Bible about "an eye for an eye".'

'Don't bring our mother into this. Just get on with it, whatever it is you're planning.'

'I couldn't have my paramour, so you can't have yours.'

'I don't see how you can stop me.'

'Six years. Yes, six years is about right, taking into account the juvenile mitigation.'

'What the hell are you on about?'

'You've to do without her for six years. If you try to take up with her before then, she'll meet with a nasty accident. Guns are so crude, don't you think?' he added, picking up his gun and waving it around. 'So primitive. A needle in the arm on a park run has much more finesse. Or how about an airport concourse? She's always hopping over to Strasbourg, I understand. All that crowded jostling. Piece of cake.'

'You vile bastard. If you harm a single hair on her head, I'll—'

'Don't get in a tizz, Scabby. If you play by the rules, then every hair on her head will be safe. Her fate's in your hands, not mine. Just like Cadi's was. Now, how are we doing on time? Ten past nine, the wedding's at eleven. Brides like to be fashionably late, so let's send this text at ten past eleven. All the guests will be there, she'll probably be lurking at the back wondering where the hell you are, and then poof! Quite the most delicious denouement. Aren't you impressed with my erudite vocabulary. A psychology degree can do that to a man.'

'What message?' demanded Bryn.

'The message I'm going to send to Theodore Kendrick, that's the guy who's giving her away, right? The pseudo father of the bride. I have him here in your contacts. I'm envisaging he'll have his mobile on silent in his suit pocket. As it gets later and later and you still haven't arrived, he'll turn it on in

case you're trying to contact him. At ten past eleven, he'll see he has a message from you. Shall I read it to you? It's quite scrumptious.'

Bryn remained silent and deathly pale.

Kraig read from the screen theatrically, 'I'm not coming, Theo. Tell Mia I made a mistake. I can't go through with it. I got carried away with the idea of it. The reality is very different.'

'Is that it? No sorry, no—'

'Of course not! Do you take me for a simpleton? No cringing apologies, no I love you buts, no you're too good for me, no get-out-of jail-free cards for you, Scabby. I want her to hate your guts. I want her to loathe and despise you, just in case you entertained any hope you could pick up with her again after the six years are spent.' Kraig slipped Bryn's mobile in one pocket and his gun in the other, before putting masking tape round his brother's mouth.

'Can't have you shouting for help after I'm gone. Check out is at 12 noon. I've put out the "do not disturb" sign. When you haven't paid your dues, some maid is bound to come along to seek you out. By then, the wedding guests will have dispersed, and your precious bride will be… well, I'll leave that to your imagination. I'll toddle off now. Goodbye, little brother. I won't hesitate to keep my part of the bargain if you welch on yours.'

'So, you see, Theo,' said Bryn, 'I had no choice. He would have killed her.'

Theo was silent with his head bowed for what seemed to Bryn an interminable time. When he lifted it, his eyes were wet. He said nothing but simply walked across to his host and put his arms round him in a fatherly hug. Bryn let his head flop onto Theo's shoulder, and then the tears came. Nearly seven years of pent-up tears burst out in stifled, gulping sobs. He had not cried like that since the day his mother and sister died almost thirty years ago.

14

Thursday, 22nd May, 2014

The afternoon dress rehearsal was going well. Anna had spotted the press reviewer at the back of the stalls. Don was sitting in one of the boxes with a special guest. She hoped he might be some bigwig from the West End. It might be that lucky break she needed. She produced her best ever rendition of her solo song and was relieved that Wayne's cutting of her catsuit, while tantalising, was not unduly exposing. Toby was warm in his congratulations, and she headed back to the penthouse tired but relieved. She could do this. She could absolutely do this. And who knew where it might lead.

It was just after six that evening when Don let himself into the penthouse suite. He had done it once before, and Anna found it unnerving. Yes, it was his apartment of course, but he had loaned it to her exclusively and it displayed a lack of respect for her privacy. She was as much at fault. It was a mortice lock, and if she had locked it from the inside and left the key in the lock, he would have had to knock, but she kept forgetting. Now that he had done it twice, she made a mental note to be more vigilant at remembering. She wondered if he had come to take her out to dinner until she spotted that he was carrying a holdall and was suddenly seized by a wave of anxiety. Surely, he wasn't planning to stay the night.

'Anna darling, you were sensational at dress rehearsal today.'

'You were right, Don. It did feel much better once we were performing it non-stop with all the lights and the costumes and everything.'

He pulled out a red catsuit from the holdall, identical to the one she wore on stage, which he laid out on the bed.'

'I don't understand,' said Anna. 'Is this to be my dressing room now? Do I go to the performance already in costume tomorrow? But what about hair and makeup?'

'You are divine as you stand, and I have all the makeup you're going to need in my pocket,' he said, pulling out a new red lipstick, discarding the cellophane wrapper on the floor and pushing up the tube to reveal a vivid scarlet red shade. 'Wasn't I clever to match it so well?' he said, planting a streak of colour across the inside of her wrist so that she could admire the match, before depositing it on her dressing table.

'I still don't understand…'

'I told you there was going to be a VIP guest watching rehearsals today. As expected, he was delighted with you, Anna. He would like an exclusive before the hordes of London get their prying eyes on you – a private performance, as it were. He's willing to pay handsomely. You'd be surprised how much some of the mega rich will pay for exclusivity.'

Anna stood frozen to the spot. 'I don't understand. What do you mean by a private performance? How can—?'

'Oh, come on, Anna. Don't try and play the schoolgirl with me. I'm sure it's charming in the right context, but you're not wet behind the ears – exquisite as they are. You know the score, so let's just cut out the crap.'

'No! No! I don't know the score. I don't understand all this. I don't understand what you think I'm supposed to know about *private performances*.'

'You get a ten per cent cut, Anna. Don't look a gift horse in the mouth.'

'A ten per cent cut of what, and FOR what?'

Don was reaching into the holdall again, this time pulling out two red silk ties and a pair of stage scissors. 'A song and a little extended role play. You're a bright girl, Anna, you can work it out. You just have to play out his fantasy. Give him a good time. It's no more than you wannabes grab at to get a leg up from the dizzying heights of your mediocrity. If you perform exceptionally well, he might even drop a word in the right ear for you, get you up that star-crusted ladder you're so keen to climb. And don't forget the ten per cent. Good money for a couple of hour's work.'

'You're out of your tiny mind!' she yelled at him. 'Do you really expect me to cavort around in THAT?' she shrieked. 'And prostitute myself to fulfil some sick bastard's fantasy? I WON'T do it. I WON'T DO IT, I tell you! You can keep your grubby ten per cent. You can keep your mucky production. How could I have been so blind to be taken in by you!'

'The vain and ambitious are blind as bats and easier prey.'

'This ends here. I want my salary to date, and then I'm getting on the next plane back to Canada. Jill is going to have to carry your opening night. Good luck with that one!'

'What salary?'

'My pay so far.'

'You haven't done a single performance yet, and your flight has to come out of your pay, so by that calculation I think you owe *me* some salary.'

Anna realised she had been so starry-eyed by the chance to be flown over to London and lodged in a penthouse suite that she had not bothered to tie down a contract. She had been such a fool. The worst kind of fool – duped by her own conceit.

'I will pay you back the cost of the flight, but I *will not* do this.'

'You *will* do it. I can't afford to hack this guy off. Nobody gets on the wrong side of him – including you, Anna. You're playing with fire. It's a couple of hours, for God's sake, what's the big deal! Swallow your pride. You'll be flaunting your body on stage for the next three weeks. This is only a smidgen more – and as I said, big rewards.'

Anna's alarm had turned to an icy steeliness. 'A *smidgen*, you sick mongrel. I won't do it, I tell you.'

'You *will* do it, Anna. He'll be here at seven o'clock, and you'd better be dressed for the part and... accommodating,' he added. He locked the door and pocketed the key. Then he picked up her mobile phone that was lying on the dressing table where he had deposited the new lipstick, and pocketed that, too. 'Even if I have to squeeze you into that catsuit myself, you WILL do this.'

'Give me my phone and room key,' she demanded.

'Technically it's *my* room key, and I'll keep your mobile for now – a little insurance policy.'

'I won't do it, I tell you. I'll scream the place down. I'll cry rape. I'll—'

'Be my guest. I rather like the idea. It will add more piquancy to the performance. Besides, no-one will hear you, Anna, the top two floors have industrial level soundproofing.'

'You can't make me do this. I'll go to the Police, I'll—'

'You really are an idiot, Anna. I got you so wrong. Thought you knew what side your bread was buttered. It's the name of the game. All those mediocre wannabes trying to claw their way up the ladder. What makes you think you're any better than the rest of them?'

'I'm not like them.'

'You want to be a star, don't you? I said I can make you a star. And I can. You just have to know how to play the game. This guy's a big fish. He's got fingers in some very big pies. He could make things happen for you. You've got a decent voice, Anna, but your best asset is your model looks. Play the game, Anna. What's an hour here and there?'

'You're a monster! You're—'

'Hardly a monster. An asset manager, yes,' he interrupted her. 'Sourcing assets, sweating assets, that's what I do – and I'm damn good at it! Animal, vegetable, mineral, whatever – if there's an angle, I'll work it. It's made me a rich man.'

'You're nothing but a sick, sordid barrow boy,' she yelled, lunging at him, trying to reach the pocket where he had stowed her phone and room key.

The lunge took Don by surprise as she wrestled him to the floor, but he was still too strong for her and soon regained his feet. 'Put it on, Anna. NOW. Or I will do it for you.'

Anna's mind was racing. Perhaps she could play along and then grab the key when he was off guard. She was an actress, after all. 'I'll do it, but I want twenty percent. I think I'm worth it. And I want the flight cost waived and payment in *cash* after every performance.'

'My, my, you're not such a schoolgirl after all. Just a moneygrubbing cunt like the rest of them.'

'Aren't you going to do the honours?' she asked, pouting sensually and pointing to the lipstick he had placed on her dressing table.

Don smirked at the transformation. They were all the same. Sooner or later, they all saw the sense of taking the handout.

When he walked across to her dressing table to pick up the lipstick, Anna grabbed the vase from the coffee table and ran at him. He turned just in time to parry the blow she was aiming at his head and, dropping the lipstick, he knocked the vase out of her hand. It smashed on the floor.

He caught hold of her long black tresses and hurled her to the floor. 'You fucking vixen!" he snarled at her. 'You stupid, fucking schoolgirl vixen!'

'You won't get away with this,' she roared. 'I'll see you rot in hell first!'

'That's exactly where you're heading, Anna darling.' He dragged her by the hair to the balcony. She struggled, kicked, and screamed, clutching at the net curtain hanging by the open French doors, wrenching it from its pole.

It was over in seconds.

Pulling her roughly to her feet, he tipped her backwards over the railing. As she descended the twelve floors, Anna let out her well-practised, colossal scream. It demanded the attention of a host of unsuspecting pedestrians on their way home from work. An actress taking her final bow, compelling her audience to look up and take note.

Don knew he had to act lightning fast. He had but a few seconds before that body hit the concrete and hordes of people would be looking skywards and reaching for their mobiles to call emergency services. He ducked down and crawled back from the balcony.

It would go down as a suicide; another homesick wannabe star overcome with fear of failure. Nonetheless, he must get himself out of there as fast as possible.

He hastily pushed the props back into his holdall and dashed for the elevator. As his car wheels screeched out of the car park, he made a call.

'Tereza, I'm heading to yours. I need an alibi. Make sure you're in and leave the door unlocked.' He was thankful it was early, and the girls hadn't arrived for their evening shift. Getting them out would have perilously delayed his getaway.

He made a second call to a number on his speed dial. 'Keep the girls away tonight. There's been a major incident at The Tower. Don't bring them in until I give you the all-clear. It will take a few days for the dust to settle. Don't worry about your commission; I'll square it with you. And I'm sure you can find other uses for them in the meantime.'

Hilda was just getting ready to go out and find a nice pub for a quiet pint and a steak pie – if they did steak pies in London, that is; and if anywhere quiet existed in such a busy metropolis – when she heard the primeval scream close by her window. So close it sounded almost inside her room.

She looked out. Directly above she could see a balcony, while four stories below she could see a body lying in a tangled heap on the block paving.

'Lord Almighty!' exclaimed Hilda to herself. 'Sum poor wretch 'as fall'n off that balcony.'

She exited as fast as her waddle and the hotel lift would allow. The weaselly receptionist was running out just ahead of her. By the time Hilda puffed to the scene, a dozen bystanders had gathered round.

Hilda stared at the body lying prostate on the ground, blood beginning to seep out onto the blocked paving. She screamed hysterically. A young man put his arm round her and tried to pull her away from the scene.

'You might be better sitting on that bench over there, Mrs. The ambulance is on its way.'

'No! Yer don't understan'! I KNOA 'er! It's ANNA! It's me best friend's gran'daughter!' Hastily she dialled Theo's number.

'Evening, Hilda. How are you enjoying the metropolis?'

'It's Anna! It's Anna!! Dear Jesus! Theo, it's Anna,' she blurted out.

In the incident room, Jemimah rushed across to Bryn's desk. 'You know we earmarked the Pearl Tower as a potential target of interest?'

Bryn nodded his agreement.

'There's been a 999 call from there a few minutes ago. A report is coming that a woman has fallen from the penthouse suite balcony.'

'I'm on my way. Can you get a message to Jake, Chrissy, and Zabhir? They're much closer. I'll meet them there.'

Theo dropped everything, but it still took him forty-five minutes to get to The Pearl Tower. On the way, he rang Jarrad, but it went to voicemail. When he arrived, Anna had already been taken off to hospital, and an area in the square had been cordoned off, marshalled by police. A crowd had gathered, but Hilda's height and bulk was easy to spot amongst them. He made his way to her.

'What happened here, Hilda? Is Anna dead?'

'I don't know. I weren't near enuff t'ear what they was sayin'. They whisked 'er off t'ospital sharpish. She weren't moving tho', Theo, and there were a lot o' blud. She weren't moving.'

Theo spotted Bryn over by the cordon and ran across to him, brushing away officers who tried to stop him. 'Bryn! Bryn!' he called out.

Bryn saw Theo trying to get to him. 'It's alright, let him through.'

'She's my granddaughter, Bryn!' He did not bother with the 'sort of', 'almost' prefixes he was used to adding. 'Jarrad's sister. Anna Adams. Is she alive? I've got to get to her. Do you know what hospital they've taken her to?'

Bryn could not remember ever seeing Theo so distraught.

'They've taken her to Kings A and E. I'm afraid she didn't survive the fall, Theo. I'm so very sorry.'

'How could this happen? She couldn't have fallen, surely? There are barriers on these kinds of balconies – and she wouldn't have... have...' Theo hesitated, remembering the shudder and Anna welling up the night before. 'She wouldn't have... jumped?'

'We're keeping an open mind at present. My team are in there, and I'm about to go in myself to see what I can find out. You get off to the hospital and I will keep you informed.'

The two men held each other's gaze for a brief moment. A new understanding had built up between them since Bryn's heart-rending disclosure. 'Trust me, Theo. I'll get to the bottom of this.'

Bryn met up with Jake in the foyer of The Pearl Tower. 'What have you got for me, Jake?'

'Jemi was right to put this on the watch list. Chrissy and Zabhir found the single rooms on the upper floors were all empty, but items they found there suggest they were probably being used for prostitution. This stacks up with the industrial level soundproofing and the separate access via the underground car park.'

'Hidden in plain sight. Clever. Have we alerted our forensics?'

'Jemi's already put in an urgent request.'

'Good work, Jake.'

'DI Wingate from Bancroft station is in charge. He's got the building cordoned off, and he's posted an officer outside the penthouse suite. I think you might have to battle him for control of this one; it's his patch. I don't think he'll take kindly to you pulling rank. He's just headed to the penthouse now.'

'How do I get up there?'

'Round the back of the building and into the underground car park where there's a lift. Those building plans Jemi rooted out have been a godsend.'

'*She's* the godsend!' added Bryn. 'I need to take a look at the crime scene first, but don't let anyone leave the building, residents or staff.'

'Noted.'

'Can you go and shake down the manager. We need to interview the owner of the penthouse pdq.'

'Will do. Good luck!'

'Good luck?'

'With Wingate I think you might need it. He's the DI at Chrissy and Zabhir's station. They say he's a brute of a boss.'

Bryn exited the lift at the penthouse floor and showed his lanyard to the on-guard PC. 'DCI Bryn Ellis from SCD9.'

'PC Rahim, sir. DI Wingate is inside, sir.'

On entering the penthouse suite, all his senses were on high alert. Before forensics got to work, Bryn liked to 'feel' the scene in its raw state.

'Who the hell are you, and how did you get in here?' snarled DI Wingate.

Bryn was relieved to see the man was at least wearing protective gloves.

'DCI Bryn Ellis SCD9. The Pearl Tower is on our watch list as part of a human trafficking investigation,' he replied, pulling out a pair of nitrile gloves and shoe covers from his pocket. 'We are going to need our specialist forensics in here.'

'This is *my* patch. She's an actress, not a migrant. It's most likely a jumper. We have our own forensics.'

'I appreciate this is your patch,' replied Bryn, 'but we will need to work together on this.'

'The last thing I need is your SCD9 nancy boys interfering.'

Bryn finally lost his patience. He could see velvet gloves were going to be useless. 'Interfering, SIR!' he boomed. 'Need I remind you that I outrank you, DI Wingate, and you will accord me due respect. I repeat, we are going to have to work together. I won't interfere in your frontline policing of this incident, and you won't interfere with the specialist nature of our enquiries. We believe this building is being used by a vice ring. I would have thought you'd be glad to offload the cost of forensics to another unit.'

'I want authorisation from my Super before I'll give this one up. Need I remind you that he outranks *you,* SIR,' he mocked.

'If you want to play rock-paper-scissors, be my guest, Wingate. I've got some pretty big boulders I can throw.'

'We'll see about that,' retorted DI Wingate as he marched out of the suite, shoulder-barging Bryn on the way.

Bryn was 'feeling' the scuffle; the broken vase, the torn net curtain. His hunter eyes quickly spotted a scarlet red tie peeping out from under the bed where it had fallen. Nor did he miss the discarded lipstick tube cellophane on the floor and the pushed-up red lipstick staining the cream carpet where it had fallen. Then he spotted them. Lying on the floor near the coffee table, still neatly folded, was a pair of white fluffy towels. He walked into the bathroom where he saw a pair of used towels hanging on the rail. He pulled out his mobile and dialled Jemi.

'How long before our forensics get here, Jemi?'

'They're on their way; ETA twenty minutes.'

He knew he needed to get to the hospital as soon as possible, so he rang Chrissy and asked her to join him in the penthouse. He waited for her in the corridor.

'I need you to stay here with PC Rahim until *our* forensics arrive, Chrissy. They should be here in twenty. It's important that no-one goes in there until our own forensics have done their sweep. This is really important, Chrissy. I'm trusting you to hold the line. You can clock off as soon as our forensics arrive.'

'Understood, sir,' she nodded.

Before leaving, he turned to PC Rahim. 'Please don't misunderstand. This is no reflection on your ability to do *your* job, but it's imperative we have our specialist forensics in there before any potential contamination. I have the utmost respect for you frontline officers, but we are in the middle of a human trafficking investigation.'

PC Rahim was surprised to have so much deference afforded him. It was not what he was used to from his bosses.

'No worries, sir, Chrissy... er, WPC Blackwell and me, we've worked together lots before.'

Meanwhile Jake had been busy interrogating the weaselly receptionist. 'And you would be?' he asked, taking out his notebook.

'Stuart Holder, sir. Pearl Tower Manager.'

'I need a name and contact number for the owner of the penthouse suite,' he demanded.

'It's Mr Kavanagh's penthouse suite. I don't have a personal number for him. If I need to contact him, I leave a message at the theatre asking him to ring me back. He owns the theatre as well.'

'Do I look like I'm wet behind the ears?' asked Jake, leaning in so that his face was only inches from Stuart's.

'I don't know what you mean?'

'You know *exactly* what I mean. So, let's start again, shall we? His *full* name would be?'

'It's Don Kavanagh, Brendon Kavanagh.'

'And the number?'

'He's very particular about who has his personal number, he—'

'The number. *Now*, Mr Holder. Or would you like me to explain to the coroner that you obstructed our enquiries.'

Reluctantly Stuart pulled out his mobile and scrolled to the number. Jake took the phone from him and dialled.

'What is it, Stuart, I'm busy,' came the reply.

'It's not Stuart. This is DS Freeman from New Scotland Yard. Where are you presently, sir?'

'I'm at a girlfriend's place, why?'

'And where would that be?'

'Peckham. What's this all about?'

'The full address, please.'

'26 Alpha Street, SE15 4GP. Now you really have to tell me what this is about.'

'Stay put, sir. We need to talk to you urgently. There's been a serious incident at The Pearl Tower.' Jake ended the call before any further protestations or questions.

Having made a note of the number, he handed the mobile back to its owner. Away from Stuart's gaze, he rang Jemi. 'Jemi, can you contact central control and get the nearest patrol car to go to 26 Alpha Street, SE15 4GP, and make sure that a Mr Don Kavanagh does not attempt to leave the property until I get there. He's the owner of the Tower Penthouse and I need to interview him urgently.'

'Is it true she's dead?' asked Jemi.

'I'm afraid so. That's why I need to speak with Kavanagh pdq.'

Theo and Hilda were sitting in a side room at Kings Hospital, still reeling from the shock. Theo had telephoned Anna's parents, Charlotte and Zak, in Canada. It was one of the hardest calls he'd had to make. Just then Jarrad rushed into the waiting room.

'I was on lates and have only just got your message, Theo. Is Anna going to be okay?'

'She's dead, Jarrad. I'm so sorry.'

'No, it's not possible. No! No! I wanted to get to know her better. I wanted to be a better brother, I wanted to…' and then he broke down.

Hilda pulled him down to sit by her and put a comforting arm around him. He sobbed uncontrollably into her ample shoulder before suddenly lifting his head.

'Do Mum and Dad know?'

'I contacted them half an hour ago. They're coming over on the first flight they can get.'

'I still can't take it in,' said Jarrad. 'And Mia!' he suddenly exclaimed. 'Has someone contacted Mia?'

'She's just finished up in Strasbourg and is booked onto an early morning flight. She was due back tomorrow in any case. She wanted to be here for Anna's opening night.'

It was almost midnight when forensics had finished their work. Bryn went back up to the crime scene on his way home. He wanted to take another look, and part of him also wanted reassurance that DI Wingate had kept to his side of the agreement and stationed an officer outside the penthouse suite overnight. Until he got some data back from forensics, he did not want to risk any possible contamination of the crime scene.

Bryn was very surprised to find PC Rahim still in post. 'Goodness, PC Rahim, it's almost midnight. When is your relief arriving?'

'I don't know, sir. I apologise, sir, but I had to relieve myself in the fire sand bucket over there. I didn't want to contaminate anything by using the bathroom.'

'You were here when I arrived not long after six.'

'Yes, sir.'

'But your shift must have finished at 10?'

'No, sir, it finished at 2pm this afternoon. I'm on earlies this week.'

'Are you telling me that you have been on duty since 6am and been stationed here for the last five hours without relief. Aren't these duties done in rotation? Who's your rotation partner?'

'He clocked off at 2, sir.'

'Have you had any food?'

'I got a sandwich at lunchtime, sir.'

'This is outrageous. What's your station number?'

'It's fine, sir, really. I'd rather you didn't. I—'

'Are you in need of the overtime, is that it?'

'I won't get paid overtime for this, sir.'

'Then why haven't you been relieved?'

PC Rahim dropped his head. Being dog-tired and hungry, and with the novelty of a senior officer according him respect, weakened his resolve. He did what he knew no Bancroft officer was expected to do – he welshed. 'It's a punishment, sir.'

Bryn was catching up fast. 'I see,' he said quietly, trying to quell the fury that was building inside. He'd seen the like often enough and it enraged him. Punishment Codes – or PCs as they were more commonly known inside the Met.' I'm guessing very few white officers are subject to PCs at Bancroft Road Station.'

'I shouldn't have said anything, sir.'

'You absolutely should. We are supposed to have a robust complaints system in the Met.'

'There's no-one to complain to at Bancroft, sir. Complaining and whining get PCs.'

'Ok. I'm going to sort this.'

'No, please don't, sir. Please, sir, it will only make it worse for me. I've got my sergeant exams coming up soon, that's why the PCs are heavier than usual. They try to make it uncomfortable so that we'll leave before we get promoted. They don't like the idea of people like us as sergeants. I can put up with this a bit longer, just till I get through my sergeant board.'

'You have to trust me. I *will* sort this. If good officers like yourself don't speak up, it's never going to get any better. You have to think of those coming up behind you as well as yourself.'

Rahim still looked troubled.

'Look, you're exhausted. Go home. Take tomorrow off in lieu. I'll stay here until relief arrives. I'll square it with your station. You'll make a fine sergeant, PC Rahim.'

'Thank you, sir. Are you sure about me taking tomorrow off? I'm due in at 6am.'

'You've just done an eighteen-hour shift, for God's sake! Go home, Rahim. Even the hardest PC-prone desk sergeant is not going to risk leaving the Head of SCD9 guarding a corridor.'

Bryn dialled Bancroft Road Station. 'DCI Bryn Ellis, SCD9. And you would be?'

'Night desk sergeant, sir.'

'I repeat, and you would be?'

'Sergeant Greenwood, sir.'

'Number?'

'Why do you need my number?'

'So, I know who to have up on a complaints charge if you don't give me the right answers.'

'What's this about, sir?'

'It's about PC Rahim still being stationed at The Pearl Tower penthouse suite after already doing an eighteen-hour shift.'

'I wouldn't know anything about that, sir. I came on duty at ten.'

'Wrong answer, Sergeant. You absolutely *should* know where your officers are and what shifts they're on. Isn't oversight and welfare of your team part of your job description?'

'I'll check the roster, sir.'

'I've sent Rahim home, and I've told him to take tomorrow off in lieu. He's done an eighteen-hour shift and God knows how much longer it would have been if I hadn't swung by. What does your roster say about who is to relieve him?'

'According to the roster, PC Khan is to relieve him at 6am. There must have been some mix-up, sir. The day desk sergeant must have thought Rahim was on nights.'

'Bullshit, and you know it. A 24-hour shift on your feet, half of which without access to food or water is a pretty steep PC, even for Bancroft Road.'

'I don't know what you mean, sir.'

'Oh, I think you absolutely do. Get someone over here on the double to relieve *me*. I'm not as patient as Rahim.'

'Yes, sir.'

15

Friday, 23rd May

Bryn felt the 10am briefing was going well, and they were getting closer. The crazy wall was crammed with Post-It notes and mug shots. 'I think we are looking at a multi-layered, sophisticated vice ring. We know that our RTA victim was probably a trafficked migrant, that her minder was definitely murdered – probably because she messed up and/or knew too much and had probably been a victim of enforced organ donation some years before. We know that the single rooms on the upper floors of Pearl Tower were probably being used for prostitution, and we have the suspicious death of Anna Adams. What else do we have?'

Chrissy reported on her interview with the cleaner. 'Her English is pretty minimal. She looked distinctly nervous, especially when I requested fingerprints for elimination purposes. She's in a holding room while we wait for a translator. My best guess is she's an illegal immigrant scraping a living on the pittance they pay her. I suspect she gave me a false name. She also gave The Pearl Tower as her address. I'd surmise it's a camp bed in the laundry room.'

'Ethnicity?' queried Bryn.

'Languages were never my strong suit. I've sent a recording of her ramblings so we can match a translator.'

'She's going to need legal aid. Can you get that arranged, Jemi?'

'Yes. As soon as we know her mother tongue, we can match her up with a lawyer.'

Jake reported on his interview with Brendon Kavanagh. 'He was charm itself. That kind of smug charm that makes you want to throw up. He has a cast-iron alibi. The girlfriend said he'd come to her place straight from the theatre and been with her ever since. His arrival time rules him out – that's if her alibi is kosher. I asked him if he felt responsible that an actress from his theatre had fallen to her death from his balcony. He said he couldn't be responsible for every actress who gets stage fright and does a jumper. Made out that she was struggling with the part.

'He's a cold bastard, hard as nails. Didn't bat an eyelid when I requested fingerprints for elimination purposes. He said it was a waste of time as he owned the place and his fingerprints would be everywhere, then he added a snide comment about wasting public money and the country going to the dogs. If Kavanagh is our man, he's very confident he's got away with it.'

'Perhaps his over-confidence will be his undoing,' said Bryn. 'Did you ask him about the sex toys in the single rooms?'

'He said the upper floors were rented out as budget rooms to backpackers and students, via a different company. He was quick to add that consenting adults' personal erotic fantasies were none of his concern. He said those rooms are the original offices from the building's former use and bring in a good enough income without the expense of converting them into the luxury studio apartments of the lower floors.'

'I've checked out the company,' piped up Jemi. 'It looks like it's a shell, so they could be using those rooms for anything – including prostitution or housing trafficked migrants. I'll need a bit more time to explore behind the labyrinth walls.'

'Brendon Kavanagh and his lady friend are coming this afternoon to give their formal statements,' concluded Jake.

'Who was scouring CCTV footage?' asked Bryn.

'That was me,' replied Zabhir. 'There are no security cameras at The Pearl Tower, which is unusual in itself for a city hotel, and the nearest CCTV is five streets away. The only thing of note from that camera is a black saloon car heading away from the vicinity. The time checks out with how long it would have taken a vehicle to reach that point from The Pearl Tower. We could only get half the number plate but we're working on it.'

'Might be worth checking if half the number plate matches half the number plate of any vehicle registered to Kavanagh,' said Bryn. 'Good work, Zabhir. Could you pull up any CCTV near to Alpha Road in Peckham, see if it throws up anything of interest?'

'Yes, sir, er… Bryn.'

'Do we have anything back from forensics yet?' continued Bryn.

'The fingerprint reports are due in soon; the other stuff will take a bit longer,' replied Jemi.

'Great work, everyone. We'll reconvene at 10am on Monday,' concluded Bryn.

After the meeting, Bryn pulled Zabhir and Chrissy aside. 'I want you to tell me everything you know about punishment codes at Bancroft Road.'

The two constables looked shocked and distinctly uneasy. 'It would be bad for us if it got out that we'd spoken to you,' said Zabhir.

'We've got to work there again after this secondment, sir. You don't understand, it's going to be difficult enough without this,' said Chrissy.

'Difficult why?'

'Because you asked for us by name. If you're female or from an ethnic race you don't get picked for these kinds of secondments.'

'That's precisely why I want to put a stop to this. PC Rahim's punishment was to be left at The Pearl Tower until 6am this morning, after starting work at 6am yesterday. He was still there at nearly midnight when I swung by, with no access to food or water since the previous lunchtime. And he was too scared to complain.'

Zabhir still looked anxious, but when Chrissy heard this, she clenched her fists in anger. 'They do it to grind you down so that you'll leave. It's been going on forever.'

'That's why it has to stop, Chrissy. Someone has to speak up.'

'Zab has a family. He needs his job. Leave him out of this, but I'll do it. This secondment has made me think about leaving the force. I don't think I could go back to Bancroft Road now, not after I've been treated so well here. I'm willing to go on record.'

'Me too,' added Zabhir. 'Chrissy's a great cop, I don't like to think of her leaving because I didn't have the balls to speak up. I've taken my share of PCs, but what they did to Rahim yesterday, that was inhuman.'

'You're *both* good cops, and it would be a travesty if either of you left the force.'

Bryn grabbed his jacket, took a deep breath, and looked around SCD9 nostalgically. It had been his best role to date, but it might be his last if he got this next step wrong. He marched up to the office of the Assistant Commissioner for Frontline Policing.

'DCI Bryn Ellis from SCD9. I'd like to speak to the Assistant Commissioner urgently,' he announced to her EA.

'I doubt she'll see you, she's very busy.'

'Ask her,' he insisted through gritted teeth.

The EA knocked and poked her head round her boss's door. 'There's a DCI Ellis from SCD9 wanting to talk to you. He says it's urgent.'

'Not now, Slyvia. Get him to make an appointment, I'm in the middle of something.'

"Whatever it is, un-middle it, Ma'am,' said Bryn, pushing past the EA and into AC Judy Purcell's office.

'I *beg* your pardon?'

'You heard me, Ma'am.'

'How dare you speak to me like that, Ellis! What's got into you, for God's sake!'

'There's very little God in this, and I *dare* because I made a judgement call that you're straight and decent and would want to know about this. If I'm wrong, then it's my career up in smoke. So, I think the stakes are high enough for you to un-middle whatever it is you're doing.'

AC Judy Purcell put down her pen and levelled a steely pair of eyes at DCI Ellis. 'And?'

'I want you to suspend the DI and the desk sergeants at Bancroft Road Station.'

'Why in God's name would I do that?

'Because they are overseeing a regime of racism, bullying, sexual harassment, and the implementation of punishment codes. I relieved a constable at midnight last night whose shift should have finished at 2pm and yet was put on solo guard duty at a crime scene at 6.30pm and was not rostered to be relieved until 6am the following morning. That's a brutal 24-hour shift, the last 18 hours of which he had no access to food or water and had to relieve himself in a sand bucket. Need I add that he's Bangladeshi.'

'There must have been a mistake with the rosters. He should have contacted his desk sergeant. It's very unfortunate but—'

'There was no mistake, Ma'am. And he didn't contact his desk sergeant because punishment codes are rife at Bancroft Road. They were supposed to have been outlawed a decade ago.'

'I need some evidence, Ellis. I can't wade in and start suspending people just because of a potentially innocent mix-up.'

Bryn hesitated for the briefest of moments. If he got this wrong, he would be selling out Chrissy and Zabhir – and Rahim. The DCI and the Assistant Commissioner eyeballed each other across her desk in some kind of truth and lies game of chicken. His eyes a dark shade of brown; hers a pale blue-grey. He spotted a hint of sadness in them and knew this was hurting her.

'I have all the evidence you need, Ma'am. WPC Blackwell and PC Ahmed are waiting downstairs in the lobby. They are willing to go on record, and I'm sure there will be others to follow once they know it's safe to speak up.'

She picked up the phone. 'Sylvia, have WPC Blackwell and PC Ahmed come up right away. They are waiting down in the lobby.' She put the receiver down. 'And you, Ellis. You can get back to your day job. I wish to speak to these officers individually – and without their minder. '

When he heard those last words, Bryn knew he had made the right call.

An hour later, Judy Purcell left her office and headed unannounced to Bancroft Road Station. She would start at the top and work down, leaving no stone unturned. She thought she'd rooted out punishment codes a dozen years ago, but chided herself for not putting in a Super over Wingate. She had cut corners on costs and was now paying a heavier price in human misery. It would need to be the right Super, though. If PCs were still rife in parts of the Met, she didn't want to entrench it by installing a Super from the same stable.

She strode into Wingate's office.

'DI Wingate, I'm suspending you with immediate effect. You're under investigation for sexual harassment, racism, and bullying. Make your way to Interview Room 2. And I'll have your badge, please.'

'What! This is outrageous, Ma'am. What possible reason could you have to suspect me of such vile conduct?'

'The sort that turns my stomach. I repeat, I'll have your badge.'

'If I'm to be interviewed, Ma'am, I have the right to representation.'

'You can have the Queen to represent you, for all I care. Just get your butt to Interview Room 2. And I'm still waiting for your badge.'

16

Later that Friday

When Bryn arrived back at SCD9, Jemi made a beeline for him. She pulled him to one side so she could speak in a lowered voice. 'I thought you'd want to know that those DNA results are back from their second test.'

Bryn was a little surprised by the unusually conspiratorial approach but did not show it in his response. 'Great, Jemi. Can you send me a copy – and can you start your database analysis straight away? Prioritise it, Jemi. This is really important.'

'I don't have them, Bryn. That's the thing,' she almost whispered.

'I don't understand. DNA results always come in via you.'

'They've been sent straight to the Chief Super.'

'I still don't understand.'

'I only know because I did a follow-up call after you said it was urgent. I wheedled it out of the clerk at the pathology lab. She told me they'd been sent to the CS.'

'This is nuts,' said Bryn, trying not to reveal his frustration. 'I'm going up to her office, find out what the hell is going on.'

'Please don't, Bryn. They'll know it was me who told you, and I wouldn't want to get the clerk into trouble.'

He nodded his agreement. 'Of course. Should have realised. My mistake.'

'I've been doing some more digging on that shell company. I should have a report ready for you within the hour.'

'Thanks, Jemi.'

'She was really kind,' Chrissy told Bryn when she came back to join him at SCD9. 'Thanked me for coming forward. She apologised to me on behalf of the Met. I told her I'd been on the verge of quitting, and she said that would have been a travesty, that they needed good officers like me, and they need more female officers.

'DI Wingate was the worst. With the others, it was just groping and sex-pesting, that kind of stuff, but he was the one calling in sexual favours. I always resisted. It's probably why I've never risen above constable. She asked me what my career ambitions were, and I said I hoped one day to join CID, that I really wanted to be a detective. She was nice, sir. I didn't think an Assistant Commissioner could be that nice. I'd have come forward sooner if I'd known.'

'You'll do well in CID, Chrissy. I know talent when I see it. Talking of talent, I need to catch up with Jemi, see if she's turned anything up from the penthouse fingerprints.'

'May I tag along, sir? I've never had sight of a forensic report before, and as I said, I'm really interested in becoming a detective one day.'

'I don't think that day is far off, Chrissy, mark my words.'

'Anything of note from the fingerprints report, Jemi?'

'There's a load of prints we can't identify from our database, which is bad news for us. All sorts of randoms could have been there on various occasions. Any one of them could have been there when Anna fell from the balcony. I've highlighted anything that has Kavanagh or Anna's prints, but all they really indicate is that they were both in the suite at some time – not necessarily the same time – and nothing to pin him to the scene at the actual time of the crime.

'I'll have a closer look once I've done some more digging on The Pearl Tower and that shell company. And before you ask, yes, I'll keep chasing the baby Miranda DNA. We're running several investigations in tandem. It's a juggling act.'

'It's what you're good at Jemi,' smiled Bryn. He handed the forensics report to Chrissy to make herself a copy and then went in search of a coffee. Coffee always focused his mind.

It was two o'clock, and Bryn was eating a sandwich, inwardly smiling on two counts. Firstly, he had heard that Judy Purcell had instigated a sweep of suspensions at Brandon Road Station. Secondly, his scrutiny of the fingerprints forensic report had given him a breakthrough. He had asked Fiona at the Pathology Lab to check if there were any traces of lipstick on Anna's body. The response had been that there was no trace on her lips, but there was a smear on her left wrist. He'd pulled in yet another favour from her to fast-track a substance match analysis with the lipstick recovered from the carpet of the penthouse suite.

Bryn really needed to know before he interviewed Kavanagh and his girlfriend this afternoon if there was a match to the lipstick tube they had found on the carpet. On the forensics report he had spotted that it only had *one* set of fingerprints – and they were Kavanagh's. A match would place him at the scene. It didn't prove he threw her off the balcony, but it would give Bryn some leverage to work with in the interview.

His email box had just pinged with the news he was hoping for. It was an exact match.

As he swallowed his last mouthful, Chrissy approached him. 'Sorry to interrupt,' she began a little nervously.

'What is it, Chrissy?'

'It's just that... well, I think I might have spotted something on the forensics, sir.'

'Oh?' he replied, lifting his head to look directly at her. 'What might that be?'

She put the report down in front of him where he could see she had ringed something with a red pen. 'It's not *what's* there,' she said. 'It's what's *not* there.'

'I don't follow,' said Bryn, playing along.

'There's only ONE set of prints – and they're not Anna's. They belong to Don Kavanagh. And the same here,' she said, pointing to the forensic entry on the lipstick cellophane wrapper. 'It was a *new* lipstick. Why aren't Anna's prints on them? It's a lady's lipstick, after all. Doesn't this prove that he must have been there during the scuffle? Doesn't it place him at the crime scene?'

'Chrissy, you're a genius!' exclaimed Bryn, 'I told you you'd make a fine detective.'

'Perhaps it just needed a woman's eyes on it,' she replied modestly.

'Great work, Chrissy. Would you like to sit in on the interviews to see how we can use this data to apply pressure? I'm on my way down there now.'

'I'd like that very much, Bryn, thank you.'

'I'll be tackling the girlfriend first. If we can break her alibi, we will have even more to hit Kavanagh with.'

Chrissy returned to her desk feeling ten feet tall and even more determined to pursue her ambitions in CID.

Tereza Quinton was none too pleased at having to attend in person at New Scotland Yard. She sat defiantly opposite DCI Ellis and DS Freeman. Chrissy sat discreetly at the back of the room.

'I don't know why I had to come all the way here when I'd already given my statement to that motherfucker,' she said, pointing to Jake. 'Since when does it take three of you to take a statement? No bloody wonder we have no bobbies on the beat, the way you lot waste money. And where's Don?'

'We take formal statements separately. We also like to give witnesses a chance to reflect independently and be absolutely sure of their facts, in case they are called to give evidence in court.'

'Let's get on with it then.'

Bryn turned on the tape and began with the formalities. 'Your full name, please?'

'Tereza Quinton.'

'Is that your real name?'

'What kind of question is that?'

'We asked you to bring some ID with you. Do you have some on you?'

'I have my passport. It's a *British* passport, if that's what you're hinting at, you racist pig.' She fished out her passport and handed it over.

'Address?'

'This is ridiculous. You came to my house, for Christ's sake! It's on the bloody passport, you moron.'

'For the benefit of the tape, please.'

'26 Alpha Road, Peckham, SE15 4GP.'

'Occupation?'

'I'm the manager of a manicure salon.'

Bryn tried not to show any reaction, but his mind was racing as he laid out a document on the desk in front of her where a yellow marker pen had highlighted one entry.

'What's this then?' she grunted.

'This, Miss Quinton, is a page of the forensic report from the Anna Adams crime scene.'

'Why has it been classed a crime scene when the most likely scenario is she jumped?'

Bryn ignored this interruption and pointed to the yellow highlight. 'This relates to a lipstick tube found on the floor of the penthouse. It has Don Kavanagh's fingerprints on it.'

'So what if he handled her lipstick. I'm sure he handled much more than that.'

'Doesn't it bother you, Miss Quinton, your boyfriend "handling" other women and their belongings?'

'We're not exclusive. I know he goes with other women. And men. He prefers men, actually. It's not a crime.'

'Look again, Miss Quinton.'

'I told you it's not a crime to play around.'

'I insist you look again.'

She glanced briefly at the paper in front of her and shrugged her shoulders. 'This is a fucking waste of time.'

'There's only ONE set of prints – and they belong to Don Kavanagh.'

Tereza looked again at the paper, her brain beginning to process the implications.

'Furthermore,' he added, pointing to another highlighted entry, 'there are only *his* prints on the cellophane wrapper that had been torn from the lipstick tube. It was a new one. The open lipstick tube and discarded cellophane wrapper were both found on the floor of the penthouse suite, where there was evidence of a scuffle. Have you caught up yet, Miss Quinton? ONE set of prints means that only *Don* could have handled that lipstick. Only *he* could have put that lipstick on our victim. Forensics have an exact substance match for this lipstick to a sample streak on Miss Adams' wrist.'

Now that the pressure was on, he went in for the kill. 'Are you sure you want to go ahead with providing this alibi – on oath and on tape? If Kavanagh killed the victim, it would make you an accessory to murder. Accessory to murder comes with a heavy sentence – up to eighteen years. So, what's it to be, Tereza?'

The witness suddenly looked very nervous. 'I'm not saying anything until I have my lawyer.'

'Very well, we will arrange that for you. We will hold you in a police cell until your brief gets here. You are now a suspected accessory in a serious crime and deemed a flight risk. Meanwhile, we will check out if this passport is a forgery. Oh, and just one more thing,' began Bryn, playing a hunch. 'Would you mind rolling up your sleeves to the elbows, please?'

'What is this! Am I going to have to strip next, you pervert?'

'Just your forearms, Miss Quinton. And we do have a female officer present.' He played his hunch. 'I have reason to believe you may have been an enforced kidney donor in a former life.'

Tereza slumped back in her chair, all her sass spent. She rolled up the sleeve of her right arm to reveal a tattoo *AC4B17D3*.

'Alright, alright! I made a mistake. I might have got the timing wrong. He might not have got to my place until an hour after I said.'

'Might?'

'Alright, alright. I lied. But he told me to. He said I owed him, and he would make it worth my while.' At this point, Tereza started to sob distractedly. 'You don't know what it was like. I had no-one to protect me. They made me do things, dreadful things – things I didn't want to do. And yes, the bastards took one of my kidneys. I had to pay my dues, they said, and if I did, they'd see me alright.'

'The passport is a forgery then?'

She nodded feebly.

'What's your real name, Tereza?'

'Tereza Nayef.'

'And you're an illegal immigrant?'

'I came hoping to get asylum. I paid them all my life savings to get passage. Will I be deported?'

'If you co-operate with us fully, we may be able to help you. I know an excellent human rights barrister. She makes it her mission to help trafficked women like yourself who've been the subject of brutal coercion.'

'Please put me in a cell. I'll be safer there. He'll do for me when he knows I've dobbed him in.'

'We'll get you into a safe house for now and into witness protection.'

Chrissy had been processing what she had heard and realised that Bryn would not have had enough time to check the lipstick substance match, so he must have already made the connection before she told him, but didn't let on. The best boss she'd ever worked for suddenly went up even further in her estimation.

Half an hour later, Bryn and Jake began their interview with Brendon Kavanagh. Chrissy sat at the back of the room again.

'I don't take kindly to being kept waiting. I'm a busy man,' bellowed Don. 'This is a bit rich. Three officers to take a five-minute statement. What's going on?'

Bryn laid out the same documents he had shown Tereza and went through the same drill about the lipstick fingerprints. Kavanagh looked a little thrown, but he kept up the bravado.

'You'll have a job making that stick in court. I was nowhere near that penthouse when she jumped. I've got a cast iron alibi. If you have any other questions, I want my lawyer.'

'No more questions, Mr Kavanagh, just a piece of information for you. Tereza Quinton reneged on your alibi half an hour ago.'

The blood drained from Don's cheeks. 'I want my lawyer.'

'By all means, but first I am arresting you on suspicion of the murder of Anna Adams...'

Don's bloodless cheeks turned deathly white as he heard the arrest mantra ringing in his ears. The arrogant swagger was replaced by raw fear darting across his eyes.

'Look here, I'm willing to cut a deal. You don't understand what these people are like. I'm a dead man walking – in or out of prison. I don't own that penthouse. I don't own any of it. I just run it for them. I can help you get to them, but I want round-the-clock protection if I cooperate.'

'Let's hear what you have to say first, and then we'll consider whether or not we can afford you any kind of "deal".'

'I want to see my lawyer,' was the only response they got.

Bryn stared at the crazy wall, processing everything that the Quinton and Kavanagh interviews had added. It wasn't enough to get to the top echelon of this putrid operation, but they were getting closer. His gut told him this was organised vice crime on a large scale. It was a further hour before the call came through that he was wanted in the Chief Super's office. *Finally,* muttered Bryn under his breath. *Finally!*

There were no flies on Chief Superintendent Martha Simmons. In her late fifties, with greying hair and round metal-rimmed glasses, she was seated at her desk, a stack of papers in her in-tray and three open reports in front of her – one of which Bryn assumed must be the Miranda baby DNA results.

'Have a seat, Ellis. I need to discuss the infant DNA results from the trafficked case you're working on.'

'That kind of data usually goes to Jemimah. Am I to assume the information is classified?'

'You are to assume nothing,' came the sharp response.

'My apologies, Ma'am.'

'There are two salient facts I need to apprise you of. DNA has confirmed the victim is *not* the mother of the baby.'

Bryn whistled. 'Wow, I hadn't seen that one coming!'

'Genetic analysis places a strong likelihood on her being Syrian, which would fit with a trafficking hypothesis. Let's not jump to conclusions just yet, because we do have two possible DNA matches to the biological father which may enable us to identify her.'

'Brilliant!' exclaimed Bryn animatedly. 'This is the lead we've been looking for.'

'Of the two matches, one of them is *yours*, DCI Ellis.'

'WHAT! That's impossible. That's insane. There must be some mistake.'

'There's no mistake. I asked for the test to be repeated and independently verified. I assume your DNA is on record from the time you spent undercover with Manchester Vice. Standard elimination contingency.'

'Yes, but I still don't understand. There has to have been a mistake. There are no set of circumstances in which I could have been a sperm donor.'

'The second – and closer – match is to your brother, Kraig Ellis, whom – I've just been reading – served fifteen years of a life sentence for the murder of your mother. The closer match means we can assume that he is the biological father of baby Miranda.' She paused while she evaluated the impact this news was having on her DCI. He was clearly in shock.

'From the records,' she continued, fingering the pages of one of the documents in front of her, 'I can see he was given a life sentence in 1986, of which he served fifteen years. He's been out twelve years; model prisoner it would appear. And there's no evidence of any subsequent convictions to date.'

Bryn was slumped back in his chair, struggling to process the information being presented to him. The very sound of Kraig's name was abhorrent to him. He detested him with a vengeance that his usually impassive face was betraying, and Martha Simmons missed nothing.

She dropped her glasses down her nose and peered intensely at Bryn over the top of them. 'What *I* have to decide is whether to take you off this investigation and pull someone else in.'

'You can't be serious, Ma'am. This is *my* case, it's—'

'I AM serious, and I take exception to any officer – whatever their rank – laying personal claim to cases. We work as a team. Is that crystal clear, Detective Chief Inspector.'

'Yes, Ma'am. I didn't mean it the way it sounded. Kraig being somehow implicated makes no difference to me whatsoever. I assure you I can be detached and professional. This is the lead we need. We can press ahead now. I'm confident we can crack this one, Ma'am. My relationship to Kraig is incidental. You can't pull me out. Not now! We've broken Kavanagh's alibi, and it's opened up a whole can of worms. We're just starting to scratch the surface of what looks like a huge international operation.'

'Are you able to consider dispassionately every aspect of your brother's possible involvement?'

'Of course, that's my job, Ma'am.'

'Full 360; a sperm donor to the mastermind behind an international vice ring – and everything in-between? From his file here, it appears he gained a psychology degree during his incarceration. How well do you really know your brother?'

The question threw him momentarily, never having contemplated it in earnest. Kraig rarely inhabited Bryn's thoughts, other than the occasional bitterness that accompanied stray memories, like an unwanted reflux bile.

'I don't really know him at all, Ma'am. I was eleven when he went to prison, and I have only seen him once since his release. That was almost seven years ago. He told me then that he'd studied psychology and that he was doing well for himself. Had his own haulage firm. I remembered as a child how much of a motorhead he was, so that didn't surprise me.'

The shrewd superintendent sensed Bryn was holding something back. 'Anything else I should know?'

'Well, he... er... he did have a gun. And he did make some threats.'

'And what was the nature of those threats, Ellis?'

'Just a private matter between brothers, Ma'am,' offered Bryn reluctantly.

Matha Simmons had never been known to let a wriggling fish off the hook. 'There can be no *private* matters, Ellis, not when they impinge on a serious crime investigation. I'll ask you again. What kind of threats.'

'He, er, well you see, he blamed me for getting him banged up. It was my testimony in court that got the conviction.'

'Yes, I've read the court report,' interjected Martha, pointing to one of the folders open on her desk. 'Pretty damning testimony from you. Without it he would probably have got manslaughter with a hefty chunk of mitigation. This is my problem, you see, Ellis. There is clearly bad blood between you and your brother that could get in the way of an impartial investigation. So, tell me about these threats.'

'He said he would make allowances for me being a child at the time I "put him away", as he claimed, but that I was not going to get off Scot free. He said it was his turn to be judge and juror. '

'And what sentence did he determine for you?'

Bryn fidgeted in his chair, seemingly unwilling to say any more.

'Bryn,' she said, more gently, 'I understand this is difficult for you, but I need to know. I need to know if I can trust you to be impartial here. I need to know if your brother has got some kind of hold over you—'

'I CAN be impartial, Ma'am. You CAN trust me. It's just that it's private and personal.'

'That won't cut it, Bryn. If you don't tell me everything, and I mean EVERYTHING, then I'm pulling you off this case with immediate effect. It's not as if I'm going to run to the *Daily Mail* with some salacious gossip about you. I only need to know so I can decide whether you stay on the case or not.'

'It's a long story, Ma'am.'

'Then you'd better get started! I have two weeks' annual leave starting tomorrow, and I don't want to be here till midnight emptying my in-tray.'

'As I said, I've only seen Kraig once since he went to prison. It was seven years ago, on the morning of my wedding. I'd moved into my fiancée's flat eighteen months previously but wanted to give her some personal space before our big day, so I booked into a hotel for a couple of nights. I'm a bit of a traditionalist that way.'

Martha removed her spectacles and, folding them neatly, placed them on her desk in anticipation of a long and painful narrative. He was one of the best she had worked with, not that she would ever let that slip – nor the fact that she had a soft spot for this staid, orphaned Welshman who was about to tip his heart out onto her regulation gun grey carpet.

Chief Superintendent Simmons returned her spectacles to their habitual home and closed the three open files on her desk. 'Much as it pains me, Bryn, it would be a dereliction of duty to leave you in charge of this case when I consider there is a clear conflict of interest. It's as I feared. There's bad blood between you two; attritional revenge, emotional persecution, and God knows what else. It will get in the way of clear-headed judgement. Ex-cons with psychology degrees wielding guns make me nervous, especially those who run their own haulage firms and are somehow implicated in fathering children of dead trafficked victims. I'm going to have to put someone else in to lead this operation.'

'*Please*, Ma'am,' begged Bryn. '*Please* don't do this. The team is gelling really well, we are on the brink of cracking this whole thing open. Bringing in a new lead will upset the team dynamics. And if it's DCI Tynan you're thinking of, he's a dickhead, Ma'am. Excuse my language, but he really is.'

'Mind your tongue, Ellis,' reprimanded Martha, even though she privately agreed with his assessment of DCI Tynan. 'Right! This is what we are going to do. I have cover for my role for the next two weeks. *I* will lead SCD9.'

'I don't understand.'

'Two weeks.'

'Ma'am?'

'Two weeks. We have to crack this case in two weeks, or I really will have to draft someone else in.'

'But you said you were starting two weeks' annual leave tomorrow.'

'Precisely.'

'But your annual leave, Ma'am?'

'It will be good to get back in the saddle for once. Life behind this desk can get pretty tiresome, I can tell you. This will be much more diverting than eulogising over salt-loving fauna with Wortley Coastal Ramblers. I'll wander down to your incident room and get a full briefing.'

'I can do that, Ma'am.'

'I'm sure Jemimah is perfectly capable of briefing me.'

'If you're going to be in charge, Ma'am, can I at least stay on the case?'

'I could use your familiar knowledge to help track down your brother and bring him in for questioning. There must be people back in your neck of the woods who have some intel on him. Tracking!' she emphasised. 'Nothing else. Is that understood?'

'Yes, Ma'am.'

'You'd better keep DS Freeman with you at all times. I can't afford you going rogue on me.'

'With respect, Ma'am, if this is covert tracking, Jake would stick out like a sore thumb back home. They know me, they're used to me visiting alone. If Kraig is anywhere in that vicinity, it would arouse suspicion and might spook him. My foster father was a police sergeant, and I still have contacts at the local station. I could call on support from them if I find him.'

'Very well, Ellis, but you put one step out of line, *one* step, and you risk your career going up in smoke.'

'I've risked that once already today.'

'Yes! I heard about your exploits over in AC Purcell's office.' And to Bryn's complete astonishment, she winked at him.

A beleaguered DCI Ellis returned to his desk, still reeling from the shock of this latest revelation. Jemi, noting his slumped shoulders, wandered over to him and presented him with a folder. 'This should cheer you up, Bryn. I've been digging up what I can on the Pearl empire. I've tracked it all to a company called Pearl Enterprises. It's a portfolio company, and Brendon Kavanagh is *not* listed at Company House as Owner-Director. In fact, he doesn't own any part of the theatre or the aparthotel. It's an empty boast. I think he just manages it and gets the penthouse grace and favour.'

'Who does own it then?'

'I'm still working on that one. Pearl Enterprises started out as Pearl Wines – fine wines imported from Lebanon, according to its website. The enterprise grew rapidly through property acquisition and development; The Pearl Tower Apartments being one of several. It's a multi-million-pound portfolio. The Pearl Theatre appears to be more of a pet project. It doesn't seem to turn a profit.'

'It could be a convenient camouflage for all kinds of illicit activities,' said Bryn. 'Imports from Lebanon provide an expedient route for trafficking, whether that's drugs or people. Lebanon has been swamped with Syrian refugees since the civil war broke out in 2011.'

'Quite so. I couldn't find a name or a listed private address for the owner/owners of Pearl Enterprises, but their headquarters are listed as an address in Mayfair. From what I can gather, it seems to be just a one-room office. I doubt that is where most of the business is conducted.'

'Great work, Jemi. Keep digging. It tallies with some of the info we've shaken down from Kavanagh. He's a bit player in this, a puffed-up pimp, and a very scared one. After he spoke to his brief, he's maintaining it was an accident, a scuffle on the balcony and she fell over the barrier.'

'Do you believe him?'

'Not for a second, but it's going to be hard to prove. I can place him at the scene, but unless we get a confession from him or an eyewitness who saw him throw her and can reliably identify him – highly unlikely, given it's twelve floors up – the coroner will judge it accidental death. Kavanagh wants to cut a deal. I don't think he's high enough up the chain to give us the silver bullet, but it will get us closer.'

'You look glum, Bryn. Everything okay?'

'Simmons is taking me off the case.'

'You're joking! But why?'

'It's complicated. She's taking over the lead for the next two weeks. In fact, she's on her way down to get a full briefing from you.'

'Well, she hasn't arrived yet, so you've still got time to get the low down on our trafficked laundry lady from The Pearl Tower. The translation match came back as Arabic, and an Arabic-speaking legal aid has just arrived. I've put them in Room 7.'

The sight awaiting Bryn in Room 7 gave him a start. The legal aid was none other than Mia. He knew she did a lot of refugee pro bono work, but it still gave him a start to see her petite form with a comforting arm around the older woman and soothing Arabic phrases emanating from her perfectly formed mouth.

'Ms Saleem.' He addressed her formally. 'Thank you for helping us with this.'

'Anna was Jarrad's sister,' she reminded him sharply. 'And I'm here to ensure there is no further maltreatment of this poor woman,' she reminded him sharply. 'Her life's been a living hell.'

Bryn nodded his agreement. Between his respectful questions and Mia's gentle coaxing, they extracted a pitiful tale of Farida, a 63-year-old Syrian refugee who had fled to Lebanon with her daughter and granddaughter following the 2011 Syrian conflict and been picked off by iniquitous traffickers about six months ago.

She recounted how the group of refugees had been taken to an empty warehouse, where they had been 'sorted' according to their usefulness. Clearly deemed too old for more profitable activity, she had been consigned to the cleaning role at the Tower. Apart from the laundry, her other duties were to clean the two upper floors, including the penthouse, and put fresh linen and towels out each day. She was aware that the rooms on floor eleven were being used for prostitution. Between bursts of sobbing, she told of sleeping on a mattress in the laundry room, located in the basement carpark. She had no idea where her offspring had been taken, or if they were still alive. Every night she hid behind a pillar in the carpark to watch the prostitutes being brought in, to see if her kin were among them.

'How does she survive? Is she given food and money? Is she locked in?' asked Bryn.

Mia translated his questions, which drew more sobs. 'She's not locked in. They know she has nowhere she can run to, and they frighten her with stories of police brutality and deportation. She's given £5 a week to survive on.'

At first Bryn thought he had misheard, but Mia confirmed that the £5 was definitely per week, not per day.

Bryn now spoke directly to Mia in English. 'Could you step out for a moment, Ms Saleem, so I can update you on something pertinent to this interview?'

'As you wish, DCI Ellis,' came the stern reply. 'Farida,' she said, addressing the older women in Arabic. 'I'm just stepping outside that door for a few moments. You are quite safe. Nothing bad is going to happen to you, and I will be back with you very shortly.' The older woman nodded her understanding.

Outside, Bryn got straight to the point. 'Mia, when I did my sweep of the crime scene, I noticed two freshly laundered towels on the floor. They looked to have been dropped in a hurry because the neat folds were slightly disturbed. When I checked the ensuite, the used towels were still hanging there. I have a hunch that Farida came up to change the towels and may have witnessed what transpired on the balcony. My hunch is she dropped the towels in shock and ran out before she was seen. I can understand why she would be frightened to disclose this. It must be very hard for her to trust the Police.'

'Are you surprised when you kept her in a holding cell overnight, for God's sake. She's a traumatised granny. What were you thinking!'

'I don't think we had any choice. Technically, she's an illegal immigrant.'

'I won't let you send her to an asylum holding centre, and I'm not letting you keep her in a cell another night. The woman has been to hell and back – several times. I'm going to seek permission to keep her with me. My spare room is as good as any safehouse you could find for her. At least I speak the same language.'

'As you know, even applying on the grounds of a serious crime, the maximum extension I can get to hold Kavanagh is 96 hours. It only gives us until this time on Tuesday to prove he murdered Anna, or I will have to release him. He'll get bail if the only thing I can pin on him is pimping trafficked women.'

'I'll get Theo involved. He's brilliant with trauma victims. Let's see if he can build a platform of trust from where you might be able to get the eyewitness account you're hoping for.'

'I'll clear it with the CS. You'll have to accept police protection. Her life could be in danger. *Your* life could be in danger,' he added softly.

'Very well, but make it a plain clothes officer, preferably female – and posted OUTSIDE, not inside, my door. Understood?'

'Understood.'

17

Saturday, 24th May

Theo and Jarrad were watching for their loved ones as the passengers disembarked through Heathrow arrivals terminal. Zac Adams was instantly recognisable because of his 6'4" height. His wife Charlotte was at his side. Jarrad rushed forward to hug his mother while Theo took her suitcase.

She blubbed into Jarrad's shoulder, unable to hold back tears that had hardly left her face for the past thirty-six hours. Both parents looked like they had not slept since they had received the tragic news about their daughter. After giving his son a lingering bear hug, Zac offered his hand to Theo.

'Thank you for meeting us, Theo. I just don't know what to make of this. I can't take it in.'

'I'm so very sorry,' began Theo, holding Charlotte in a tight hug. 'Mia sends her love. She's busy reassigning her caseload to focus on this.'

Charlotte merely nodded wearily, thankful but unable to find any words.

A figure had been hanging back while these reunions were happening, but now Rosie Aldridge stepped forward, parking her over-sized rucksack to the side of the huddled group. 'Hello, Jarrad. Hello, Theo.'

'Rosie!' exclaimed Jarrad. 'I had no idea you were coming, too!'

'She's my best friend of twenty years, Jarrad. How could you think I wouldn't come!'

There was an awkward silence. Jarrad was looking at the limp sleeve of her jacket and the scar down her left cheek. 'I was sorry to hear about your accident,' he blurted out, not quite knowing what to say, or whether to shake hands with her good side or give her a hug without crushing the bad side.

Theo saved the moment. 'Rosie Aldridge! Well, I never. It must be ten years or more since I saw you. It's a great pleasure to meet you again.'

'Thank you, Theo. I'm very pleased to see you again, too. I hear a lot about you from Charlotte.'

Theo wanted to ask, "Not Anna?" but knew that it would have been an insensitive query. 'Let's get you to your hotel. I have the car waiting in short-term parking.'

'I can manage from here, thanks, Theo. You'll have a full load with four of you and all that luggage,' said Rosie.

'Not a bit of it!' protested Theo. 'It's an estate car. There's plenty of room.'

'It's a kind offer, Theo, but I prefer to be independent. It's a time for family to be together. I'll ring tomorrow and arrange to catch up with you all.'

'But where will you stay?' asked Jarrad.

'I'm staying at a Travelodge in Stratford. Don't worry about me, I've been to London before. I know my way around.' With that, she swung her rucksack onto her back with her good arm and set off in the direction of the underground.

Jarrad stood open-mouthed. He had not seen Rosie for six years, and even then only briefly, because she had already been away at university for two years when he left for London. Anna hardly ever talked about her. He had never really taken any notice of the friend who seemed to be some kind of limp appendage to his pushy sister. Yet here she was, a feisty one-armed backpacker with a big heart and an even bigger backbone.

Wretchedly, he realised he knew precious little about his older sister or her life. They had never been close. He had not even heard about Rosie's car accident from Anna. The news had come from his mother. Firemen had had to cut her from the wreck, and she had lost her left arm above the elbow. Contritely, he acknowledged there must have been more to Anna than he thought to have a best friend like Rosie. He had been too judgemental, too dismissive of her conceited ways, and now it was too late to make amends.

Rosie checked herself into the budget hotel she knew well. It was near the Olympic swimming pool where she had competed in the 2012 Paralympics. She had swum a personal best and got as far as the semi-finals in her classification event. She was a relatively unknown newcomer on that stage and had not broadcast her participation. Only her mother and Anna knew.

It had been a healing time for her. Swimming had been the lifeline that pulled her through the painful recovery after the car accident. It had strengthened her stub arm and restored her fitness. She still swam regularly but had no ambitions to go to Rio. The 2012 Paralympics had provided a fitting closure to enable her to move on with her life. Teaching was her passion, and that was where her ambitions lay.

As soon as she had unpacked, she headed for the pool. She found the rhythm of the strokes calming and the released endorphins exhilarating. Out of the water she felt like an ugly duckling, skinny and plain – even before the disfigurement to her left cheek. In the water she felt like a beautiful dolphin, streaking through some vast ocean.

After 1500 metres, the weariness of the flight eased away, her spirits lifted, and her mind cleared. She would need a clear head to deal with whatever ugliness lay ahead.

When she had showered and changed, she headed to The Pearl Tower. She wanted to see the place for herself. She wanted to see the spot where Anna had died. She was convinced it must be murder. There was no way Anna would have jumped. Not Anna! And it couldn't have been an accident, because she remembered the balcony from the FaceTime video. The barrier was much too high for her to have accidentally fallen over.

She would not rest until Anna's memory was free of the stigma of suicide. It was no more than Anna would have done for her.

She pulled out her mobile and sent a text to Theo. 'You must promise me if there is anything I can do to help, ANYTHING, you must ask me.'

A text came back almost immediately. 'I promise. Thank you.'

PART THREE

BROTHERHOOD

18

Sunday, 25th May

Bryn was driving out to South Wales, towards the town of his childhood, his head still whirring with a myriad emotions. He had packed for an indeterminate stay, whether that was two days or two weeks. He did not relish the prospect of coming up against his brother again but was determined to find him and bring him in. It was the only way he could prove to Martha that he should be given back SCD9.

He would stay with his old neighbour Mrs Matthews, as he always did. They had become firm friends since her only son died. He had joined the army after the pit closed, like a lot of the younger miners did, and been killed on active duty. She was long widowed and in her late seventies now.

The regular visits to his family graves and Mrs Matthews were the only touch points Bryn had left with the town of his childhood. He made sure he always did some DIY jobs when he stayed and took her for drives round the valleys to lift her out of her lonely humdrum existence.

It was fittingly grey and drizzly when Bryn approached the outskirts of Aberfor. He could never shake off the sadness that descended on him each time he took in the giant spectre of the disused mine shaft straddling the deserted colliery site, with its ugly slag heap stretching out behind. A ghostly primer to the derelict town opening up before him. Once a close-knit, thriving community, only a tenth of the population had stayed, trapped in their ramshackle houses, the streets lined with boarded-up shops.

Bryn parked his car and began to walk the rest of the graffitied route, picking his way round empty cans and discarded needles – hallmarks of the broken lives of a forsaken community engulfed by tedium, bitterness, and despair.

The cemetery was always his first port of call whenever he visited. Everything that was dear to him lay buried in two graves. One grave housed his foster parents and was in a part of the cemetery chosen by their children in the vicinity of two other generations of Edwards. Bryn would always spend a few moments in quiet reflection and gratitude for the sacrifices they had made welcoming him into their family. Owen had died ten years ago, and Ffion had followed him three years later.

The other grave was in a different part of the cemetery. It was older, its headstone beginning to show a little weathering, although the crowded lettering that depicted its multiple occupants of mother, sister, and father, was still entirely legible. He was pleased to see how well tended it was, not a weed in sight, and some beautiful flowers had been planted which he not seen before. He must remember to thank Mrs Matthews, whom he knew still came to pay her respects on her chapel visits.

Bryn knocked loudly on her door, knowing she was a little deaf these days.

'Bryn!' she exclaimed. 'How wonderful! Come in, come in. I'll get the kettle on.'

He kissed her on the cheek. 'You sit down, Mrs M, *I'll* make the tea. I brought some bara brith and chocolates.'

'It's so good to see you, Bryn. How've you been?'

'It's certainly been an eventful few months! I'll bring you up to speed once I've got you settled with a cuppa.'

Once the last crumbs of the bara brith had been polished off and they had updated each other with their news, Bryn finally came clean. 'This isn't entirely a social visit, Mrs M, although it's always great to see you. I'm here for work reasons.'

'Cuff me now, Officer, I'll come quietly,' she joked with him, holding out her hands. 'Might be the most exciting thing that's happened to me in a decade!'

Bryn smiled at the jovial bravado of this plucky lady fate had not been kind to. 'I need to find Kraig.'

'I see,' came the quiet reply, tinged with sadness. 'I'm guessing it's police business, not a thawing of the bad blood between you.'

'He might be innocently implicated, I don't know for sure, but his DNA has turned up in a big investigation. We need to bring him in for questioning, and they've sent me to track him down.'

'I see,' she said again. 'I haven't set eyes on Kraig in a long time, but I do hear things about him from time to time.'

'What kind of things?' asked Bryn hopefully.

'You'll remember how smitten he was with Megan.'

'Yes, I remember,' said Bryn, not wanting to reveal just *how* smitten he knew his brother was from the revenge wrecking ball Kraig had wielded on Bryn's wedding day.

'When Kraig went to prison, she married the colliery electrician, Dave Jones – and in a hurry. He was ten years older. She hid it very well, but the gossip was she was pregnant by Kraig. Anyway, she lost the baby, so no-one ever knew for sure. It's proved to be a good marriage. Dave's a top guy, salt-of the-earth type; must have been to be prepared to take on another man's child. As a qualified electrician, he was luckier than most of the men round here when the mine closed. He did freelance work for a while and eventually set up his own business about twenty miles up the valley.

'I think they still live there. I hear they have three kids of their own – the youngest must be about sixteen or seventeen by now. Rumour has it Kraig tried to get her to run off with him when he got out, but she wouldn't leave her family.'

'He told me he owned his own haulage business.'

'I don't know anything about that, but I remember how much he loved motors, so maybe. I only hear stuff about Kraig if it relates to Megan, nothing about the rest of his world. I just hope your investigation isn't anything bad.

I wouldn't want to see him back in prison. He was a bit wild as a teenager, but I don't think he's bad in his heart.'

Bryn did not want to disavow her charitable view of humanity by revealing the details of Kraig's vindictive revenge he had exerted against his younger brother and the cruel barbs against his dead sister, so he half nodded a polite response.

'Do you happen to have Megan's address?'

'No, but it's only a small town, and there can't be that many electricians up there. You could try Yellow Pages.'

'Yes, I'll do that. Now, how about I take you on a jaunt up the valley before I go? It can't be a long one, but I know how much you love to get outdoors when you can.'

'That's kind of you, Bryn, but if you're here for work you should prioritise that. There'll be plenty more chances for valley jaunts. I've put fresh linen on your bed, so it's all ready for you when you get back.'

'You're too good to me.'

'You've been good to me, Bryn, especially since Ray died.'

'Well, if you're sure?'

'I'm quite sure.'

Bryn got up to take his leave when he suddenly remembered he hadn't thanked her for tending the Ellis family grave. 'By the way, thanks for the lovely flowers you planted on the grave. They look champion. Mother would be made up that you take so much care.'

'I haven't been able to get up to their grave these past few weeks. I was laid up with a chest infection. It might have been the minister or…' she stopped suddenly just as Bryn was having the same thought.

'Or Kraig?' he jumped in. 'Do you think it could have been Kraig?'

'Whatever you think of your brother and whatever bad blood there is between you, he's a son just the same as you, who lost his family tragically. So, yes, I do think it's possible – even likely – that Kraig visits the grave from time to time. And now you must run, you have work to do.'

※※※※※

It was as Mrs Matthews had predicted, and Bryn easily found the address in Yellow Pages. He parked his car well away, not wanting to announce the presence of a stranger, and then knocked on Megan's door.

'You won't remember me, Megan. I'm Bryn Ellis.'

Megan peered at him. 'I wouldn't have recognised you, but now I look hard I can see some of Wynne in you. What do you want, Scabby?'

Bryn expected nothing less; the man of the boy who put her boyfriend away was hardly going to be a welcome sight.

'I need to find Kraig urgently, and I thought you might be able to help me.'

'Why would you think that?' she stiffened.

'Because he sought me out seven years ago, and he kept on about blaming me for losing the love of his life. *You*, Megan. He adores you, so I thought he might have kept in touch.'

She softened a little at this declaration, echoing as it did the deep love she had carried in her own heart for thirty years. 'You'd better come in.'

Bryn followed her into the living room where her husband, Dave Jones, was slumped, semi-conscious, in a worn armchair, hooked up to an oxygen cylinder.

'It's advanced emphysema,' she said bitterly, 'he hasn't got long.'

'I'm sorry,' replied Bryn with a catch in his voice. He stood transfixed, taking in a scene which could easily have been his own father, had he lived. A scene that had widowed so many Aberfor wives.

'That's one small mercy. Prison saved Kraig from the miner's curse. Prison saved Kraig from a lot of things – including himself,' she added.

'How do you mean?'

'He got an education. He grew up. He left the hothead behind him.'

'That's not a description that concurs with his visit to me seven years ago,' replied Bryn angrily. 'He held a gun to my head; he imprisoned me in my hotel room and threatened to kill my fiancé if I didn't give her up. And he did it all on the morning of my wedding, just to twist the knife more cruelly.'

Megan suddenly burst out laughing, loud baying cackles. Her husband stirred slightly but did not wake. 'You prize idiot. God, you're an easy play. Kraig always said you were a dumb ass.'

'I don't understand…'

'That's because you're a dumb ass. You're no match for Kraig. The man certainly played the boy there good and proper.'

'I still don't understand?'

'It was a replica, you moron! The gun – it was a replica! And those were idle threats. He would never have harmed her. An Oscar performance that you fell for, Scabby, hook, line, and sinker.'

Bryn's cheeks reddened as he replayed the scene over and over in his head. 'But he stole my mobile and sent a vindictive text to discredit me, to get my fiancé to hate me to—'

'Of course he did. He wanted his revenge, but he's no killer. You fell for it, dumb ass, because you *believed* he was a killer, you *believed* he meant to murder your mother, so you believed he was a bad man who would do evil things. Maybe he was a hothead once upon a time, like so many in their teens, but he was not a bad man, and he did not do bad things. Bad things were done to *him* – and by you, Scabby. You're the one with the bad thoughts. *You* got him put away for fifteen years. So, what are you trying to pin on him now?'

Bryn felt himself reeling, his head spinning as he processed the awful truth unfolding. He tried to gather his thoughts, recover his equilibrium, remember that he was there with a job to do.

'Kraig's DNA has turned up in a human trafficking investigation. Suspicion fell on Kraig because of his haulage business – possible people smuggling.'

Megan was looking angry now. 'What haulage business?'

'He said he had his own haulage business, that he was his own boss, that—'

'My God, you really are a gullible simpleton. It's a man and a van, Scabby! It's all he could get with his criminal record. He has a psychology degree and couldn't get a decent job. There aren't many options for an ex-con with the stigma of murder still hanging over him, even less for an ex-con with the stench of *matricide*. He makes a living but it's a hard one, and he's on the road a lot – and NO, it's not illegal immigrants he's carrying; it's plants! He does bits of man and van work locally when he can get it, but his main job is a regular contract doing deliveries for a big nursery down the valley. Their main sales are online. Kraig does those deliveries. He covers a big patch out as far as Bristol. As I said, he's on the road a lot. But I warn you, Scabby, if you're planning to frame him for something else, you'll have me to answer to.'

'How come his DNA is all over a trafficked victim's baby then?'

'I have no idea, but you can ask him yourself. He usually calls in on a Sunday, brings me some vittles and helps me with Dave.'

'Does Kraig live here now?'

'What kind of impertinent question is that, you scumbag? You really do have a low opinion of us, don't you? Kraig must have asked me a dozen times to take off with him when he got out of prison, but I wouldn't. That boat sailed long ago. Dave's a good man. He's been a good husband and a good father, and I owe him big time. Perhaps I don't love him in the way I love Kraig, but I'm not the black-hearted bitch you think me, Scabby.

'Kraig gave up on trying to coax me away yonks ago. He's stayed in touch like some guardian angel watching over me. Now we know Dave's emphysema is terminal, we might get a chance to be together in the future – after a decent interval. I have the boys to think about and how they would take it, and my youngest still has a year to finish at school. So, in answer to your filthy question, NO. Kraig doesn't live here, and NO, we don't carry on behind Dave's back. Kraig lives in a caravan. I've never been. I think it's a few miles down near the nursery.'

'Can I wait for Kraig then?'

'You bet you can. I want to be here when you confront him. He needs a witness. He needs protection from scabby cops with trumped-up charges.'

'I just need to talk to him, Megan. I'm not going to judge him till I've heard what he has to say. You need to know what he has to say about this DNA business, too.'

It was three hours later before Kraig turned up. Bryn occupied the time deep in thought, reflecting on the last thirty years and where he might have gone wrong. He watched Megan tend gently to Dave, who only woke for short bursts when she would take the opportunity to try and feed him. He didn't ask after the stranger sitting in his living room. He seemed oblivious to all but gasping for air between painful swallows until he could get re-hooked to his oxygen supply.

Kraig had arrived with a box of groceries which he put in the kitchen and a bunch of flowers for Megan. She smirked at Bryn as she received them lovingly, as if to say *'I told you so'*.

'What the fuck do you want, Scabby,' railed Kraig when he caught sight of his younger brother. 'How dare you sully Megan's home. Is *nothing* sacred to you?'

'It's alright, Kraig,' interjected Megan. 'Hear him out. He wants you to unravel something for him, and I'd quite like to hear it, too.'

The DNA conundrum was far from Bryn's mind when he opened his mouth to speak. The words tumbled out inelegantly, clumsily. 'I got a lot wrong, Kraig. Megan has shown me that. I hope you can forgive me I... I...'

'Well, well! The boy has finally found his manhood. You've done your time, paid your dues, I'll give you that, but as for forgiveness – I can only forgive the boy, not the man. So, say what it is you have to say and then get the fuck out of my life.'

'I'm in the middle of a human trafficking investigation.'

'That's got nothing to do with me. I don't do that kind of shit.'

'I'm not saying you do, but I need you to explain how your DNA is all over a dead woman's baby. A trafficked dead woman. There is no DNA match to the mother. We assume she was a surrogate, possibly an enforced surrogate. Your DNA is the only link we have to go on.'

'Look, I don't know anything about enforced surrogacy or trafficked women. All I know is I did a sperm donation when I did a drop at a fertility clinic out towards Bristol way. It had extensive grounds, as I remember. It was a big order. Ten specialist Japanese acers at 350 quid a pop. And I quite liked the idea of helping some couple somewhere get the baby they yearned for. I won't ever get that chance.

'Besides, I reckon I was a good catch: a good looking, educated bloke like me, fit and healthy. Some lucky couple would think they'd won the pools. It was a proper licensed clinic and all. How was I to know they were into dodgy stuff?'

'You see, Scabby. I knew there would be a simple explanation. You don't know your brother like I do,' she crowed.

'How did she die?' asked Kraig. 'The mother. How did she die?'

'She was hit by a lorry, trying to escape her captors. A nearby medic performed an incredible caesarean in the street.'

'You mean the baby survived?'

'Yes. She's very premature but is hanging in there.'

'It's a girl then,' mused Kraig, casting an affectionate glance at Megan, who blew out her cheeks.

'So, I'm the father? Is that what you're saying?

'The sperm donor, so biologically yes. But there will be judicial transfer orders already in place. The baby will already have elected parents once we trace them.'

Kraig was momentarily lost for words before blurting out, 'You always wanted a girl, Megan, after losing our little lass. Not that you'd change any of your boys, of course. Feels a bit cruel, somehow.'

'We need your help, Kraig. Can you remember the name and location of this clinic? Heaven knows what we'll find, but I'll lay odds there'll be something related to human trafficking lurking beneath their squeaky-clean veneer.'

'Why should I help you? Why should I help cops who stole fifteen years of my life?'

'Because you wouldn't be doing it for me or the cops. You'd be doing it for those abused women who can't help themselves.'

Kraig looked at Megan. She shrugged. 'It's up to you. You don't owe them anything.'

'I wouldn't be doing it for them.'

'As long as you remember that, and as long as those plods don't try and pin anything on you.'

'I've done nothing wrong and I've nothing to hide.'

'Doesn't count for anything with those idiots.'

Kraig turned to his younger brother. 'What would you need me to do?'

'Come to New Scotland Yard to give a statement and let us take a DNA swab. We have your DNA on record from your…' Bryn hesitated, 'from your…'

'My time inside, that's what you're trying to say. Spit it out, man. Call a spade a spade.'

'But my Chief Super will still want a confirmatory DNA test. If everything you've told me is true, I would put my job on the line to guarantee your—'

'Of course it's true,' interrupted Kraig angrily. 'Even now you—'

'I DO believe you, Kraig. I DO,' insisted Bryn earnestly.

'Right well, let's get on with this and put those shitheads... out of business.'

Kraig's hesitant choice of words was not lost on Bryn. Even now it must be hard for him to say 'behind bars'.

'I've got local jobs tomorrow, and I don't like to let the locals down. I could shift things round on Tuesday. Yeah, I could do Tuesday.'

'I'll pick you up at 7am on Tuesday then,' said Bryn, aware he was going against Martha's express orders not to bring Kraig in himself. But surely this was different? He was coming as a witness, not a suspect.

'No way. I'm not sitting in a car for hours with you, Scabby. This changes nothing. I told you, when I've done this, I want you to get the fuck out of my life. I'll follow you on my bike.'

Martha Simmons reluctantly agreed for Bryn to escort Kraig to the Met without backup.

'Now that we know Kraig is not intentionally implicated, can I come back as SIO?' asked Bryn.

'Are you absolutely sure you're not being played again?'

'I can't win with you,' replied Bryn irritably. 'You're either saying there's bad blood between us and it will affect my judgement, or I've gone soft on him and it will affect my judgement. What in God's name do I have to do to convince you, Ma'am?'

'I'll ignore that insubordination this once, Ellis, but tread carefully. I'm on your side here, however my patience is not infinite. I'm in charge for these two weeks. I'll have ample time to satisfy myself you're not going to crack under pressure at a critical moment in this investigation. Then, and only then, will I agree to let you return to full SIO duties.'

'What pressure? This is unjust, Ma'am. I've never given any cause to suggest mental instability.'

'Till now, Bryn. Trauma, bereavement, guilt – they all sit very deep in the psyche and can surface unexpectedly, even decades later. From the account you told me yesterday, you've had a bellyful of all three.'

'You seem to know a lot about it.'

'I have a good friend who's a psychologist and specialises in this stuff. He's helped me over the years with some of our more traumatised victims. First up, we need to get as much information as we can from your brother. I'll do the interview with DS Freeman. I can't have you anywhere near that formal statement. It needs to be squeaky clean, no hint of bad blood, coercion, or any other hook some smart-arsed defence lawyer might grab onto.'

'Understood, Ma'am. Have we got enough to do a raid?'

'Let's wait and see how the interview with your brother goes. His information needs to be one hundred percent accurate. We can't afford to make a mistake and raid the wrong clinic. You can imagine what the dailies would make of that!'

'Do you think these cases are linked? The nail bar, The Pearl, the clinic?'

'Possibly. You'll know as well as I do that expert traffickers sweat their assets, get the best price for each human commodity. This is no amateur outfit. My hunch is it's a large cell with a sophisticated distribution structure, which is another reason why we need to proceed with caution. We want the whole loaf, not just the clinic crumbs.'

19

Monday, 26th May

Jarrad had arranged to meet Rosie for a coffee. He wanted to get to know her better, but primarily he wanted to get to know his dead sister better, and her best friend was a good place to start. Rosie said she would be swimming at the Olympic pool first thing, so they arranged to meet at the café there.

When Jarrad arrived early, Rosie was still in the pool. He could see her from the balcony window of the café and could scarcely believe his eyes as he watched her power up the 50-metre pool. With her stub arm she would still easily beat him, despite his tall, athletic build. She could probably even give him a 10-metre start.

When she joined him in the café, her short hair still damp, he got up admiringly to greet her. 'I saw you swimming just now, that was awesome! I had no idea you could swim like that. You looked really at home in that pool.'

'It's nostalgic for me. I swam here in the 2012 Paralympics,' she replied, a little shyly.

'You did what?' he asked incredulously. 'But I was here. I was two years into my training at King's. I could have come to support you. Why didn't you tell me? Why didn't Anna tell me!' he added angrily. The goodwill he was feeling towards his sister was taking a dent.

'Because I made her promise not to. I made Charlotte promise the same. They and my mum were the only ones who knew I was competing. I was an unknown, you see, and I only made it to one of the semi-finals, so no pundits would have followed it.'

'But who was there to support you?'

'No-one.'

'Not even your mum – or Anna?'

'They both wanted to come, but I wouldn't let them. You see, this was for me. Just me and only me. Swimming is what got me through my rehabilitation after the car accident, and it was like some personal goal I wanted to achieve. I just wanted to see if I could qualify for the Paralympics, and when I did all I wanted was to swim a personal best. I knew I was nowhere near medal standard.'

'And did you? Did you swim a pb?'

'Yes, in my heat. I didn't better it in the semi-final. But it didn't matter; the pb was as good as a gold medal to me and it gave me closure, helped me move on with my life. I was always a bit plain – certainly compared to Anna – but after the car accident, with a stub arm and this scar on my face, I felt like a real ugly duckling. When I get in the water, that all melts away. I felt like a dolphin. It helped restore some of my self-esteem.'

'You're not plain or an ugly duckling, Rosie. I think you're amazing.'

'Goodness, I don't know why I'm talking about myself like this when you're here to talk about Anna. What would you like to know about your sister?'

'Everything. But I want to know more about you first. Even though you've always been around since I was a kid, I don't think I ever really knew you, with you and Anna being two years older than me. We never moved in the same circles.'

'There's not a lot to tell. I majored in English at Uni, and I teach at a high school in Edmonton – and I swim. That's about it really. I sometimes get out on my bike. I love books and I cook pretty well – Mum taught me that. What about you?'

'I've just qualified, and I want to specialise in surgery eventually. I like books, too – and I cycle. If it hadn't been for what happened to Anna, I was about to start a chunk of leave before I take up my first post-qualification post. I was going to take my bike up to our family cottage in Silecroft. Grandma left it to us. I've visited there every year since I was fourteen, and I'd like to do some touring round the wider Lake District. It's really beautiful. Not on the scale of our lakes in Canada, but very beautiful all the same.'

'And what do you want to know about Anna?'

Jarrad looked a little awkward. What he wanted to ask was how such a quiet, modest, intelligent woman could be best friends with his pushy, selfish, vacuous sister; like some lap dog always at her bidding. But he didn't know how to phrase it tactfully.

'I think what you're wanting to ask me is why someone like me would be best friends with someone like Anna. You probably think we're chalk and cheese.'

'Well, I—'

'It's alright, Jarrad. I get your drift. There is... was... a lot more to Anna than you know.'

'Clearly!' admitted Jarrad.

'We've been friends since Elementary School. Being from a single parent family, of modest income, and me with glasses and buck teeth, well, I was a prime target for the bullies. Anna was the tallest in the class, taller than a lot of the boys even, and she was *very* confident. Boy, was she confident. She took me under her wing, and I never had to worry about bullies after that. We've been as close as sisters ever since. I've always been in her shadow, but I never minded. Over time I developed my own confidence and my own bit of sunshine, until the accident. She was amazing after my car accident.'

'Anna never told me anything about that. It was my mum – and she didn't give me any details. I'd no idea you'd been so badly injured,' he said, nodding towards her stub arm. 'What happened? Do you mind me asking?' he added uncertainly.

'We were hit by an oncoming car that skidded on black ice. My boyfriend was driving. He was killed outright, as was the other driver. I got crushed against the car door, which was wedged into the rock face. They had to cut me out.'

'Oh my God, Rosie. I had no idea. No idea at all. That's too awful.'

'Anna visited me every day in hospital. Sat with me for hours. Read to me – from books she hated but knew I loved. Then she helped me through the depression that swamped me. *Made* me buck up. A bit like she'd done when I was being bullied at school. *Made* me grow some backbone. I'm not sure I could have got through it without her.

'It was Anna who suggested I go big on the swimming. Swimming and schoolwork were the only things I was better at than her. She helped me get my confidence back. She wanted me to succeed. She pushed me. She was so thrilled when I qualified for the Paras and was furious when I wouldn't let her come to watch me, but she kind of knew I needed to do it by myself. We spat from time to time, like all friends do, and have different – *had* different – paths we wanted to follow, but we never lost that closeness. We told each other everything.

'We FaceTimed every day. That is, we did until a couple of days before that balcony fall. I *knew* something was wrong, Jarrad. I could feel it in my bones. She wasn't calling me, and she wasn't picking up, and I didn't like the sound of this musical she was supposed to be starring in. I even phoned Theo to ask him if he'd seen her and if she was alright. That's when he told me you were meeting her for dinner on Wednesday night – the night before her death. Anna could be brash and cocky sometimes, Jarrad, but she was fiercely loyal.'

'I've clearly got a lot to learn about my sister.'

'You were always too quick to judge her, too critical – and I hope you don't mind me saying this, too nerdy. You need to lighten up, Jarrad Adams.'

'Perhaps I need to think a bit more deeply before I judge people.'

'Reserving judgements is a matter of infinite hope.'

'That's pretty profound.'

'I wish I could lay claim to it, but F Scott Fitzgerald said it first.'

'The novelist?'

'Yes. It's a quote from *The Great Gatsby*.'

'Perhaps I should get myself a copy. It's passed me by. Like so much else,' he added sadly.

※※※※※

Theo had spent much of the weekend at Mia's apartment. He had done three short sessions with Farida on the two previous days, and three more today. He felt that he was making headway. Once Farida got over the shock of being treated like a human being and housed and fed like a cherished grandmother, she started to relax a little. She had begun to hope again, and with that hope had sprung the green shoots of trust. But Theo knew they were running out of time. While he and Mia cleared away the supper dishes, they conversed in English about their progress.

'We're running out of time, Theo,' said Mia, echoing his own thoughts. 'The Police can only hold Kavanagh until tomorrow afternoon.'

'I'll try a different tack tomorrow morning, Mia. It will be our last chance. They have to release Kavanagh by 3pm.'

'Yes, and I was thinking I might try something this evening when you've gone.'

'What would that be?'

'The pulling power of family.'

When Theo had left for his own apartment, Mia began to tell Farida about her own Iraqi background and the atrocity that had wiped out not just her whole family but her whole village. Farida put a comforting arm around her. 'I had no idea you had experienced such pain,' she said. 'Family is everything.'

'Yes, that's why I'm so grief-stricken about Anna Adams dying. She was the sister of my best friend, and she was Theo's granddaughter.'

Mia didn't try to explain the complication of the 'almost' granddaughter part. In her mind, Beth's kin would always be Theo's. She put her head in her hands despairingly. 'And on top of everything else, they have to suffer the stigma of her suicide. It besmirches her memory. It's too cruel.'

Farida looked away as if she was struggling with something and then blurted out, 'She didn't jump.'

'How do you mean, Farida?'

'The lady in the penthouse, Theo's granddaughter, she didn't jump. The boss man was on the balcony. I saw him push her over the barrier.'

'Farida!' exclaimed Mia. 'How could you see them?'

'I had a lot of laundry to do that day, and the fresh towels weren't dry when I cleaned the penthouse, so I had come up later to collect the used towels and put out the new ones. I knocked but no-one answered. I saw the red outfit laid out on the bed, the smashed vase on the floor, and the torn curtain. I could hear voices on the balcony, which was why they must not have heard me knock. I peeped out, and that's when I saw it.'

'What did you see?'

'I saw him tip her backwards and push her over the balcony.'

'Did he see you? Is that why you've been so frightened to say anything till now?'

'He didn't see me. I dropped the towels in fright and got out as quickly as I could. I'm sure he didn't see me.'

'What is it you're so frightened about, Farida? Why didn't you say anything sooner?'

'I think the prostitutes he brings in at night are captured migrants. I keep thinking that my daughter and granddaughter might be among them. I hide behind a pillar in the carpark every night when they are brought in, to watch in case I see them. If the boss man knows I've testified against him, he might take revenge on them.'

'Would you know this "boss man" again if you saw him?'

She nodded nervously.

'Listen carefully to me, Farida. I deal with these kinds of cases and these kinds of brutes in my day job. They are cowardly. They will do anything to save their own skin. If this vile man thinks he is facing a murder charge rather than a human exploitation charge, he is likely to squeal and dob in his sources. The best chance of finding your loved ones is to get to those sources, and the best way to do this is to keep this man behind bars and squeeze him. If he's charged with murder, on top of the other offences, he won't get bail. Do you understand what bail is?'

Farida nodded.

'The Police already have evidence that places him at the scene of the crime but nothing to prove he *actually* killed her – until now. Would you be willing to talk about this to that nice detective who let you stay here with me?'

Farida looked about her anxiously, as if someone was peering over her shoulder.

'I would be with you the whole time, and I promise I'll keep you safe. You would be helping to catch a bad man. You would be helping a bereaved family come to terms with the loss of a *daughter*, a sister – a *granddaughter*. Your testimony might save hundreds of women. Women like your own kin. It's our best chance of finding them.'

At the mention of her family, Farida looked up and nodded firmly. 'Yes. I will do this.'

Mia pulled out her mobile immediately and dialled Bryn's number.

Bryn had spent Monday doing some jobs for Mrs Matthews and taking her on a jaunt up the valleys.

'I'm glad you've come to see your brother in a different light,' she said as they sat eating their sandwiches, taking in the beautiful valley vistas. 'The bad blood between you two near broke your dad, and goodness knows what your Mam would have made of it all.'

'Kraig hates my guts, and I can't say I blame him. I don't think we'll ever be close, but I hope I might be able to make things right with him one day.'

Their chat was interrupted by Bryn's mobile ringing. His heart missed a beat when he saw it was Mia's number. She conveyed her information formally in perfunctory, clipped tones. If the mode of delivery was cold, the news was feverishly welcome.

20

Tuesday, 27th May

DS Freeman organised the identity line-up for the next morning, and Farida confidently picked Kavanagh out. Mia and Theo had accompanied and stayed with her behind the screen while she scrutinised the six men in the line-up. Five hours before they would have had to release him, Kavanagh was charged with the murder of Anna Adams. Two hours later, he had given up his sources in the hope of a plea bargain.

It was meagre fare. Kavanagh turned out to be a bit player, a ruthless pimp who had no conscience about trading in human misery. The only useful information he was able to provide was where he had sourced his 'pearls', as he liked to call his prostitutes.

Jemima tracked this to another shell company trading behind the fortress of Pearl Enterprises. It was another brick in the wall, and with Jemimah on the case there was a high degree of confidence that SCD9 would be able to make inroads into some of the higher echelons of the vice ring.

The founder company, Pearl Wines, provided an ideal route to smuggle in trafficked migrants via its shipments of fine wines. It was a clever plan, operating in plain sight. The much sought-after Lebanese wines, retailing at over a hundred pounds a bottle, were luxury goods which attracted high customs and came in smaller shipments. Smaller shipments that paid their custom dues in full and on time rarely attracted the same attention, unless they were being checked for small contraband like drugs or diamonds. The Lebanon was not known for a proliferation of either. Even if sniffer dogs were deployed, they are trained to detect certain drug smells which would not be present on migrants. Illegal migrants were more commonly smuggled in on large lorries carrying volume goods, where human cargo might more easily be clandestinely stowed.

Jemimah was tracking the next shipment of Pearl Wines, and SCD9 were on high response alert to intercept it when it docked.

While Kraig was helping SCD9 with their enquiries, under the direction of CS Simmons, Bryn whisked Jemimah off to the canteen for a coffee. He wanted to pump her for information about what had been happening on Martha's watch.

'She hasn't changed,' began Jemi.

'How do you mean?'

'I've been with this unit fifteen years, Bryn. I was here when Martha did your job. She always was a bit maverick. Sailed close to the wind. Don't quote me, but I think she sailed too close a bit too often and got pushed upstairs.'

'You think she's taking risks?'

'I can't work out exactly what she's got planned. There's a big SCD9 meeting this afternoon, so we'll know a bit more then. I wish you were back in charge, Bryn. She makes me uneasy.'

'We only have to suck it up for another week-and-a-half. She's back upstairs after that, and hopefully she'll give SCD9 back to me. It could be worse. She could bring in Tynan over me.'

Jemi shook her head, muttering 'Bonkers!', as she headed back to SCD9.

When they were finished with Kraig, Bryn escorted him back to his parked motorcycle. The silence was palpable. Kraig did not want any unnecessary interaction with his scabby brother, and Bryn did not know how to break through the wall of indifference that separated him from the brother he would like to reacquaint himself with – indeed, in all honesty to *acquaint* himself with.

'Thanks for doing this, Kraig. You may well have saved a lot of women from a heap of misery.'

Kraig said nothing, just climbed astride his motorcycle. Before putting on his helmet, he turned to Bryn and addressed him sternly. 'I want to see her.'

'See who?'

'My daughter. I want to see my daughter.'

'Technically she's not your daughter. We have yet to locate the parents and—..'

'I don't give a shit about the legal loopholes. I'm no dummy. I know the score, and I've checked this all out on the internet. Nothing's set in stone until after the birth, and the surrogate has to agree to the parental transfer order. The surrogate is dead. I have more claim to that baby than a set of parents who wanted to buy her to order, like some goddamn Harrods hamper.'

'It's not that simple, Kraig. Really it isn't. The courts won't see it that way—'

'I *want* to see her,' he butted in fiercely, 'and you're going to fix it for me. Phone the hospital and tell them I'm coming in. Get whatever clearance you need. Before I leave London, I want to see my daughter.'

'She's in an incubator, Kraig. She's on breathing apparatus and being fed through a tube. You'd only be able to see her from behind a screen.'

'I don't care. I want to see my daughter, and you're going to fix it for me.'

'Very well, but I'll have to come with you.' Bryn made the call to the hospital.

'Thank you,' said Kraig, nodding to his brother. They were the first civil words the older brother had addressed to the younger in thirty years. 'I'll follow you.' Clearly not enough of a thaw to sit in the same vehicle together.

At the neonatal ward, Bryn watched as Kraig studied baby Miranda through a glass screen that separated visitors from the incubators. His huge frame dwarfed the viewing window. He placed both his hands on the glass and leaned in, as if that would get him closer to her. He stood motionless for a good five minutes.

Bryn could not fail to notice the mist in his brother's eyes. Then, quite suddenly, Kraig turned and left at a pace suggesting he was grappling with his emotions. There was no goodbye, no word of any kind. He simply walked out of his younger brother's life. Bryn did not know if he would ever see him again. All he knew was that he *wanted* to see him again, have a chance to get to know him afresh, put the past behind them.

As a boy he had set his mind against him, deaf to all the pleas of his father for compassion and understanding. He had been hell-bent on revenge. Now in his manhood he had to face the uncomfortable truth pricking his adult soul. He had known he could turn the jury, but he had wanted to punish Kraig. It had taken him nearly thirty years to realise that a brother living with the daily torment of losing his mother by his own hand was a far greater punishment than Bryn or any jury could ever have conferred.

Bryn made his way to his incident room – technically the Chief Super's incident room for these two weeks. The room was more crowded than usual. SCD9 were huddled round the meeting table. Three lay figures were also seated at Martha's table. Bryn recognised two of them instantly.

'Ah, there you are, DCI Ellis. Pull up a chair,' said Martha breezily. 'This is Professor Theodore Kendrick, who's helped me from time to time with specialist trauma support, and Ms Amira Saleem, a human rights QC with expertise in asylum and trafficked victims who comes highly recommended by Professor Kendrick. They both speak fluent Arabic and are already involved through the support work they are providing for our trafficked laundry granny that resulted in the arrest of Kavanagh for Anna Adams' murder this morning. They are joining us as external consultants.'

'I can see I have a lot of catching up to do,' said Bryn, trying not to look at Mia or Theo and grateful that he had not referred to them by name during his recent soul-baring chronicle to Martha. The visitors did not appear to have divulged their past acquaintance with him to her either. Even so, this was going to be a very awkward passage of time.

'And this is Miss Rosie Aldridge. She's the best friend of the victim and has agreed to be a stalking horse for us and gather some triangulated information from the fertility clinic.'

'WHAT!' yelled Bryn. 'This is madness!'

'I volunteered, DCI Ellis,' said Rosie. 'She was my best friend. She would have done the same for me.'

'I don't like it. I don't like it one bit.'

'It's not your place to like or dislike anything, Ellis. *I'm* running this operation for these two weeks. You're helping from the sidelines, as I recall,' declared Martha.

'Why can't a trained police officer go undercover? Why put a member of the public at risk?'

'Because even the best undercover officers lack the authenticity that Rosie can provide. She'll be wearing a T-shirt, just as she is now and – forgive me saying this, Miss Aldridge – but it's hard to fake a missing lower arm. It's just as hard to fake being a Paralympian who competed here in London only two years ago. If any dodgy offers are going to be made, they're bound to check her out. She will come across as entirely genuine and above suspicion.'

'I wouldn't let Rosie do it if there was any danger – and I'll be undercover, too,' confirmed Theo. 'Rosie's going to pose as a cash-strapped single woman needing a surrogate and see if the bait attracts an "under-the-counter offer". If it doesn't, she just walks away and we're no worse off than we are now. I'm playing myself too. A 65-year-old retired grandee. A famous, well-heeled psychologist.

'There's no point pretending otherwise, as the briefest Google search would turn up my profile. I'm exactly the kind of fodder they feed on. Rich and desperate. I haven't fathered a living child of my own. I'll eke out the story of my wife dying in childbirth. How time is closing in on me and now that I'm retired, I want to grab my chance of fatherhood with no strings attached.'

Mia was listening to this explanation with a pained expression. More than anyone in the room, she knew how closely the undercover story resonated with Theo's wounded heart.

'This really is madness! Please tell me you're not going undercover, too,' said Bryn, turning pleadingly to Mia.

'No, I'm too high risk. A Google search would turn up my human rights work, which might spook them. I'm here to help with the legal labyrinth, although this whole thing has made me think seriously about freezing my own eggs,' she added cuttingly.

'Jake took a statement from Kraig Ellis earlier today,' said Martha, 'and while it enables us to pinpoint the clinic, it's not enough to secure a search warrant. I need a credible premise that dodgy dealings are going on there. As Theo says, we've nothing to lose and everything to gain.'

'I must protest my opposition in the strongest terms,' declared Bryn. 'The whole charade is far too risky. With respect, Ma'am, it's a long time since you've been in the field. I beg you to reconsider.'

'The die is cast, Ellis. Nothing more to be said.'

21

Wednesday, 28th May

Theo stayed with Farida while Mia had a catch-up day back at her Chambers. Almost imperceptibly, the therapist-client relationship seemed to have flipped, and it was Farida who was quizzing Theo about his time in the Middle East, about his Lebanese mother, and about how he had rescued Mia in war-torn Iraq. Before long Farida had his whole life story at her feet, and Theo realised it could not have been better therapy for her even if he had planned it.

When Mia arrived early evening, she found them both in the kitchen singing songs from their childhoods, while Farida prepared a dish of lamb meatballs with lentils and fava beans and Theo assisted as her sous chef.

'My goodness!' exclaimed Mia. 'It smells like I'm in for a treat tonight. I'm glad I only had a sandwich for lunch.'

'We've been food shopping,' beamed Theo.

Farida retired early; her body clock still had not adjusted from its habitual 5am start in the laundry room. Theo and Mia sat sipping their green tea and coffee contentedly.

'It's been a very positive day,' mused Theo. 'The only therapy Farida needs now is to find her daughter and granddaughter safe and well.'

'And to be granted refugee status,' added Mia. 'I'll take their cases myself, right up to the European Court of Human Rights if I have to, but they are not being sent back to the hell they came from. Not while there's breath in my body,' she proclaimed fiercely.

'Are the Police making progress with the investigation?'

'I'm sure they are. DCI Ellis said—'

'DCI Ellis?' interrupted Theo, dismayed. 'Why so formal? Since when did he stop being Bryn?'

'Since six years, nine months, three weeks, and five days ago,' she replied bitterly.

Theo put his coffee cup down with a thump. 'That's it!' he said angrily. 'This farce has gone on long enough! I'm not in the habit of breaking my word to anyone, but sometimes a sense of justice has to trump a word of honour. You are going to sit there, Amira Saleem, and I am not letting you move until you have heard the truth about your ill-fated wedding day.'

'Not that again!' said Mia impatiently, standing up to take her mug to the kitchen.

'Sit!' commanded Theo sternly.

A little taken aback, Mia sat down again and dutifully listened to the astonishing narrative that unfolded.

Theo took a deep breath when he had finished, as if the effort of breaking his word to a friend had knocked the stuffing out of him. Mia was very still. She sat with her head bowed and her hands tightly clasped. She looked up at Theo but did not comment on his narrative.

All she said was, 'Would you stay with Farida please till I get back? There's something I have to do.'

Bryn had been home about half an hour and had just put his stir-fry pan in the sink to soak when he heard the doorbell. Wiping his hands on the kitchen towel, he opened the door. Mia was standing there!

Before the door was even half ajar, she had pushed through. She was in a rage, and she was shouting. 'How dare you! How DARE you, Bryn Ellis. How DARE you keep it from me!'

'Woah, woah. What's all this?'

'How *dare* you cheat me. How *dare* you steal my free will. It was MY choice to make! How **DARE** you choose for me like I'm some five-year-old kid.' The crescendo of her ranting increased with every repetition of 'dare'. 'You BRUTE! You arrogant NEANDERTHAL brute! Theo told me everything.'

'He had no right; he gave his w—'

'He had EVERY right.'

'I couldn't let you take that risk, Mia. He threatened to kill you.'

'LET me? How DARE you talk about *letting* me! I'm not yours to *let*. I'm not your possession. I'm a grown woman with a mind of my own to take the decisions *I* want to take.'

As the crescendo of rants waned, she took to pummelling his chest with her tiny hands. 'You're a thief, Bryn Ellis. A choice thief. Theo was right to tell me. We could have faced it together, Bryn. I would have wanted to face it *with* you, even if my life was on the line. You *were* my life, Bryn. You stole—'

Mia got no further. Bryn gently took her wrists and pulled them away from his berated chest. Then, much less gently, he crushed his mouth against hers. Almost seven years of longing and despair spilled out in a passionate embrace that left them both breathless.

'God, I've missed you, Mia. Forgive me. Please forgive me.'

'Not for at least seven years,' she moaned, as he picked her up in his arms.

22

Thursday, 29th May

Mia crept into her apartment in the small hours to find Theo fast asleep on her sofa. She did not wake him. Exhausted but elated, she flopped into bed and did not stir until she heard Farida rustling up breakfast. Having quickly showered and dressed, she wandered into the kitchen to find Theo sitting at the table, coffee in hand, humming along to a song that Farida was singing.

'Good morning, Sleeping Beauty. I trust you had a fruitful outcome from your late-night assignment.'

'I'm sorry I was late, Theo. You were fast asleep on my sofa when I got home and looked so peaceful I didn't like to wake you.'

'And I'm glad you didn't, otherwise I might have had to wait another whole day before I found out what transpired at your mysterious assignment, or should I say *assignation*?' he teased.

Mia did not answer. Instead, she returned to her bedroom and rummaged at the back of her dressing table drawer. She pulled out a ring that had been unceremoniously wrapped in kitchen roll and placed it on her finger.

Back in the kitchen she snuggled up to her 'almost father' and waved her left hand in front of his face. 'I told him I would not forgive him for at least seven years, but I might wear this in the meantime to soften the blow.'

Theo beamed broadly.

'What's the happy occasion?' asked Farida.

Mia waved her ringed finger at Farida who gasped, 'No! Surely, he is too old!'

Theo and Mia burst into hoots of laughter. 'No, not Theo!! The nice detective who got permission for you to stay here with me.'

Then it was Farida's turn to laugh, until she stopped mid-chuckle, suddenly remembering that laughing could not have a place in her life until she had found her daughter and granddaughter. 'I... I need to tidy my room,' she said, and departed quickly before the tears began to flow.

The atmosphere had turned solemn, and Mia decided to ask Theo's advice about something Bryn had mentioned when she was with him last night.

'It must be so hard for Farida, Theo. The longing and the not knowing.'

'Yes, I can see that she has a great capacity for happiness but won't let herself.'

'I need your professional advice, Theo.'

'What about, *ma petite*?'

'Bryn reminded me of something we may have missed, and I'm conflicted. It may be a long shot, and it has the potential to help the wider investigation, but also the potential to cause Farida profound grief.'

'Tell me.'

'We should have thought about the unidentified surrogate who died in the RTA. We should have asked Farida if she recognised her. She might have seen her on the trafficked transport, or... or...'

'Or it might be her daughter,' finished Theo. 'She'd be about the right age. It couldn't be her granddaughter.'

'You can see why I'm conflicted. If it is her daughter, well, I can't imagine the pain it would cause her, and she has been doing so well. She's even been singing in my kitchen.'

'But it would bring closure. There's only one thing worse than losing a loved one, and that's never knowing if they are alive or dead, if they are in pain, if they are cold or hungry. All those needs that a mother nurtures in her child.

Without closure, grief is eternal. With closure, healing can gradually come, and if it's *not* her daughter, she will still have hope.'

'Shall we ask her then?'

'Yes, let's talk to her together.'

Farida was shocked by the account of what had happened to the RTA victim, but she was determined to find out if it might be her daughter. Mia called Bryn, who contacted pathology. Everything was arranged for that afternoon.

The Syrian grandmother had never been to a pathology lab and was surprised that the body had been laid out with so much respect in a peaceful side room, not just wheeled out from a mortuary freezer. When she indicated she was ready, the pathologist pulled back the cover sheet.

Farida gasped and then wailed. Mia put a comforting arm around her while Farida stroked the cheek of her youngest child. A husband and two sons lost to the conflict, and now she was staring at the dead body of her only daughter.

When she was calmer, she nodded. 'Yes, this is my daughter. This is Yasmin Farah Al-Hakim, thirty-eight years old, mother of Leila, who is seventeen. We must find Leila! She's the only blood relative I have left in the world except for Yasmin's baby. You said the baby survived?'

'Yes. She was eight weeks premature and is still in an incubator. She's a fighter and is holding her own, but you must understand, Farida, Yasmin was an enforced surrogate. The baby is not biologically connected to her. The baby was created from another woman's egg and a sperm donor. The woman whose egg was used is the elective parent and will want to claim the baby once we trace her.'

'Yasmin carried that baby in her womb for seven-and-a-half months,' Farida argued. 'The baby may not be blood-related, but I will always think of her as my granddaughter. May I see her? May I see my granddaughter?'

Mia looked at Theo who nodded. The psychologist knew how important this was to Farida's continued wellbeing. 'I will talk to Bryn, and we will arrange it. There is something else you should know, Farida.'

'What is that?'

'The sperm donor was Bryn's brother. It was a philanthropic act. He thought he would be helping a childless couple have the baby they longed for.'

'That makes me happy. Bryn is a good man. I expect his brother is a good man also. It connects this baby even more closely to me. Please let me see her – and soon.'

23

Friday, 30th May

It was 8.45am and Jeff Lawson was sitting in his palatial office, sipping his first coffee of the day. His Executive Assistant, who was also his wife, was seated opposite with the day's schedule in one hand, a half empty cup of Earl Grey in the other.

'And what delights does the day hold for us today, my dear?'

'You're in theatre all afternoon and two appointments this morning.'

'Anything interesting in the appointments?'

'Your first is at 10am. Professor Kendrick. He's in his sixties and childless, looking for a surrogate. Says he's just retired and will have the time to devote to the child he's always wanted. He told me his wife and unborn child died several decades ago, and I got the impression he's never really got over it.'

'He's fertile then. That's a good start, but if he's in his sixties we'll need to do a sperm count to make sure it's still high enough. Did you Google him?'

'Yes. He checks out. He's a professor of psychology who made his name working with veterans with PTSD. Has written several influential books.'

'Good. What's next?'

'You've got an 11am with Miss Rosie Aldridge. She's a Paralympian swimmer – competed here at the London 2012 Games – looking to freeze her eggs and is asking for information about surrogacy. She checks out. She swam for Canada in the 800 metres freestyle, got as far as the semis.

She's over here to train at the Olympic pool with a British coach she's teamed up with. I imagine she won't want to interrupt her training schedule for Rio and beyond, to carry a baby. Could be a good prospect for us.'

'We need a few more if you want that yacht I've promised you. And I needn't remind you we still have a loss to make up from that unfortunate RTA.'

At ten o'clock exactly, Theo was escorted into her husband's office by Pamela, who had already been won over by the chivalrous gentleman with the gorgeous voice. She nodded approvingly at her husband as she closed the door on the two of them.

'Professor Kendrick, do have a seat,' Jeff beamed, proffering his hand. 'Jeff Lawson, Director and Senior Consultant here at Brampton Clinic.'

'Thank you for seeing me,' said Theo congenially, taking in the grandness of the office and the sumptuous leather of the chair he sank into.

'My pleasure, Professor. Now, how can we help you?'

'I'm sixty-five, recently retired, and reached that stage in life where I've achieved almost everything I wanted to.'

'Almost?'

'Yes. I never managed to have a living child of my own, and time's marching on, so I thought I ought to think about going it alone. My wife and unborn child died in tragic circumstances over thirty years ago, and I haven't been able to get past that. Till now, that is. Perhaps it's Old Father Time catching up on me.'

'I'm sorry for your loss, Theodore – may I call you Theodore?'

'By all means, but I prefer Theo. No need for condolences. It was a long time ago.'

'Quite so, Theo, quite so. But a loss is a loss.'

'I'm looking for a surrogate with no strings attached. I need it to be watertight. At my age I can't afford to risk having a surrogate change her mind and want to keep the baby. I've digested all the information on your website, and I think you might be the best clinic to provide the solution I'm looking for.'

'We can certainly do that for you, and the good news is you've already fathered a baby, so you are fertile. But we will still need to test that your sperm count is high enough.' Jeff coughed politely as he added, 'It can sometimes wane with age, you understand.'

'I anticipated you would ask that, so I had my sperm count checked beforehand.' He plucked the mocked-up data sheet SCD9 had furnished for him from his inside jacket pocket and showed it to Lawson. 'I'm informed that the sperm count is in the normal range. Would that be your interpretation, Mr Lawson?'

'Yes, I would concur with that,' replied Lawson, having briefly scanned the numbers. 'I can see you are very serious about this, Theo. May I ask if you already have a willing egg donor, or do you need a donor for that part, too?'

'As long as you can guarantee a no-strings solution, then yes, I would be interested. I prefer that the egg donor is not the surrogate, for all the reasons I have already outlined.'

'We can certainly arrange that for you, Theo.'

'Can you explain the legals to me? As I said, I need to know I have a watertight solution. I don't want any complications with the surrogate, especially as I'm basically just renting a womb.'

'We have an inhouse legal expert who ensures our clients have ample protection. There are parenting court orders to be drawn up, of course, and the final parent transfer order cannot be done until after the birth. But we will sort all that for you, unless you prefer to engage your own lawyer.'

'No, seems sensible to keep it all in one process. Assuming the legal side is covered, what is the surrogate situation?'

'We have a number of surrogates on our books. Some are philanthropies, some are volunteers who just love being pregnant. Others find the remuneration advantageous. The law states you are not allowed to pay a surrogate; they are only entitled to expenses. The expenses are always very generous and a welcome bonus for surrogates who are on modest incomes. In your circumstances, the former two options might be riskier, as those surrogates who love being pregnant might suddenly decide they want to keep the baby. It hasn't happened here at Brampton, but there is always that slight risk. Indeed, if you are seeking the most watertight solution, I would go for our "D" option.'

'The "D" option?'

'The Dispassionate. We screen surrogates for the most dispassionate who prefer not to get involved with the future parents, and who avoid the kind of surrogate bonding that often goes on with some parents-to-be, which in my view can lead to separation issues later on.'

'But surely the would-be-parents will want to follow the progress of the pregnancy, be there at the birth. All of that.'

'Yes, naturally, but we do it in a hands-off way. No interaction with the surrogate. If you go for this option, you would see the implantation of your fertilized egg from behind a screen, have access to all the scans and pregnancy reviews, and watch the birth – again from behind a screen. The baby would be given to you to hold within minutes of the birth. From that point on, the surrogate has nothing to do with the baby. All the procedures, including the birth and the postnatal care, are undertaken here. We have state-of-the-art labs, birthing suites, and an infant nursery. I can get Pamela to show you round, if you like.'

'Yes, I would like that. And how soon before the parent can take the baby home?'

'If the baby is healthy and there have been no birth complications, then as soon as the last part of the legals are sorted.'

'And how long is that?'

'One to two weeks. The parent transfer orders can then take three to nine months, but we pride ourselves on rarely taking longer than three. Nominated parents are allowed to have the baby with them during that period unless a judge has due cause to object. That couldn't happen in a case such as yours.'

'How could I be sure the baby is mine? Mix-ups do happen.'

'DNA verification is part of the end-stage legals.'

'And how much would your "D" option set me back? A ballpark figure is good enough for now.'

'With the lab fees, the embryo implant, ongoing pregnancy reviews, scans etc, the birth, infant post-natal care, the legals, and of course the surrogate expenses, you are probably looking at…' Jeff wrote a figure down and passed it to Theo and was pleased to see his client did not balk at the quoted figure but merely nodded.

'I perform all the D options myself,' Jeff added. 'My wife, Pamela, assists. We met twenty years ago when she was a theatre sister. She's added midwifery to her credentials since then.'

'My goodness, and she's also your PA? What a talented lady-wife you have!'

'You might say we're a dream team, Theo. I couldn't have done any of this without her.'

'It must be a very heavy workload.'

'Not really. And we have the convenience of a state-of-the-art operating theatre in our own home.'

Theo's mind was racing. Lawson had said 'operating' theatre. *Did he really mean operating theatre and not birthing suite? Was it a careless slip?* Unless all of the surrogacies were planned caesareans, why would they need a separate operating theatre, lest its real purpose was performing other surgical operations. *Kidney transplants perhaps?* He quickly pulled himself back into the moment.

'Three plus months after the birth is longer than I was expecting to be certain of becoming the legal parent.'

'That's the law, I'm afraid. It's why we recommend our D option for clients in your position. It makes the judicial stamping very straightforward.'

'Your D option it is then. How soon can you arrange it? Now that I've decided, I just want to get on with it. Age is not on my side, Mr Lawson.'

'I would need to check our surrogate register, but I think we could probably arrange this for... let's see, it's Friday, so I can arrange for in vitro fertilisation and surrogate implantation on the same day. So, yes, we could get this sorted by next Thursday. Is Thursday convenient for you?'

'Thursday is perfect.'

'Pamela will be in touch with all the arrangements. There's just the small matter of payment. You will need to outlay one-third of the cost when you come next Thursday, one-third at the birth, and the final third when all the legal parenting orders are completed. We do have low-cost finance options, if that is a problem for you.'

'Not a problem at all.'

Pamela, having applied fresh lipstick, escorted Theo on a tour of the clinic. Theo kept his eyes peeled for any clues he might pick up on the way, while keeping up the charm offensive in case she dropped any pointers. The vainglorious are always easy prey.

'It's *Mrs* Lawson, isn't it?' he asked innocently.

'Yes, Jeff and I set up this clinic together eighteen years ago, and it's gone from strength to strength.'

'I knew you couldn't be just an ordinary PA. You're much too clever, and if I may say, much too attractive.'

'Oh, I don't know about that,' she replied, patting her hair and blushing ever so faintly.

'Behind every successful man... as the saying goes.'

'Well, without sounding arrogant, I don't think Jeff could have done it without me.'

'Oh, I'm certain of that.'

'And I do assist him with some of the procedures. I am a qualified midwife and a theatre sister from an earlier life. It's how Jeff and I met, actually.'

'Multi-talented, Mrs Lawson,' he said admiringly. 'Trade must be good, given the clinic's reputation. Aren't you ever tempted to pack it all in and retire to a sun-soaked villa somewhere?'

'We need one more good year, and then we might be tempted. Jeff has promised me a yacht.'

'My, you *must* be doing well. Good for you.'

Pamela checked her watch and realised she had to get back for the next appointment. 'I'm afraid I'm needed back in the office, but I do look forward to your next appointment visit with us, Professor.'

'As do I,' he smiled. 'What a beautiful day. And what beautiful grounds you have here. May I take a short stroll before I head back?'

'By all means, Professor. We take great pride in our gardens. It's important to create a stress-free ambience for our clients. We have a mindfulness Japanese garden with some beautiful acers, if you care to meander through it.'

'I certainly will. Thank you, Mrs Lawson.'

'Oh, Pamela, please,' she insisted.

'Thank you, *Pamela*,' he repeated gallantly. 'And it's Theo.'

Once Pamela was safely back in the clinic, Theo eschewed the gardens and headed in the direction of the Lawsons' detached house. It was a large, three-storey Victorian building. From the outside, he estimated there must be a substantial basement. Perhaps that was where the operating theatre was sited? He reckoned the other three floors housed at least twelve rooms. Temporary housing for trafficked surrogates perhaps, or trafficked organ donors, or both? He must ensure Martha understood that any search warrant she applied for had to include the private residence.

At five minutes past eleven, Pamela showed Rosie into her husband's office.

'Do have a seat, Ms Aldridge. How can Brampton Clinic be of service?'

'I was badly injured in a car accident some years ago,' she began. 'My boyfriend was driving. He was killed outright.'

'I'm very sorry for your loss, Rosie. May I call you Rosie?'

'Yes, please do. I lost most of this,' she said, nodding mechanically to her left arm, 'and suffered some internal injuries. I am still ovulating, but I am told that my uterus is too damaged to sustain a pregnancy, which is why I have decided to freeze my eggs in the hope that I could have a child of my own via surrogacy.'

'I see. And do you have a partner who would like to co-parent with you?'

Rosie shook her head. 'Rob – my boyfriend – was very special. I've not found it easy to move on from him. I've decided I'd like to go it alone. My mother was a single parent, and she managed admirably.'

'So, would you be looking for a sperm donor?'

'Yes. I understand from your website that you have a premium sperm bank.'

'We do indeed, and although our donors have to remain anonymous, we are able to share with you some of their attributes so that you can choose a donor that best meets your needs.'

'How much would it all cost?' she asked timidly.

Lawson went through the same calculations he had done with Theo but added another 9k for the egg freezing, then passed the sheet of paper over to Rosie.

'Oh, my goodness!' declared Rosie, displaying the disappointment she had been coached to show from her

SCD9 brief. 'I had no idea it would cost so much. That's completely beyond my reach. I'm going to have to wait until I get a gold medal and some serious sponsorship to be able to afford that.'

'We do offer a finance option with very low interest rates.'

'Thank you, Mr Lawson, but I really can't commit to any ongoing debt. Not until I get some better sponsorship.'

Jeff Lawson was weighing up his options and mulling over whether or not to dangle the bait.

'There might be another affordable way.'

'Oh... you really think so? It would mean so much to me.'

'We do have some surrogates who are on low incomes, and therefore their out-of-work expenses are very much less. It would mean very little choice over the surrogate, and they don't have any ongoing contact with you during the pregnancy. It cuts down the overhead expenses, you see. But if you really only want to rent a womb, it might be worth consideration.'

Jeff smiled kindly. 'I would like to help you Rosie, and as long as you promise not to broadcast the hefty discount we could offer you – otherwise we would be inundated with requests we could not accommodate – I could see my way to lowering those costs considerably.' He wrote down another figure and passed it to her.

'Oh, Mr Lawson, that would be wonderful. Oh yes, please. What would I need to do?'

'Normally, one egg is released into the fallopian tube during ovulation. Because we need to retrieve as many eggs as possible, we work to encourage the ovaries to release multiple eggs at the same time. We do this by matching a fertility medication to your hormone levels, and you self-inject the medication for a couple of weeks. Blood tests and ultrasound will tell us how well the medication is working. When we detect there are sufficient eggs in the ovaries, a "trigger injection" is administered, which causes the body to release the eggs for retrieval.'

'I see. And if you harvest multiple eggs, I can freeze the others, just in case – or would that be additional cost?'

'No, you would only be charged once for egg freezing. Obviously, if you wanted a second child, there would be the other costs to find.'

Rosie put on her best beaming smile. 'In which case, I would like to go ahead. When could I choose my sperm donor?'

'We could do that now, if you like. Pamela can go through it all with you.'

Rosie agreed eagerly, as she hoped it was giving Theo more time to snoop around.

With the intel that Theo and Rosie provided, Martha was able to get the search warrant they craved. The 'Brampton Sting', as she liked to call it, was planned for the coming Thursday, when they were confident at least one trafficked surrogate would be on the premises. In the meantime, covert surveillance would track vehicles entering and exiting the clinic, and a small, armed response unit was on standby for the day of the Sting. It consisted of two unmarked vehicles that would be stationed a short distance away, ready to move in when Theo pressed green. Theo had been fully briefed on what the green code was. SCD9 officers and forensics would follow in unmarked cars.

24

Thursday, 5th June, 2014

Preparations were being made at Brampton Clinic ahead of Theo's scheduled arrival at 10.30am. Pamela was wearing her best silk blouse and had squeezed in a visit to the hairdresser the day before. Theo arrived admirably promptly and was offered a coffee before their planned decamp to the Lawsons' private residence.

'Is everything ready with the surrogate?' asked Theo, as he sipped his coffee.

'Everything is ready for you, have no worries on that score.'

Theo smiled. It was the confirmation he was looking for, and he pulled his phone out on the pretext of turning it off. 'Can't have any unwanted interruptions on such a momentous day,' he said theatrically.

It was a simple green code. Before he switched off the phone, he pressed send on a pre-prepared text. It was done in a microsecond and went unnoticed.

Theo eased back into his chair to finish his coffee when the door to Jeff Lawson's office suddenly burst open, and Kraig Ellis charged in, wielding a gun. Pamela screamed, and her husband spilt his coffee down his crisp white shirt.

'Stay perfectly still or she gets it,' commanded Kraig, pointing the gun at Pamela, who screamed a second time. 'I want the file on the baby I've fathered. The one that survived the surrogate RTA. Don't try and fob me off with obfuscations. I know what your game is. I'd never have given you a sperm donation if I'd known what filth you were up to.

'The surrogate is dead, and I want to know who the so-called "parents-to-be" are so I can go and have a cosy chat with them about my rights. I'm the only one left with a biological connection to that little girl. Get it for me, NOW!' he ordered.

Jeff got up gingerly from his armchair and sat at his desk and fired up his laptop. 'I'll need your full name, if I'm to trace this for you. I'll have to cross reference it from the sperm donor register.'

'Ellis, with two L's. Kraig Ellis, spelt with a K.'

On hearing this, Theo instantly realised that the man wielding the gun must be Bryn's brother, and if history was repeating itself the gun was very probably a replica.

With shaking fingers, Lawson typed the words into his search directory. A few moments later he had the details which he started to read out.

'Print it out for me,' insisted Kraig.

Lawson did as he was bid and passed the sheets across. Once Kraig had them firmly in his pocket, he pulled the cable out of the laptop and pushed it into his backpack. 'I'm sure this will make interesting reading,' he said.

But before he was able to make his escape, the door burst open a second time, and in stormed three police officers with firearms.

In a flash Theo remembered Bryn's painful account of his brother's staged vengeance.

'Don't shoot!' he yelled. 'It's a replica! He's unarmed! Don't shoot!' Theo leapt up and shielded Kraig in a desperate attempt to avert disaster. 'Give me the replica, Kraig,' he entreated. 'I know all about it from Bryn. Please give it to me before there is a misunderstanding and someone gets hurt.'

Stunned both by the arrival of armed Police and Theo's apparent knowledge of his weapon, Kraig handed it over, and Theo placed it in his pocket.

'Hands in the air, down on your knees,' came the command from the senior officer, just as Martha, Bryn, and Jake appeared.

'What's happened here?' demanded CS Simmons.

'It's alright, Martha. It's just a misunderstanding. Kraig came here to get some information on the nominated parents of baby Miranda so he could go and talk to them.'

'He had a gun!' squealed Pamela. 'He threatened to kill me!'

'It was a replica, Martha. You know the backstory to that as well as I do. It was just a replica, like before. No harm done. There are more important matters to attend to, as I recall,' pressed Theo.

'Quite so. Discussions about replicas will have to wait. Mr and Mrs Lawson, I am arresting you on suspicion of profiting from human trafficking. You do not have to say anything, but if you do it may be taken down and used against you in a court of law. I have here a warrant to search this clinic, its grounds, and your private residence. We will do so with attendant respect and due care for any patients currently in attendance. All staff will be detained for questioning.'

At that point, Jake came forward to handcuff both suspects and remove them to a waiting police van.

'Forensics can start in here,' concluded Martha.

Theo nudged Kraig, who was back on his feet, and gave him a meaningful stare. Responding to the prompt, Kraig held out the laptop and printed information sheets.

'I was borrowing these to help me trace my daughter's so-called parents. They should make interesting reading.'

Bryn stepped forward to take them from him. The two brothers exchanged poignant glances that quelled a lifetime of bitterness.

'I'm just in the way here,' said Theo, 'so if you've no objection, Martha, I'd like to get home. It's been quite a morning,'

'Yes, of course, Theo. Jake, can you radio the officer on the gate and instruct him to let Theo through.'

Once Theo was well clear of the gate and surveillance cameras, he pulled over into a layby and breathed a huge sigh of relief. He pulled out Kraig's weapon from his pocket. As soon as he had taken it from Kraig, he had known it was not a replica. It was far too heavy. He removed the cylinder and tipped out six bullets. He put the bullets into one jacket pocket and placed the empty pistol in the other jacket pocket. As he drove home, he kept his eyes peeled for a suitably remote stretch of water. He pulled over, checked there was no-one around, and then threw the pistol as far as he could into the deepest part of the river. He drove three miles further along the snake of the river and then disposed of the six bullets in the same way.

The raid on the Lawson's home uncovered a fully functioning operating theatre situated in the basement. A trafficked woman was being held in an upstairs bedroom, seemingly awaiting the first stage of an enforced surrogacy for Theo. Two other migrants were also discovered; a man and a woman, both with tattooed codes on their forearms, presumably waiting for kidneys to be forcibly removed.

Interviews with staff and clinic patients showed them to be innocent parties, with the exception of one medic. He was the anaesthetist for the illegal basement operations.

Jemimah's deconstruction of Lawon's laptop unlocked the identity of all sperm donors, egg donors, and elective parents. The majority were expected to be legitimate, but all would have to be checked.

Martha pulled in a small army of reinforcements to begin the intricate work. Just as Kavanagh had done before them, the Lawsons gave up their sources in the hope of leniency.

SCD9 were getting closer and closer to the top echelons of the vice ring, so Martha was too busy to worry about a stray replica gun that Theo had commandeered. When quizzed about it, she readily accepted his explanation that toy guns were a menace, and he had thrown it in a skip to avoid it causing any more havoc.

Theo played his PTSD card, arguing that Kraig had been traumatised by the discovery of a biological daughter and had only been trying to find out information about her. He suggested that six mandatory PTSD sessions with himself would be of more use than charging Kraig for possession of a replica weapon with intent to threaten others. The esteem in which Martha held Theo was ultimately persuasive.

'You knew, didn't you?' said Kraig, in the first of those mandatory sessions. 'You knew it wasn't a replica. What did you do with it?'

'I disposed of it somewhere it will never be found. I need an undertaking from you not to get hold of a gun, replica or otherwise, ever again. You must dispose of that replica gun if you still have it, at your first opportunity.'

Kraig nodded compliantly. 'Thank you, Professor Kendrick. I realise you took a great risk on my behalf and saved me from a certain return to prison.'

'We need to talk about your prison years and your childhood, but first you must call me Theo.'

'Very well, Theo,' he replied stiffly. He was clearly finding the whole process uncomfortable. Being subjected to mandatory therapy sessions, having someone else pulling the strings – it all felt like another form of incarceration.

However, it was not long before Theo's skilful techniques had broken down his defences, and Kraig was baring his soul. New understandings were forged between the brilliant professor and his highly intelligent client – a slighted mother's son, a detested brother, a displaced lover. Overlooked and over-punished, this victim – of others, but mostly of himself – weighed heavily with Theo's sense of justice and humanity. He brought Bryn into the final session to engender a long overdue rapprochement between the two brothers. There was another expiation that Theo was targeting, but he was going to need Mia's help for that.

Friday, 6th June, was Martha's last day as SIO. Her two weeks were up, and she had agreed to hand the reins back to Bryn. SCD9 had gathered in the incident room. There was cake and booze, lots of cheering, and a rendition of *For She's a Jolly Good Fellow*. Rousing applause accompanied her exit. Bryn had not joined in the singing, and he kept his hands firmly in his pocket when everyone was clapping around him. He followed Martha up to her office and shut the door quietly behind them.

'What is it now, Bryn?' she asked, still flushed from the animated celebrations. 'I've reinstated you as SIO. Clearing the rest of this up will be career-defining for you.'

'If you ever pull a stunt like that again,' began Bryn in quiet, measured tones, 'I will get you kicked off the force.'

'How dare you, Ellis. What's got into you!'

'What you did was unforgivably irresponsible. You're lucky no-one was killed. How could you put a Canadian tourist, a disabled female no less, into that viper's den? You already knew we'd had one woman thrown off a tower balcony, another woman's throat slashed, not to mention the unfortunate RTA victim. If Rosie had been rumbled, we could have had another murder on our hands. And Theo, your feted white knight. How could you let him put himself at risk like that? Not to mention Kraig being nearly gunned down, by all accounts. It was reckless, Martha, utterly reckless. This is SCD9. We have trained undercover officers, for God's sake. We have protocols. You broke every rule in the book.'

'Don't worry, Bryn. You won't have to hound me out. I've decided to retire. This was my swan song, and it was very stimulating. I couldn't go back to this tiresome paperwork after that. The Chief Constable already has my resignation. I'm retiring on a high, so don't spoil it for me. If you ditch that broom handle you've got stuck up your backside, you might make a good DCS yourself one day.'

A large contingent travelled down from Cumbria for the inquest of Beth's granddaughter. Rhianne and Eithan came with their three children; Keira and Matt with their two little ones. Hilda, making her second journey to the big city, carried a photo of her longtime employer-friend in her capacious handbag and brought Ruth with her to swell out the Bakery ranks. Mia and Farida were there with Theo – and of course, Beth, who was ever present in her toy soldier that Theo kept in his trouser pocket.

The Adams family were grateful for the tangible outpouring of love and support. Zac and Jarrad each had an arm around Charlotte as they guided her into the court room. Rosie followed respectfully behind. Mia had assured the family this would not be a suicide verdict. It was an open and shut case since Kavanagh had confessed to the murder. Nevertheless, Charlotte's face was contorted with anxiety.

It was as Mia predicted; the coroner returned a verdict of unlawful killing. Family and friends then retired to a pre-arranged memorial service before Anna's coffin was transported to the airport. Charlotte and Zac were taking her home. They had considered the option of burying her next to her grandmother in Silecroft, where they had a cottage and spent a month there every year. They had also considered the tug of her brother being based in London. But Canada was Anna's home. She was born there. She grew up there, and they decided that even with her brother in London and her grandmother in Cumbria, she should be buried in Edmonton.

Jarrad had made no secret of his love of London and his surgery ambitions at King's College hospital. So, he surprised everyone when he announced he was returning to Canada. His parents needed him more than ever now. He had not been close to his sister in life, and he did not want to be thousands of miles away from her in death. He would try and obtain a junior surgical post in Edmonton, and if he was unsuccessful, he would join his father in General Practice.

Before then, he was going to spend a last few weeks with Rosie. She was not returning to Canada until the start of her school term in September. He wanted to show her the splendours of the English Lake District, his grandmother's bakery, and the Adams' family cottage. He hoped he might be able to tempt her back the following summer.

Rosie Aldridge had been another consideration in his decision to go back to Canada. He wanted to get to know her a whole lot better.

PART FOUR

FATHERHOOD

25

Mid-June, 2014

Back in the saddle, Bryn had quickly got SCD9 humming again. Word was put out across all MET stations to check every pop-up nail bar on their beats. This net caught a dozen rogue operators and around fifty trafficked migrants. Testimony from them and Kavanagh's rescued 'pearls' told a similar tale to Farida's; of being driven from the docks to an empty warehouse, where they were grouped according to gender, age, and health, and whisked off to different locations. This tallied with the sources Kavanagh and Lawson had given up.

It was all pointing to a large international operation radiating out from Pearl Fine Wines. Bryn resolutely awaited the next wine shipment, due in three days, when he hoped to close the loop. The interception would not only unclasp another group of migrants but should lead to the identification of the original overseas source point. Meanwhile, Mia worried over Leila. If she was seventeen and still alive, she would most likely have been put to work as a prostitute.

The interception of the Pearl Fine Wines shipment went according to plan. Thirteen migrants were rescued. The small number was what Bryn was expecting. Thirteen naively cooperative migrants were easily secreted behind the luxury wine cases, and the frequent shipments provided a safe, steady flow of human fodder. The fees extracted from the migrants' meagre savings for the cost of their passage, plus the cash from the regular buyers who took them for their own nefarious ends, provided a long-term lucrative income for

Pearl Enterprises. With the information extracted from commodity buyers, Jemimah was able to track down the owner behind the multiple shell walls. His arrest and interrogation yielded data that enabled the transnational police network to trace the overseas source. Before long, the powerful international vice ring was smashed open and high-profile arrests followed.

There was, though, much still to do, and Bryn needed Mia for most of it. The legals surrounding outstanding parent orders were a minefield, and they still had not found Leila.

Mia prioritised tracing the elective parents of Baby Miranda. The egg donor, Belinda Melkin, was a celebrity model at the peak of her career. Mia had made a prior appointment and was shown into the reception room of a luxury home in W8.

Belinda's wife was also a model, albeit with a less illustrious profile. They were one of the first celebrity couples to take advantage of the new law that legalised gay marriage. When Mia proffered her business card and explained the purpose of her visit, Belinda was shocked. She had assumed the baby had died in the RTA, along with the surrogate. Brampton Clinic had led her to believe that at the time.

'You need to know that the baby was born eight weeks premature by emergency Caesarean at the scene of the road accident. She is still in an incubator and is likely to have to remain there for the next two or three weeks, until she is strong enough to be discharged. I also need to inform you that the surrogate was a Syrian refugee who was the victim of human trafficking.'

'But that's impossible! Brampton Clinic seemed entirely legitimate. Mr Lawson was very charming. He offered me what he called his dispassionate option as the best protection against a surrogate changing her mind and deciding to keep the baby. I had no idea that meant he was going to use a trafficked surrogate.'

'Jeff Lawson is currently in police custody. He's under arrest for profiteering from human trafficking via enforced surrogacies and the illegal removal of kidney organs.'

'What! Oh my God! Are you telling me he was forcibly taking kidneys from migrants as well?'

'I'm afraid so. I understand the black market for kidneys is very lucrative since the explosion in Type 2 diabetes.'

'I can't be associated with this. I can't afford any scandal. I have a celebrity profile to maintain. If anything came out about me being connected to any of this, it would be disastrous. I would lose half my contracts at a stroke.'

'With regard to your public profile, I'm afraid there is one other piece of information which might leak out. You know how clever these gutter journalists are at prising things out.'

'What other information?'

'It transpires that your sperm donor has a criminal record. He was given a life sentence for murdering his mother.'

'Fucking hell! This just gets worse. If even a whiff of this came out, it would ruin me. Besides, I'm not comfortable with the thought of a child of mine having a biological father who killed his own mother. It's perverse. It's… ugh… it's totally unacceptable. I don't want anything to do with that baby. They can't make me, can they?'

'If you instruct me to rescind your surrogacy parent application, I can make this all go away. It's a simple legal matter, and once that is done there is no way anyone can tie your name to this unfortunate turn of events.'

'Yes, yes, do it.'

'Are you engaging me to act for you in this matter, Ms Melkin?'

'Yes, is there a form I have to sign or something?'

'Just leave everything to me. You're in safe hands. I'm a very experienced QC,' replied Mia smugly.

'Whatever it costs, just do it as quickly as you can.'

Mia reported back to Bryn on the first part of her Kraig Ellis renaissance mission, as she liked to call it. 'So far so good, although the second part might not be quite as easy.'

'If the egg donor has revoked her rights, and the surrogate mother is dead, does that clear the way for Kraig to be able to claim his daughter?' asked Bryn.

'A criminal record does not preclude you becoming a father, although it would definitely prevent you adopting. The route to fatherhood for Kraig is via proof of DNA, and proof that all other claims are void. A judge may still want to assure himself that he is a fit parent. By all accounts, he was a model prisoner and has not been in trouble with the police since.

'Theo managed to parry that replica stunt he pulled at the clinic. Plus, he has assisted in the successful overthrow of an international vice ring. Apart from Martha, only you, Theo, and I know about the other replica gun stunt. I don't think Martha is going to spoil the party. She's getting up close and personal with baby gorillas in equatorial Africa, from what I heard.'

Bryn smiled at the image this news manifested. 'He lives in a caravan. Is that going to be a problem?'

'Ah, I had assumed he was living with Megan.'

'It's only three weeks since her husband died. They said they want to wait a year before they move in together, out of respect for Dave – and also, Megan has to consider her three sons. It would understandably rankle if a new man moved in with their mother before their father was cold in his grave.'

'I think this might be one of my unforeseen snags. Health visitors aren't going to be too keen on this. They might make a referral to social services, and that could plant us back at square one.'

'If you're still okay about me moving in with you, Kraig could have my flat.'

'Yes, that would work, but what about his job? He needs to show a good work record, and he would lose the nursery delivery contract if he moved away. That's been steady work for him for several years.'

'Surely he'd have to give that up? It's not a great start to fatherhood being on the road so much.'

'We'll mull that one over, but I'm sure we can come up with a solution. If he moves to London, we can showcase his past work record, but he will still need to prove he has a steady job here. Let's put our thinking caps on for that one.'

Mia hesitated slightly before continuing. 'There's something else I want to do for Kraig. Theo has learned a lot about your brother in the therapy sessions. He struggled with Cadi supplanting his place as the golden son, and it coloured his attitude to her during her short life. He sees things differently now. He has huge regrets about a lot of his early life. Theo says he really is a tortured soul. He thinks the chance of fatherhood could be very healing for him. Theo also believes he has been over-punished for a momentary loss of control. He never intended to harm his mother.'

'It's the kind of punishment that has no parole.'

'I've scrutinised the court documents from his case. My Head of Chambers and I agree it was entirely your testimony at the trial that got the murder conviction.'

Bryn bowed his head and wrung his hands. 'Don't you think I know that now, Mia? It haunts me.'

'If you were willing to sign an affidavit that your testimony at the original trial was coloured by your grief for your mother and sister, then I could get Theo to provide expert testimony that your state of mind and young age would have rendered you an unreliable witness. I think I could persuade the Crown Court of Appeal that the original trial was unsafe and the sentence erroneous.

'If I am granted leave to appeal, the prosecution only has seven days to notify the court if they are going to oppose, and I doubt any CPS would risk its reputation on this one. The court papers are pretty damning. Dozens of mistakes were made in that trial. Kraig's barrister should have picked up on the animosity between you two brothers and absolutely trounced you in the witness box. By opting to appear in person rather than via video, you forfeited your right to be afforded undue deference on account of your age.'

'What would that achieve?'

'It could lead to the murder charge being set aside in favour of manslaughter. Theo said that Kraig was dreading the day his daughter found out her father was a convicted murderer.'

'What would a likely sentence for manslaughter be?'

'It could be anything from community service up to ten years, depending on what mitigation is applied.'

'Baby Miranda is going to need to stay in hospital another month or so. Is that enough time to do this before Kraig's parent appeal?'

'Only if CPS decide not to oppose my application. Remember, they only have seven days to decide. Then it's down to how quickly we can get it onto the court schedule. Three judges sit on these kinds of cases. Even if it takes a while, we would be able to demonstrate that CPS have not opposed the application, which will be a huge step forward in Kraig's bid for fatherhood. A good character reference would be helpful.'

'I'm sure Mrs M would do that. She's delighted the Ellis brothers are reconciled, and I think she has a soft spot for Kraig.'

Bryn wasted no time in contacting Kraig. 'I have a suggestion to make that may help you in your fight to gain parenthood of Miranda.'

'I need all the help I can get.'

'Mia thinks you living in a caravan would be a big drawback. It's not an ideal environment for a tiny baby who's spent the first two months of her life in the Neonatal Unit.'

'I can't ask Megan. It wouldn't be decent, I've explained that.'

'I know that, Kraig. I totally understand.'

'I've been looking at selling the caravan and using the money to put a deposit on a rented place.'

'I have a better idea. Mia has invited me to move in with her, so you could have my flat. I rent it, but you could live there as my long-term guest for as long as you need. It's only one bedroom, but it's all you need for now. In a year, you and Megan might get a place of your own.'

'I couldn't afford London rents, Bryn. They're prohibitive.'

'Don't be daft, Kraig, you could live there free of charge. It's the least I can do. In any case, I can't charge you rent without getting permission from the landlord to sublet.'

There was no answer.

Bryn waited in silence, not quite knowing how Kraig had reacted. He might not take too kindly to charity from his kid brother. Then he heard the faint noise of a broken sob.

'Are you there, Kraig? Kraig, are you there?'

'I don't know what to say, I—'

'Just say, yes. That's all you have to say.'

'Thank you, Bryn. Thank you.' And then the phone went dead.

26

Late June, 2014

As Mia had predicted, CPS did not oppose her application for leave to appeal against Kraig's murder conviction, and she immediately set to work preparing the case. Kraig was in raptures at the prospect of impending fatherhood *and* the possibility of his murder conviction being commuted. Megan tried to temper his euphoria. She could not bear the prospect of Fate dealing him another, possibly two more crushing blows.

The wheels of SCD9 kept on turning, and more and more migrants were being rescued from rumbled captors. Each morning, Farida hoped it might be the day there would be news of Leila. The longer it took, the more hope faded that they would find her alive. Mia had seen a crumpled photo of Leila that Farida kept by her bedside. She was stunningly beautiful, and Mia wondered if Leila had been singled out as an exclusive for one of the top brasses rather than put into the prostitute mix. They doubled their efforts and Farida doubled her prayers.

The breakthrough came in the last week of June when they received intelligence from the international central network that they had found someone answering Leila's description during a drugs raid on a villa in the south of Spain, owned by an Englishman. She spoke a little English but was too traumatised to say anything about her ordeal. They sent over a photo, and Bryn took it straight to Farida with every digit crossed. In an instant, Farida recognised her granddaughter and fell to her knees to give thanks to Allah.

As soon as possible, Bryn arranged for Farida to speak to her granddaughter on a video phone link alongside Theo. On seeing and hearing her grandmother, Leila's terror began to melt, and they spoke animatedly in Arabic.

'You're safe now, Leila. The English police have helped me, and they are going to help you. We will bring you back to England. This is my dear friend, Theo. He is a professor who specialises in trauma. He has offered to accompany the English police to bring you back to me. He speaks fluent Arabic. His mother was Lebanese. You can trust him, Leila. He has a great soul. He is blessed by Allah.'

'Where is Mother? Is she with you? Is she safe?'

Farida had been expecting the question, but when it came, she floundered. Theo stepped in. He judged the news about her mother would be too distressing for Leila in the present circumstances.

'Your mother's resting, Leila. We can talk about everything you have missed when you are back here, but there isn't time now. This is only a short call. There will be plenty of time once you're here with your grandmother.'

He had fallen back on a euphemism. Yasmin *was* resting. They would need to explain the essence of what that 'resting' actually meant in a gentler cocoon.

'I have to get to the airport now. A lovely lady police officer called Chrissy is coming with me to bring you back. Not long now, Leila. Be brave.'

'Soon, Leila, very soon. We'll be together very soon,' said Farida, blowing Leila a kiss, and then Theo wisely ended the call.

❈❈❈❈❈

As soon as planning permission for the Lotus Hub in Sycamore Avenue had been approved, Mia had involved Farida in the preparations for the first intake of trafficked women. Farida had asked if she could be among the first residents, arguing she could be more use there than being pampered in Mia's apartment. Mia had grown very fond of the spirited grandmother and had enjoyed sharing space with her, but she knew the Lotus Hub was a better solution. Besides, Bryn was itching to move in with her, and this would pave the way for them to co-habit again and for Kraig to take up residence in his brother's flat.

149 Sycamore Avenue was ready to take its first female residents. The bedrooms were large enough to take two beds but had been set up for single occupation, as Mia knew the traumatised victims would need their own safe space. Farida was assured there would be a place for Leila. That left six bedrooms and the difficult task of selecting the most in need from the dozens of women who had been rescued in the recent SCD9 operation.

'Leila and I will share,' insisted Farida. 'We are family. We cannot take two bedrooms if it means another wounded soul misses out.'

'Thank you, Farida, as long as you're sure it won't be detrimental to Leila's recovery.'

'I'm sure.'

'I can see you're going to be a great help to the other seven women when they arrive. They will be traumatised like Leila.'

'We will be a Lotus Hub family. Everyone will help everyone. After a while you might find others offer to share, too, when they understand it gives other women like them a chance of sanctuary.'

'In time I hope to be able to open more Lotus Hubs, as long as the Foundation funds keep growing.'

'You and Theo, you are good people. Allah has blessed you with great souls.'

'There are a lot of good people in the world. Many more than bad people. We mustn't let evil prevail by doing nothing.'

'Will we get permission to stay in this country? Will we be granted residence?'

'I have successfully represented dozens of traumatised trafficked women in circumstances like yours and Leila's. I would stake my career on it.'

149 Sycamore Avenue was soon buzzing with its new occupants. Theo spent every afternoon there doing therapy sessions. Mia was too busy with Kraig's appeal case to give much of her time, but the small army of volunteers that had clustered around her Foundation were there in force. All kinds of classes – English, IT, yoga, relaxation, gardening, to name but a few – were made available. A nurse was stationed on the premises, and volunteer medics ensured there was always a female doctor on call.

Beneath the protective mantle of sisterhood were chasms of grief, rivers of torment, and the all-too-frequent nightmares that Theo tried to dispel. Leila, in particular, needed a lot of help. She had been hit hard by the news of her mother's death. Theo judged she would be in therapy a long time if she were ever to overcome the trauma of a seventeen-year-old virgin forced to be a cruel man's plaything.

❈❈❈❈❈

Bryn telephoned Mrs Matthews to tell her about Kraig's hopes of fatherhood and asked if she would be a character witness in Mia's efforts to get a retrospective commuting of his murder conviction to manslaughter.

'Well, I never!' said Gracie. 'This is wonderful news. Of course I will write a character reference for him. He's a good man deep down, and he's knuckled down to make the best of things since he got out. It cut me to the quick how harshly he was punished for what he did. He and my William were good mates at school, and they started down the pit together. They'd probably still be mates if the Iraq war hadn't claimed my baby in '89.'

Bryn knew all too well there had been no work for the miners when the colliery closed, and like many of the younger men, William had joined the army. 'It's been hard for you, Gracie. War claimed your only child, and then emphysema claimed your husband.'

'I'm a survivor,' she replied, 'like my mother before me, and my grandmother before her. We're no strangers to hardship.'

'I'm moving in with Mia and letting Kraig have my apartment. He and Megan are waiting a year before they get together – out of respect for Dave and for her youngest, who still has a year to finish at school. Mia thinks that living in a caravan will count against him. The health visitors might take against a single father in a remote caravan bringing up a newborn just out of neonatal unit. Mia doesn't want to risk it getting referred to social services.'

'Oh dear, he will be a fish out of water in London, Bryn. It will be hard on Megan, too. She'll be so far away. We can do better than that. Why doesn't he move in with me – and I can help him with the baby? Megan will be near at hand, too. He'd need to have your room, of course. So if you visit, you'll have to make do with the little bedroom – and when the wee one needs that, you'll be relegated to the sofa!'

'Mrs M, you're an absolute treasure! I don't quite know what to say. Kraig will be over the moon. Mia will be over the moon. Megan will be over the moon.'

'And *I'll* be over the moon. It will be a new lease of life for me having a baby in the house again.'

27

July 2014

By mid-July, baby Miranda had reached a healthy enough weight to be discharged into the care of her father. There was great excitement and an outpouring of love for this tiny infant who had survived against the odds. Kraig had traded in his cherished motorbike for a second-hand car and the highest spec baby car seat he could find. Farida felt a connection to the baby her daughter had carried for seven months, and she had been busy knitting a cardigan with matching socks and bonnet, while Gracie Matthews had crocheted a crib blanket. Even the nursing staff had clubbed together to buy her a Babygro with 'small but mighty' brandished across the tummy. Theo bought the cot, Jarrad a Moses basket, and Megan sorted all the bottle-feeding equipment.

Bryn insisted on buying the pram. He and Mia went on a shopping expedition to buy an all-terrain one, given where the infant would be living. It took longer than expected, because Mia was distracted by all the pretty baby clothes and had five outfits in her basket before they even made it to the pram section. They wheeled several up and down, asked for advice from the nursery assistant, and finally settled on a top-of-the-range all-terrain model, with removable carrycot that converted to a three-position reclining pushchair.

'We will need to ask Kraig to road-test it.'
'I'm sure it will be fine, Mia. It gets a five-star review.'
'Not for him, for us!'
'I don't understand?'
'Miranda is going to have a cousin.'
'You mean… you mean…?'

'Yes, you dummy! We are going to have a baby of our own.'

'Mia! Mia! Oh, this is so amazing! I can't believe it.'

'It's hardly rocket science, Bryn. Didn't they teach you about the birds and the bees?'

Bryn picked her up her and swung her round, almost knocking over a display of Disney soft toys. Then he shouted at the top of his voice, 'We're going to have a baby!' to the great amusement of nearby staff and customers, because surely that's why most young couples test-wheeling prams in that department were there!

Before he left London, Kraig went to register his daughter's birth, along with Mia. He wanted legal counsel on hand in case there were any complications. Other than Megan, Kraig had not discussed with anyone his plans for naming his daughter. Until this point, everyone had referred to her as baby Miranda. When the registrar asked for the name(s) and spelling(s) of the infant, Kraig produced a piece of paper on which he had written his chosen names. He requested three copies of the birth certificate.

Bryn was waiting for them at the neonatal ward for the planned discharge of his niece. He was eager to tell his older brother that he too was going to be a father. Before he could deliver his news, though, Kraig thrust an envelope into his hands.

'Keep it safe. You're the custodian of the Ellis family name. I forfeited that right a long time ago. I was not a good son and a worse brother – particularly to Cadi. I hope I can be a better father.'

Bryn unfolded his niece's birth certificate. He saw it straight away: *Catrin Wynne Ellis*. Bryn's heart almost burst with pride. He was not surprised to see their mother's name; he had half expected it. But Catrin was their dead sister's name!

The diminutive Cadi she had been known by in her younger years suited her so well that Catrin was only ever used on formal occasions. Kraig had named his daughter after a sister he had maligned the whole of her short life. It was testament to the huge steps he had made in the mandatory therapy sessions where Theo had gently excavated and banished the deep-seated childhood resentment that had mired relationships with both his siblings.

'Don't worry,' said Kraig. 'Megan and I have agreed she'll be Catrin from the off. We're not trying to replace Cadi, just honour her.'

'I think it's wonderful, Kraig. Dad would be so proud of you. I have exciting news of my own. Mia's pregnant. Catrin is going to have a cousin sometime in early March. I hope they'll grow up to be close.'

'We'll make sure of it, Bryn. We most certainly will.' He proffered his hand to shake his younger brother's, but Bryn thought it was high time, however awkward, that they learned how to do a brotherly hug.

'While we are busy celebrating your fatherhood duo, I think we should make this a triple celebration. Theo is also going to be a new father,' announced Mia.

The brothers looked on in astonishment. 'Goodness, Theo, you kept that liaison close to your chest. How long have you known her? She's a lucky lady, whoever she is. When do we get to meet her?' quizzed Bryn.

'Theo's not got a girlfriend,' laughed Mia. 'He's adopting *me*. The papers have just come through. I don't think I'll ever get used to calling him Dad; he's been Theo far too long. But it's legal now – he's not my "almost dad", anymore and he won't be an "almost grandfather" to my baby.'

28

September

Mia's morning sickness was only slight, and she was able to keep on top of her caseload, preparing trafficked women's asylum cases and schooling her juniors to be able to take them forward while she was on maternity leave. Her main focus was Kraig's Crown Court appeal, which had been scheduled for Monday, 22nd September.

The Lotus Hub at Sycamore Avenue was humming with purposeful activity. Farida worked tirelessly to support her granddaughter and the seven other new residents. Theo still had contacts from his old journalist days and managed to get some media coverage of the successful SCD9 operation that had brought down such a large international vice ring. He made sure that The Lotus Hub Foundation got mentioned, and a stream of donations had followed. It set Mia thinking.

'Penny for them?' asked Bryn, over dinner.

'We need to consider how we are going to refer to the Lotus Hubs when we eventually have more of them. I don't think we can keep referring to our first one as Sycamore Avenue. It needs a name. They will all need a name.'

'Have you any ideas about what you might call it?' asked Bryn.

'Yes, I've been mulling it over. I'd like to name it Yasmin House.'

'Farida will be made up.'

'We should have a naming ceremony. Have a board made. Get our patron, Baroness O'Neil, to open it.'

'That's a splendid idea. Talking of names, we should start thinking about some for our baby. Have you given it any thought now the scan has confirmed we're having a girl?'

'I'm not going to marry you, if that's where this is leading. Not ever. One trashed wedding day is more than enough for any self-respecting female. Even if I were – which I'm not – I wouldn't change my name. Our daughter will have my family name; she will be a Saleem. So I think you should have first pick of a forename. A Welsh forename and an Iraqi surname will be an unusual combination but a very fine one.

'My first pick would be Efa," he replied. "Its English equivalent is Eva or Eve and originates from the Hebrew meaning "alive". It's a kind of celebration of the miracle of life, of survival.'

Mia jumped up from the table and returned from their bedroom with a long-eared, cuddly rabbit in her hand. 'You told me how special this Efa is to you because Cadi gave it to you.'

'Yes, this was Reesa Rabbit, her favourite cuddly toy. When my dog, Efa, died she gave her to me and told me to rename her Efa. It was a precious gift. At the time I didn't realise just *how* precious, because Cadi died soon after. Efa has journeyed with me my whole life since I was a boy, keeping *me* alive, helping me survive the aftermath of being orphaned at eleven.'

Mia kissed Efa and passed her to Bryn. 'She will need a good clean, and then she can be Efa Ellis Saleem's first cuddly toy.'

'I have other plans for Efa. Mia... hang on... did you just say Efa *Ellis* Saleem?'

Mia smiled mischievously. 'Don't get excited, it doesn't mean I'm going to marry you. I don't want to saddle her with a double-barrelled surname, but if it's her middle name she will always have options and can make her own choices. You know how much of a stickler I am about *choice*! And you never know, I might even change my mind one day and agree to marry you, after all.'

Bryn took her in his arms. 'If she's anything like you, I can see I'm going to have my work cut out with two bossy women in the house!'

29

29th September, 2014

The day of Kraig's Crown Court appeal arrived. Mia had been schooling Kraig for his appearance before the three judges who were to hear the case. Bryn knew that the outcome would depend on his testimony, and he knew exactly what he had to do. Theo needed no schooling; he was well versed in providing expert testimony in court.

Kraig arrived, looking very smart in his only suit. Mia had primed them all to avoid mentioning anything other than the circumstances of Wynne's death. She especially cautioned Bryn not to volunteer the wedding day stunt that Kraig pulled, or the replica gun incident at Brampton Clinic. Mia had submitted a comprehensive dossier of all the relevant facts, but the last thing she wanted was Bryn to over-volunteer information during his soul-baring.

Bryn was first to testify. The judges seemingly accepted submissions about his youth and unreliable emotional state of mind, as collaborated by the expert opinion of psychologist Professor Theo Kendrick. However, they did probe timing and motivation.

'The original verdict was pronounced twenty-eight years ago. Why have you suddenly decided to come forward with this change of heart now?'

'As has already been explained, Your Honours, I was a mixed-up kid, still grieving for my mother and sister and looking for someone to blame. Kraig is ten years older. We were never close as boys. Once he went to prison, it's like he just disappeared from my life. It was only the happenchance of him helping us with this vice investigation that we got reacquainted, and I realised how wrong I had been about him.

'It made me rethink how I had thrashed about trying to blame someone, and how much I must have exaggerated his goading of my mother. Kraig is my only blood kin. My mother, sister, and father had all died by the time I was twelve. I feel shame and guilt that it was my actions that robbed him of so many precious years of freedom. I wish I could put the clock back, but I know that is not possible. I desperately want to put things right now.'

Mia was surprised that Kraig received very little grilling. The judges seemed to have accepted a lot of her dossier submission at face value. There was much probing, however, around timing and financial motivations.

'You've been out of prison twelve years, why haven't you appealed before now?'

'I couldn't see any point. I assumed there was still the same enmity between me and my brother. I couldn't see that he would want to change his testimony. It's only since we've become reacquainted as adults that this has become a possibility.'

'Have you given any inducement to this new buddy brother of yours to testify? If your conviction is commuted, you stand to gain significant compensation.'

At this point, Mia jumped up. She had anticipated this. 'The appellant has waived all rights to any compensation, Your Honours. He just wants to clear his name of the matricide charge. He has recently become a father and does not want his young daughter to have to live with the stigma of her father's murder conviction.'

'I see,' said the senior judge, raising his eyebrows and scribbling some notes.

The judges retired to consider their verdict, and Mia advised everyone to go home and get some sleep. She did not expect to hear anything for a day or two. When the ushers called them back first thing the next morning, Mia wasn't quite sure whether to be hopeful or not. It had been a very short deliberation.

Kraig stood up to his full six feet height while the senior judge addressed him. Bryn looked on anxiously; he had picked up on Mia's nervousness.

'Mr Ellis, we have considered your appeal carefully. It is an unusual case. My colleagues and I agree that the original trial was strewn with errors and a prey for every manner of emotive outpourings. There was more than enough evidence from expert witnesses that you did not act intentionally or with malice. We accept that the boy's emotive testimony was unduly affected by bereavement and bitterness towards his older brother. It was unsafe testimony, and it went unchallenged.

'We judge that a verdict of involuntary manslaughter should have been an appropriate sentence. In view of that, your original conviction of murder is quashed and will be replaced with involuntary manslaughter. The circumstances of the case would probably have attracted a two-year sentence, with a minimum term of twelve months. You served fourteen years in prison longer than you should have. Taking off the cost of board for those years, we calculate you are due compensation of £850,000.

'We respect your offer to waive your rights to any compensation, but you have been the victim of a miscarriage of justice, and for that we are awarding you this compensation. If you choose to give some or all of it to charity, that is your prerogative. It is *our* prerogative to administer justice.'

Kraig could hardly contain his relief and elation until the judges had retired, and then he turned to find Bryn and gave him one of those brotherly hugs they were beginning to get the hang of. They all retired to the nearest pub to celebrate.

'You're a rich man now, Kraig,' said Theo, shaking his hand. '£850k will buy a mansion in Wales.'

'Or set me up in my own business. I've always dreamed of owning my own garage. I love motors, and it would keep me closer home for Catrin. I've talked to Megan, and we've agreed that it's way more than we need – or ever dreamt of having. Megan will have some money from her house and Dave's life insurance, so we have decided to give half the compensation money to charity. We want that charity to be Mia's Lotus Hub Foundation.'

'That's a very generous gesture,' said Mia. 'It's the largest single donation we have received. It will buy at least half another Lotus Hub. With what's in the funds already, we have more than enough to proceed with a second. I think such a large donation earns you the right to choose a name for it.'

'That's a very generous gesture, too, Mia. I've never been asked to name anything before. It's a no-brainer. If I am to have the choice, I would name it after the person who has turned my life around, shown me where I went wrong, and how to fix it. I would want to name the next Lotus Hub, *Kendrick House*.

There were loud cheers and applause at this declaration, and Theo, blushing a little, called for another round of drinks.

Epilogue

Spring 2015

The successful operation covered SCD9 in glory. Additional funds flowed in to bolster a unit that was viewed as a major cog in the MET's fight against human trafficking. Its success led to a promotion for Bryn to Detective Superintendent, and Jake to Detective Inspector. Allocation of additional resources enabled Bryn to employ Zabhir and Chrissy. Having passed his sergeant's exams, Ahmed Rahim also joined the ranks.

Mia went into labour a week early, and Efa Ellis Saleem was born on 24th February, weighing 6lb 7oz.

Early April was fittingly sunny, with blue skies and warm air. It was the perfect time to make the trip to Wales for Gracie Matthews to meet little Efa. As had always been his wont, Bryn's first stop was the graveyard. Mia carried Efa, snuggled in a quilted pramsuit. They stood quietly at the grave for a few respectful moments before Bryn formally introduced Efa Ellis Saleem to her grandparents and her aunt. Then he carefully positioned the spike of a glass case into the ground to ensure it never moved in the wind. There was something sealed inside the glass.

Bryn knelt beside the grave. 'Efa has journeyed with me through my darkest days and into the brightest sunshine. Her job is done now. It's time to bring her home.'

About the author

Efa is R P Salmon's second novel, and the sequel to *Toy Soldier*. The mother of three grew up in a Lancashire mill town where her grandmother was a cotton weaver. She describes her life as a series of fortuitously joined-up dots, with careers in social work, teaching, and academia. She draws on all of them in her writing. Renowned for academic publications that challenge the status quo, she writes fiction under the pseudonym R P Salmon, tackling gritty issues and the complexities of human relationships. She is fascinated by the power of story that can reach different people in different ways – and stay with them for different reasons.